Baptism of Fire

Virginia Crow

CROWVUS

First Published in 2020

Crowvus, 53 Argyle Square, Wick, KW1 5AJ

ISBN: 978-1-913182-11-3

For comments and questions about "Baptism of
Fire" contact the author directly at
daysdyingglory@gmail.com

www.crowvus.com

To Mimsy,

for patience where my writing is concerned and belief in all I do

Part One

The First Weekend

"I don't believe in curses. It comes with the job."

Sally-Anne nodded at the vicar's words. She didn't really care what the priest thought about curses, jinxes or hexes. The fact remained: she hadn't believed in them until she had met Kevin Alderman.

She'd been a social worker for eight years, as long as Kevin had been alive, and she'd worked some really tough cases. But, after careful handling and occasional police involvement, she'd resolved them all. Reverend Roberts was a last resort for Kevin, and she'd only considered the priest's request because she was really beginning to believe the child was cursed. Four foster families had suffered fatalities after taking in the boy. Six deaths to his name and he was not even a decade old.

"I don't think he means for it to happen," Sally-Anne explained, sighing as she looked out of the window to where Kevin stood. He was trying to reach the apples from the lower branches of the tree in The Vicarage garden. The boy looked the image of innocence.

"I'm not afraid," Alistair Roberts replied. "It will just be nice to have a child in the house again."

Sally-Anne walked to the French windows and called Kevin indoors.

"Am I staying?" Kevin asked, his green eyes twinkling in his thin face. "I like Reverend Roberts, and I really like his garden."

"Well, you've had your long stays, Kevin," Sally-Anne began, as she had four times before. "Looks like you and the vicar are going to really hit it off."

"Thanks, Sally-Anne," Kevin said, the faintest smile on his pale lips.

"I'll see you out," Alistair added, beaming with a smile Sally-Anne was afraid would be short-lived. "You make yourself at home, Kevin," he added, calling over his shoulder to the boy. "I won't be a minute."

"Don't let him near the hob," Sally-Anne blurted out as they reached the door. "He has a bad track record with burning."

"He doesn't seem like the type to self-harm," Alistair muttered.

"It's not self-harm, Reverend Roberts. All his," she paused and tried to find the right word. Unable to do so, she continued. "They've all had burns."

"It's not hellfire," Alistair stated. "He just

needs a home."

Sally-Anne almost screamed at the naivety of the man before her. She had watched three experienced foster carers buried because of this boy. Another had lost her mother prematurely, while Kevin's adopted father had been found in a burning car on a straight, empty road. There was something about the boy. But, if the priest was happy with the arrangement, she was more than happy to say goodbye to Kevin Alderman.

Alastair turned back to his living room and frowned thoughtfully. Kevin was still standing at the window, staring out over the autumnal garden. It was difficult to imagine a more beautiful sight. The child turned an excited face to him, pointing out of the window.

"I saw a squirrel," he shrieked. "It was a squirrel!"

"Yes," Alastair smiled. "They come quite often. I think they have a nest somewhere in the garden," he continued, walking through to the kitchen and setting the kettle on the gas hob. "But I don't know where."

"Have you ever looked for it?" Kevin asked, watching intently as the flames caressed the base of the kettle.

"No. Sometimes it's best to just leave things in peace."

"I'd have gone looking for it," Kevin replied, turning from the kitchen and walking back to the large windows.

Their first day together was uneventful. By eight o'clock, Kevin was lying in a new bed, staring at the unusual ceiling in an alien room. There were glow-in-the-dark stars stuck to the blue ceiling. Planets, some with rings circling them, others just balls of putrid yellows or burning blues, dangled down from the roof on invisible threads. Kevin studied each one as he lay in the bed. He was used to sleeping in different rooms, but he had never been in one like this. The curtains, which were pulled closed, showed smiling astronauts, and rockets shooting up towards crescent moons. The walls were painted a light blue, with silhouetted space shapes stencilled onto them. There was a lamp next to his bed, and even the shade was space themed.

Alastair had said goodnight to him, leaving him alone in the strange room. Kevin could hear him whistling a tune downstairs. Except for this, the house was quiet. Occasionally, he could hear the vicar moving from room to room, carefully closing doors after him. Kevin thought Alastair must do everything carefully. He seemed to ooze calmness. He was not like any of his other foster carers, or his adopted parents. He couldn't remember his real parents, just knowing them as figures of his past who were little more than names. Melanie and Harry Alderman. That was the order in which they had always been referred to. His mother's name was spoken with an air of apology, while his father's was whispered, almost as though people didn't want him to know who his father had been. This was the only way Kevin had ever heard them referenced, so now, without even meaning to, he would refer to them in the same way.

When Kevin awoke the next morning, it was to muffled light coming through the spacemen curtains. He was alone in the room. Not like in Foster Home Three. She had always been there when he woke up, apart from the morning after the fire. He had never seen her again after that. Kevin got out of bed, his feet slipping into a pair of slippers. He looked down in surprise at finding them there, before he walked from the room and across the landing to the toilet.

By the time he had made his way downstairs, Alastair had already set the toaster on, and he ushered Kevin to a seat at the breakfast bar. It faced the window which looked out over the garden and the vicar smiled across, pushing two slices of bread into the toaster.

"See if you can spot the squirrel again," he began. "I put some more nuts out this morning."

"Have you named him?" Kevin asked.

"Yes. But it's usually a her who visits. I call her Ysolde."

"Ysolde?" Kevin repeated, his mouth stumbling over this name. "I thought you'd call it Jesus or something."

Alastair gave a slight chuckle before he picked up Kevin's plate and pressed the release button on the toaster, sending two barely brown pieces of bread shooting out of it. "Jesus didn't have squirrels. I call her Ysolde because of the legend. Here," he added, pushing the plate of toast towards Kevin. "What do you want to put on it? I've got butter, jam, marmalade or golden syrup."

"What's the jam?"

"Raspberry, with seeds."

"That's my favourite," Kevin squeaked.

"Mine too." Alastair moved over to the

cupboard and pulled out a jar, which he opened and handed over.

"Don't you eat breakfast?" Kevin dipped the spoon into the jar. "Helen said everyone should eat breakfast."

"Who's Helen?"

"She was my last foster mum."

"Well, she's right. But I've already eaten mine." Alastair poured out a glass of milk and offered it to Kevin. "But this is your stay-at home now."

"That's what Liam said," Kevin responded. There was no sorrow in his eyes, only doubt. "None of them believed it would happen to them."

"What?"

"The fire, the crash, the explosion." Kevin's face furrowed. "But it happened."

"You're safe here, Kevin," Alastair said, walking around to face the boy. "Nothing will happen here. Only good things."

Kevin nodded and scrubbed his hand across his mouth, wiping away the milk mark on his upper lip. Alastair walked over to the French windows and stared out over his garden. There was a thin veil of rain separating him from the apple tree where the squirrel feeder hung. He stared out feeling a strange chill take the back of his neck, gripping his nape with icy talons. It was not fear, but sorrow. He did not believe in the curse Sally-Anne had spoken of, but he was distressed that Kevin clearly did. There seemed to be little doubt in the boy's head that he was responsible for these terrible deaths, and Alastair was unable to reconcile with the manner in which the poor boy seemed to believe he was cursed. He jumped as a small hand slotted into his own, and he looked down to find Kevin staring up at him.

"What shall we do today?" Alastair asked. "It's Saturday, so there's nowhere I have to be."

"Can we go out into the garden?"

"In the rain?" Alastair asked doubtfully. He was met by an enthusiastic nod of the head. "I haven't got you any waterproof clothes."

"That's okay. I don't mind rain."

Alastair was torn but nodded. Kevin's mouth turned up in a smile, but it didn't reach his eyes. He was such a serious child, Alastair felt it was a fitting challenge to try and make the boy smile genuinely. He smiled down at Kevin.

"I just have to make a couple of phone calls. Can you give me a few minutes?"

Kevin nodded. "I'll go upstairs."

"You don't have to," Alastair replied, eager not to let the boy feel he was being sent away. "Why don't you stay here and keep an eye open for Ysolde?"

"Okay."

Alastair walked through to his study and pushed the door closed. Giving a ragged breath, he reached his hand to his face, rubbing his eyes. He had managed his first night with the child. He walked over to his desk and sat down looking at the papers which were arranged neatly, little souvenir paperweights resting on each pile. Alastair gave a sniff and tried to dismiss the panic that he could smell gas. He rushed to the door and pulled it open, walking through towards the kitchen. Unwilling to walk past Kevin, he went through the other door, but when he reached the kitchen, it was to find he stood alone. The gas hob was silent and cold. He walked back to the study, still hiding from Kevin, and rebuked himself as he reached for the phone. Sally-Anne had done this to him. He refused to believe Kevin Alderman would bring any harm upon either of them.

His phone calls took far longer than he had meant them to, pleased to talk to other adults, people who knew him and who he did not have to work hard with. When he returned to the French windows, he expected to find Kevin had wandered off, but the child still stood there, staring out at the rain and the ripened apples on the tree. As the vicar walked over, Kevin turned an apologetic face towards him.

"The squirrel hasn't been," Kevin muttered. "I don't think it's coming back."

"She'll come back," Alastair replied with certainty. "She always does come back."

Kevin nodded but did not offer any answer beyond going through to the front hall and pulling on his shoes. He waited as Alastair sauntered through, helping Kevin into his dark blue anorak before pulling on his own waxed jacket. The rain was not heavy, and it was not enough to dampen Kevin's spirits as he rushed off, determined to find Ysolde's home. There was a disc of the sun in the sky, like a pale watch face, measuring the passage of time.

Alastair watched as Kevin darted from tree to tree looking for the squirrel, but never finding her. Unable to keep up with the exhausting and excited manner in which he ran hither and thither, Alastair contented himself with gathering some of the windfall from the ground.

Having collected all the suitable fallen apples, and there being a fraction more room in the bag, he reached towards one which was hanging low on the tree, about to pull it free. He stopped as he heard a child's laugh. His hand closed and pulled back, away from the fruit. He looked over his shoulder expecting to see Kevin, but he was not there. Was it a trick of echoes? Or was it that other child, hidden from him through the thin curtain of rain?

Alastair carried the bag back to the house and sat on the step at the French windows. He watched Kevin running through the trees, leaping as high as he could to try and see whether Ysolde was inside the holes in the trunks or scurrying along the upper branches. But as his search continued to come up empty-handed, he tired and trudged back towards the house. His shoes squelched as he walked over to Alastair and his face had a sinking, disappointed expression to match. Alastair reached his hand out to the child, but Kevin ignored it and stood before the vicar, his bottom lip trembling and his tears lost in the rain which ran down his face.

"I didn't find her."

"I know," Alastair replied, standing up. "But think how cold and wet you are, even with all your clothes. She will be curled away somewhere keeping warm and dry. She'll come again."

He and Kevin walked to the door in silence, but as soon as they were inside Kevin turned to look at the vicar as he helped pull the soggy trainers from Kevin's feet.

"I can take my own shoes off." It was the dismissive tone with which he spoke which made Alastair lean away.

"Because you can do something doesn't mean you have to."

"What do you mean?" Kevin asked, watching as Alastair struggled with a series of knots which had gathered in the shoelace. Kevin never undid them, he just pulled them on or off.

"You can run in front of a car, but you don't have to. We call it 'Free Will'."

"I watched that film once," Kevin replied, bringing a slight smile to Alastair's face.

"Well, just remember," he continued, trying to hide the amusement in his voice. "Sometimes we all have to do things we don't want to, but we don't have to do all the things we can do."

Kevin slid his feet from the shoes and pulled off his soaking socks, burying his toes into the slippers he had discarded there earlier. He walked through to the living room and sat staring out of the French windows. Alastair picked up the boy's shoe and continued struggling with the lace for a minute before he walked through to the study and, collecting a large pair of scissors, cut through it. He wove the lace out of the shoe, feeling suddenly sick as the thin cord snaked through his fingers. Had it been a mistake? Should he have got home earlier? Should he never have looked to adopt the child?

He spun to the door of the room as he heard a shuffling sound behind him.

"How am I going to wear them with no laces?" Kevin demanded, seeing the cord wrapped tightly around Alastair's hand.

"I have some more laces somewhere," Alastair replied, shaking the sodden one from his hand

and into the bin. "In fact, I think I have some better shoes for you somewhere. Come on."

Hurriedly, Alastair ushered the child from the study and closed the door, opening another one directly opposite. It was a cupboard, big enough to walk into, but small enough so that it didn't have its own window. Kevin hung back, his mind flashing to a memory of his first foster home. He could remember the cupboard under the stairs, the large skeletal spiders which tucked under each step, still far above him, looking down when he had been sent there because he had done something wrong.

Alastair's cupboard was tidy, though. As soon as the light was switched on, there was nothing scary about it. A single spider hung from a thread, so small Kevin had barely noticed it, and he watched as the vicar hooked the thread with his hand and moved the spider into the corner of the room. He began rummaging on the bottom shelf, stretching behind two pairs of shoes to pull out a pair of children's shoes made of shiny leather.

"Here," Alastair said, rubbing them with a duster which rested on top of a storage cabinet behind him. "I hope they fit. You might want to give them a bash, too. They've been in here a while."

"I don't like spiders," Kevin whispered. "They have eight eyes."

"Eight?" Alastair asked, holding onto the shoes and leaving the cupboard. "That does sound quite scary. What's your favourite animal, Kevin?"

Kevin watched as the man hit the two shoes

together and a cloud of dust flew up in his face, but no spiders.

"A zebra," he replied.

"Well, maybe in spring, when the weather's better, we can take a trip to the zoo and see one."

Kevin's mouth turned up into a smile, catching his cheeks but still failing to reach his eyes. The expression changed abruptly as the telephone in the study rang. Alastair handed him the shoes and walked across the hall, leaning over the desk to pick up the phone. Kevin listened to the one-sided conversation for a while, but Alastair walked over to the door and looked down at him.

"Sorry, Kevin. I have to take this, and it's private. Why don't you go and watch TV?"

Kevin nodded as the door was closed in his face. There was a quiet resolution to his steps as he walked back into the living room and stretched up to reach the TV. It was attached to the chimneybreast and he had to reach across the empty hearth to get to the switch. He recoiled from the opening and left the TV switched off. He walked instead to look at the alcoves on either side of the fireplace. One of them was filled with books, much too big for Kevin to safely pull down, but on a lower shelf there were some children's books. He pulled one of these out and began looking through the brightly coloured pictures. The pages had been turned often by little hands, some fingerprints were still clear on the corners, and at the front the name Leo had been scrawled in purple crayon. Kevin returned it to the shelf and pulled out another one. It had the same name at the front, this time with a little piece of paper saying he had been gifted it at a church event.

Kevin read the story, smiling in places, and eager to know how it ended. He turned a page and looked down in disappointment at where the ending should have been. The page had been torn out. He closed the book and looked across at the window, wondering who would spoil the ending of a story in such a way. Something caught his eye out of the French windows, and he crawled over to find two jet black eyes meeting his own. Ysolde stared at him through the glass before she bounded over to the apple tree and, in one fluid motion, leapt into the lower branches. Kevin reached his hand out to the window and rested it on the glass, smiling slightly as she wove in and out of the twigs, picking up the nuts Alastair had put out for her.

After a time, she leapt into another tree and disappeared from Kevin's sight. Still with the book in one hand, he moved over to the second alcove and looked at the ornaments which sat there. Most of them were made of wood in swirling grain, so they looked stripy. One was of a horse, and the stripes made it look like a zebra. He reached his hand up to it and carefully lifted it down, stroking its side and feeling the slight bump of the grain as he ran his fingers over it. He stretched to return it again and, in doing so, found himself staring into the face of another child. It was a photograph of a boy who looked to be his own age. He had an enormous smile on his face, and he was reaching towards the photographer. He was being held by a woman with a mass of blond hair, who was smiling too, although there was something in her eyes which made her look sad. Perhaps it was just the reflection of the camera's flash, but Kevin thought there were tears there, waiting to be shed. But it was the clear tube which ran from behind the boy's ear to his nose which Kevin stared at.

"Sorry about that," Alastair's voice began, and Kevin turned around to face the vicar as he entered. "Last minute preparations for tomorrow."

"What happens tomorrow?"

"Church," Alastair said, looking at the two objects in the boy's hands. "Biggest day of the week for me. It's Eucharist here at nine, then a quick drive across to Little Golforth for the three o'clock family service. I think you'll like that one."

"Do I have to go?" Kevin asked, boredom creeping into his voice.

"Yes," Alastair replied. "You might even enjoy it. If I can find someone to look after you, then you don't have to, but it's a bit short notice for tomorrow."

"Okay," Kevin sighed, turning back to put the wooden horse on the shelf. Alastair's eyes never left the book in his hand as Kevin presented it to him. "How does it end?" the boy asked. "Someone tore out the last page."

"It ends with the boy and his dog climbing the hill and looking down over the castle."

"Why did someone rip out the ending? That's the best ending there could be."

"Accidents happen," Alastair replied dismissively. "What do you want for dinner?"

"Do you cook?" Kevin asked. "I've never met a

man who could cook."

After sending Kevin to change into dry clothes, they prepared their own dinner of pork chops, potatoes and salad. Kevin prepared the salad, refusing to go near the flames of the gas hob, while Alastair did the rest. Next, he set the breakfast bar for the two of them, making sure that he would be able to look out the window while he ate. As they cooked they talked of everything and nothing. Kevin told the vicar that Ysolde had come to the window, to which Alastair replied that she was very well-mannered and would have been saying thank you. The rejection Kevin had felt when he had been dismissed from the study was gone, and he was loving being with the man before him. Alastair knew so much about so many things. It didn't matter if Kevin wanted to talk about maps or animals, history or books, Alastair knew about it all. As they sat down for dinner, Alastair put his hands together and looked across at Kevin who stared blankly back.

"We'll say grace," Alastair explained. "All this food came from somewhere, and I'm really grateful it did."

"Me too," Kevin replied.

"Amen," Alastair prompted, and listened as the boy whispered it after him.

They ate in silence, except for when Kevin pointed out different birds landing on the feeders. At the end of the meal, Alastair invited Kevin to come and sit down beside him on the sofa. The boy sat at the end furthest away from Alastair and pulled his feet up. Curled up like this, Kevin hugged his knees to him. Alastair frowned at this body language, before he corrected himself and smiled across.

"We have a few things to talk about."

"Do you want me to go?" Kevin whispered. "I've only just come."

"Go?" Alastair choked. "No, of course not. But we have a few rules to go through. Really, I should have talked to you about them yesterday, but I was just so pleased to have your company I forgot all about it."

Kevin let go of his legs and nodded.

"Firstly, every room in the house is in part yours. But since there's an en-suite in my room, you can keep the bathroom."

Kevin smiled slightly.

"But the study is where I go to work, and meet people, and take phone calls, all of which can be quite private. So because you have the bathroom to yourself, I'll have the study as my room. Seem fair?"

Kevin smiled again, a little deeper this time, and nodded.

"On Tuesdays and every other Saturday, Jilly comes in to help me clean the house. She goes everywhere."

"Is that Jilly?" Kevin asked, pointing to the picture he had found before dinner.

"No," came the thoughtful reply, as though Alastair had forgotten all about the picture. "I'll introduce you to Jilly tomorrow. She's lovely and looks after twins just a bit younger than you."

"Like you are going to look after me?"

"Not exactly," Alastair replied. "Benji and Tom are her nephews. Their dad works abroad and, when their mum is at work, Jilly looks after them."

"So she gets to go everywhere?"

"Yes," Alastair replied, relieved to be back on track with the conversation. "Next rule: bedtime is nine o'clock."

Kevin nodded and let his legs slide from the sofa.

"And no Christmas music until after the holiday."

Kevin's face lifted in a smile. "I love Christmas," he conceded, whispering as though he shouldn't be saying it. "It's my favourite time of the year."

"Mine too," Alastair whispered back, a cheeky grin appearing on his face. "But my parishioners tell me off if I start Christmas too early."

"What's a parishioner?"

"People who go to church. Like Jilly."

Alastair smiled across as he watched Kevin shuffle on the sofa. He was sitting normally now. The priest tried to imagine how unsettled the boy must feel, that each time the need to have a conversation was mentioned, he worried he was going to be sent away. He was still playing through these thoughts as he left Kevin's room that night, wishing him a goodnight, and switching off the centre light so that only the space lamp lit up the astronautical room. Each word Sally-Anne had told him came back to haunt his thoughts as he washed the supper pots, staring out at the apple tree which was lit up by the light from the French windows. He whistled the tune of a harvest hymn, trying to focus on the plans he had for tomorrow's homily, but he kept thinking of Kevin's bitter background.

He walked through to the study and opened

the middle drawer of his desk, pulling out the envelope Sally-Anne had given him the month before. It was full of legal documentation, psychologist's assessments, and scanned copies of newspapers he had tucked in. In each of the fires and deaths which had been suffered by his carers, Kevin had remained unharmed. Even in the case of the third foster family, whose detached house had been destroyed in a gas explosion, Kevin had been at school at the time. Alastair flicked through the papers and his frown grew deeper and deeper. Kevin Alderman had appeared, unannounced to the world, a little over eight years ago, at the start of October. His birth was registered by his mother, Melanie, and his father's name was given as Harry. Melanie, cast out of her family for having fallen pregnant so young, had died when Kevin had been two. She had been at a friend's flat when the apartment next door had caught fire. It was found it had been an electrical fault, but it had cost the lives of both Melanie and her friend. Kevin had been saved, his mother having sheltered him as she struggled through the smoke and flames. She had died a few hours later in the hospital. And that had been the start of Kevin's curse. Harry had been in prison since before Kevin was born, and had moved from establishment to establishment after starting fights and, on one occasion, a riot. He had died in a crash on the journey between two prisons.

"Poor child," Alastair whispered.

He closed the file, not wishing to remember the other gruesome deaths which had followed the young boy around. Sally-Anne may have believed he was cursed, but Alastair was determined to see him as blessed. After all, he had survived all the fires. He returned the file to the desk and rose to his feet. As he left the room, his eyes rested on the coiled shoelace in the bin. He gave a long sigh and forced himself to stare at it, imagining the feel of cord in his hand once more.

Alastair closed the door on the study and walked upstairs to bed. On his way, he called in at the kitchen, checking again that all the gas jets were quiet and clear. He didn't believe in curses, he reminded himself. And he certainly didn't believe a child as fragile as Kevin could be cursed. He needed to be loved, that was all. And Alastair needed the same thing.

Eight o'clock on Sunday morning, Alastair poked his head around the door to Kevin's room and announced it was time to get up. Kevin appeared downstairs ten minutes later, his hair like a tangled mop and his eyes half-closed. He ate breakfast without tasting any of it and he found himself staring blankly into the garden, his sleepy senses finally coming around to the waking world. He looked across at Alastair and frowned as his eyes took in the clothes he was wearing. It was a long black cape which reached down to the floor, with sleeves which opened at the cuffs, and he looked both slim and swamped in it. At his neck, he wore the broad white collar which Kevin knew denoted his role in the community.

"I thought you could come along early, with me," Alastair said cheerfully. "And if you don't want to sit by yourself, I'll see if Jilly will let you sit with her."

"Can't I sit with you?"

"Not today, Kevin."

Kevin nodded and shuffled off the high stool. He walked to put his shoes on and smiled slightly at the shiny leather ones which had replaced his trainers. He slotted his feet in and knelt down to tie the laces. They were almost a perfect fit, just a little narrow, but Alastair promised he would buy Kevin some new shoes of his own tomorrow. There were only little grocery shops in the village, and the town was a thirty-minute drive away. The shoes gave Kevin a renewed confidence, though. He had never had a smart pair of shoes before, always wearing either trainers or plimsolls, and he walked through the house with a straighter back and a jaunty swagger.

Alastair grabbed a leather satchel from the hall stand and ushered Kevin out of The Vicarage. It was not a long walk to the church, but it wove along a little-used footpath, which was penned in on either side by thick beech hedges. They loomed over the top, meeting in some places. Different houses lined the other side of the hedges, and at one house Kevin rushed to hide behind Alastair as angry barking broke out. Alastair swapped the satchel into his other hand and offered Kevin his now free hand which the boy took as they walked past the dog house, but let go of as soon as the dogs were left behind.

The weather was dry, but at times the wind whipped at them both as they continued toward the church. The path led directly into the churchyard and, as soon as they were there, Kevin hung back from the vicar.

"I can't leave you outside," Alastair began. "Come into the vestry."

Kevin kicked his feet as he entered the small room. It was lined in wooden panels along the first three feet of the wall, and peeling white plaster rose up to the wooden beams of the roof. It was as dismal as Kevin had imagined it would be, improving only a little as Alastair switched on a light. Kevin jumped as he heard a scream and he ran to Alastair, clutching at the cassock he wore.

"Vicar, you scared the life out of me!" a woman exclaimed, clutching her chest as though she thought her heart might have exploded. She was much older than Alastair, her rich chocolate hair turning to grey around her face, which was as round as a penny. She looked doubtfully at Kevin before she continued. "It looks like I gave you a similar fright, young man."

Alastair wrapped his arm around Kevin and gently pushed him forward, presenting him to the woman.

"This is Kevin, Mrs Henderson. He's staying with me."

"Ah," she said, her face lighting up in a smile which could rival Alastair's as the warmest gesture Kevin had ever seen. "I've been bursting to meet you, young man. We all have."

"Are you Jilly?" Kevin asked, and was met with an amused laugh, while Alastair stumbled over himself to apologise.

"Sorry, Mrs Henderson. I told him he could sit with Jilly if she didn't mind."

"I'm sure she won't," Mrs Henderson replied, the corners of her mouth twitching upwards once more. "I'll be your teacher, Kevin," Mrs Henderson went on, turning her attention back to the boy. "I'm the headteacher at the school."

"Sorry," Kevin muttered, feeling confused by what exactly the woman before him found so funny.

"The candles on the altar need replacing, Vicar," she continued, talking over Kevin's head now. "Have you got your key for the cupboard? I left mine at home."

Alastair nodded and dipped his hand into his satchel, bringing out the biggest chain of keys Kevin had ever seen. They were all different shapes and sizes, and he tried to imagine what each would unlock. Mrs Henderson picked the cupboard key immediately, without seeing the sense of fun and imagination which flared up in the boy. When she had collected the candles she walked out of the vestry, pausing just long enough to smile back at Kevin.

"Mrs Henderson is the churchwarden," Alastair explained softly. "She and Mr Pitt run the church."

"I thought you ran the church?"

"They make sure everything is where it should be, so that I can talk to people and teach them."

"They're like caretakers?"

"Yes, exactly." Alastair smiled at the boy as Kevin sighed. "Today's Harvest, Kevin. Have you ever had a Harvest Festival?"

"In school we talked about Harvest. Last year."

"Great!" Alastair said jovially. "I just have to get my vestments on, and then we can go and meet people as they come into church."

Kevin watched as Alastair unlocked a

cupboard next to the one Mrs Henderson had used, and he saw a row of the most beautiful garments he had ever seen. He reached forward and took one. It was silky and soft, and even the embroidered patterns were delicate and light. Alastair was pulling one of them over his head when the door opened, and a fiery-haired woman stepped in. She laughed as she saw Alastair, reaching forward and pulling the voluminous garment into place.

"Good morning, Vicar," she laughed. "I wondered where you were hiding."

"Hello Jilly," Alastair said, his voice caring but well measured. Kevin looked across at her at the sound of this name and studied her thoughtfully while Alastair continued to talk. "No Benji and Tom this morning?"

"They'll be here," she assured him. "But Trish is off work today so they're coming with her. But, hello!" Jilly went on, ignoring Alastair for a moment and looking at Kevin. "You must be Kevin."

"Yes," he answered.

"I'm Jilly," she replied, matching his serious tone as well as she could, but her face was not made for sobriety and a smile flashed right through every one of her features. "I'm the organist."

"I thought you were the cleaner."

Jilly laughed as Alastair blushed. "I will be cleaning your house, so do me a favour and don't be as messy as your dad." She motioned over her shoulder towards the vicar.

"My dad's dead," Kevin stated.

"One dad," she answered, not at all shocked

by the boy's response. "But you're so lucky, you've got another dad now. When mine died, I never got another."

Kevin stared at the woman as though she was mad. She just smiled at him and ruffled his hair before she began walking into the main part of the church. She stopped as Alastair said her name.

"Yes, Vicar?"

"Can Kevin sit with you today? He's not sure about church, and I think he'll be happier hidden from view."

She lowered her head slightly and nodded. "Yes, of course. Come on, Kevin."

Kevin sat beside Jilly on the long organ stool. It was the most uncomfortable seat he had ever sat on and he twisted repeatedly. Jilly gave him her coat to sit on, but it made little difference. The service was long and, except for the singing, it meant nothing to him. He would have been lost entirely if it hadn't been for Jilly pointing out where they were in a small service book. It might have been boring if it had not been for the opportunity to admire the chancel. Everywhere he looked he saw something different, and everything was new, exciting and beautiful. He loved the echoes his voice made as he sang up to the ceiling. He knew none of the songs, but they all had catchy tunes and several verses, so he was singing confidently by the end of each one. Jilly smiled across at him, but most of the time she watched Alastair in a mirror on the organ. Alastair never sang any of the songs, so Kevin's voice was the only one in the chancel.

When Jilly went up to the altar near the end

of the service, she offered Kevin her hand, but he shook his head quickly.

"Maybe next week," she giggled, her voice scarcely a whisper.

Kevin watched as Alastair gave her, and every other person who came forward, a small biscuit. Mrs Henderson followed him, giving a silver cup to each person in turn. There were so many different people, old and young, men and women, suited and casually dressed. There were no two people the same until two boys, who Kevin correctly guessed were Benji and Tom, walked forward. They saw him at once and began pointing and whispering to each other. One of them waved across, but the woman who was with them tapped his hand down. Kevin was sure this was Jilly's sister, for she had the same wild red hair and a nose full of freckles. The only difference he could see was that her face looked thinner and sterner. She didn't have the bright blue spectacles like those which sat on Jilly's nose, either.

When the service ended, Jilly pulled out all but two of the organ stops and the instrument thundered out its music, filling the church.

Kevin waited until she had finished playing before she and he climbed down from the bench and she guided him into the nave. The building was filled with colour from where the sun caught the south and east facing windows, and Kevin looked at his hand as it caught a red ray of light. Alastair was at the door, shaking hands with everyone who left, but before Kevin could walk over to him, one of the twins appeared before him.

"I'm Thomas," he announced.

"Hello," Kevin ventured.

"This is Kevin, boys," Jilly said, smiling as Benji came to join his brother in staring at the child before them. "Trish," Jilly continued, calling to her sister. "The vicar's off to Little Golforth this afternoon. Can we take Kevin to see Mum? I think the Golforth crowd might be too much for him."

"And these two terrors won't be?" Trish laughed, her detached appearance thawing in the warm sound. "Sure."

Jilly walked over to Alastair while Kevin turned back to the twins. Both wore hand-knitted jumpers, one with a sheath of corn and one with a basket of apples, but he couldn't remember which one was which.

Alastair watched Jilly approach with a neutral smile. Her own smile was more than wide enough to make up for it. She took his outstretched hand and shook it.

"We can take Kevin to see Mum, if you want."

"Doesn't he want to go to Golforth?" Alastair asked.

"I think it might just be a bit too much for him," Jilly laughed. "And Tom and Benji would love his company."

"Okay." The assent felt as though it was being pulled from his mouth. "Can you drop him back at The Vicarage, Jilly?"

"No," she laughed. "I thought I'd let him walk back." She brushed her red curls behind her ear and laughed again. "Of course I will!"

"How is your mum? I missed her this week."

"She's fine," Jilly replied. "She'll be home for

Christmas."

"Really?" Alastair asked, surprise and disbelief in his voice. "They said that?"

"No," Jilly admitted. "But I know she will be. It won't be Christmas without her."

"I'll make sure I get to see her this week," Alastair promised. "I've got to go and get Kevin some new shoes tomorrow, so I'll call in then."

"I thought those shoes looked familiar," Jilly whispered. She smiled up at him and squeezed his hand a little. "I'll tell Mum you'll see her tomorrow."

Alastair smiled across and nodded. He watched as she walked back over to Kevin, announcing to her sister's family that Kevin was to join them for the rest of the day. Alastair watched Kevin's face turn up in a smile and the boy rushed over to him.

"Is it really alright for me to go?"

"Just be careful, Kevin," Alastair said after nodding his agreement. "And be gentle. Benji's and Tom's grandma is very ill. If she needs to sleep, stay quiet so she can."

Kevin nodded and walked sedately back to the family. Alastair was unsure whether he should warn Jilly and Trish about the boy's past but, as he stepped over the threshold and into the church once more, he reminded himself that he did not believe in curses. Kevin Alderman had been unlucky, not cursed. Jilly and her family would be as safe having Kevin with them as they would have been without him.

It was nearly five o'clock by the time Alastair arrived home after his service out in Little Golforth. Jilly had been right. The service might have been too much for Kevin. The churchwardens in Little Golforth had begun a campaign two years ago to try and get as many young people involved in the church as they could, and the effect had been a fantastic number of families arriving for every family service, but so few of them having any inclination to partake in the religious aspect. Instead, the church had become a meeting hall where children played, and parents chatted while he was trying to hold a service. He never wore vestments, and only a handful of the congregation even came forward for communion.

He closed the door and hung the car keys on the key hooks, then walked through to the kitchen. Here, he poured himself a glass of wine and stared out at the fading garden. Another Harvest brought in. Another year passed by. He realised suddenly that he was alone again, as he had been before Kevin's appearance as a Godsend. Outside in the garden, he could see shadows moving which he took to be cats or birds, but he was so exhausted they could have been anything. He walked over to the sofa and slouched into the corner, staring at the empty fireplace but seeing nothing. A million questions trickled into his head, dancing through his consciousness, keeping him awake with their constant nagging. Was Kevin safe? Were Jilly and her family safe? Was the boy really cursed? Were there even such things as curses? Was there even such a thing as God?

This question had gnawed at his soul with an alarming ferocity over the last two years. But every time he came close to thinking the answer was no, he felt so lifeless and lost he could not reconcile with it. As a child, God had been a father. As a teen, He had been a guide. As an adult, He had been a comforter. Alastair could not bear to consider he might lose any of these things.

He must have fallen asleep for he was woken up by a pounding on the French windows. Alastair muttered a word he had taught himself not to say on a Sunday as he felt the wine seep through his white shirt but set the glass on the small coffee table and walked to the window, flicking the light on as he did so. At once, the image of Jilly and Kevin appeared at the glass, amid a host of fluttering moths. Jilly looked shocked and scared as he pulled open the door.

"Vicar?" she stammered, reaching her hand out and resting it on his stomach. "Alastair?"

Alastair felt his face burst into colour as he stepped back. "It's fine, Jilly," he explained, ushering them in and closing the door on the few moths which had remained outside. "It's wine."

"Oh," she whispered, her own cheeks turning slightly red. "I think your doorbell isn't working," she went on, trying to return to a calm normality. "We rang it three times, didn't we, Kevin?"

Kevin nodded.

"So, I'll head home," she went on, seeing neither man nor boy wanted to make conversation. "Thank you for sparing him for the day, Vicar. See you soon, Kevin."

"You can go out the front," Alastair said, but she only laughed and shook her head.

"No thanks, Vicar. I'm sinfully superstitious."

Alastair watched as she carefully slipped out

the French windows, disappearing into the night. Kevin looked across at him and smiled sleepily.

"Did you have a good day?" Alastair asked. He gained a nod in return.

"What's the matter with their grandma?"

"She's got cancer," Alastair said. "I'm going to see her tomorrow."

"Will she die?"

"The doctors aren't sure," he said honestly. "They're trying a new treatment for her."

"I hope she doesn't," Kevin muttered.

"Early bed. It's the first day at your new school tomorrow," Alastair said as cheerfully as he could. "You need to be bright-eyed and bushy-tailed for then."

When Kevin was ready for bed, Alastair came into the room. He had changed from his wine-stained shirt into his usual jumper and corduroy trousers.

"Why does Jilly come to tidy our house?"

Alastair smiled at the boy's choice of pronoun. "When her mum went into hospital for the first time, she needed some extra money to help pay for everything she suddenly had to do. So I gave her a little job to earn money. She's happiest when she's working. She's just one of those sort of people."

"How was your afternoon?"

"Fine, thank you," Alastair answered, genuinely surprised by the boy's question. "Are you looking forward to school?"

Kevin shrugged his shoulders and snuggled down under the covers. He watched as the planet above the radiator spun a lazy circle in the upward draught.

"You'll do great," Alastair said, willing the statement to be true. He had hated his own schooldays. "And Mrs Henderson is a lovely teacher."

"I've been to so many schools," Kevin sighed. "Sometimes I lose track of them."

"Have you stayed in touch with anyone from your other schools?"

"No," Kevin replied, no hint of any emotion in his voice. "They all knew I was different." He looked across at the gentle, calm face of the man before him. He wanted to trust him. He wanted it more than anything. But everyone he had trusted had died. Reluctantly, he muttered, "Do you think I'm cursed, Alastair?"

"No," came the resounding reply. "I don't believe in curses. Or else, I believe God conquers all such things."

"But Sally-Anne thinks I am."

"Don't worry about Sally-Anne," the vicar replied, leaning forward to take Kevin's hand. "She is afraid, that's all. Fear makes people say and do all sorts of crazy things. She doesn't really believe it."

Kevin gave him half a smile. "Trish knows everyone at the hospital," he said, changing the subject and relieved to do so.

"She's a nurse there," Alastair said, straightening up as he let go of Kevin's hand. "She's worked there a while now."

"And Benji and Tom are going to be in my class."

"Yes," Alastair said, deepening his smile for the sake of the boy before him. "There are only two classes in the school."

"Why is it such a small school? The last school I was at had fifteen classes."

"Fifteen?" Alastair asked in mock disbelief. "Well, in our little country schools we don't usually have more than four or five. But there are two schools in this village, so one of them is very small." He rose to his feet and pointed to one of the planets, setting it spinning. "This one's Saturn. It's the only one I ever used to be able to remember, and that was only because of its rings."

"Is it your favourite?"

"I suppose."

"Was this your room?"

"No," Alastair whispered, looking across at Kevin, and willing himself to talk to the boy as though he really was his son. "I grew up a long way away."

Kevin nodded and muttered, "Me too."

Alastair watched as he turned over onto his side and curled into a ball ready to fall asleep. He took this as his cue to leave and walked to the door.

"Goodnight, Alastair," Kevin murmured.

"God bless, Kevin."

He latched the door and trudged downstairs, his hand tapping the banister as he went. In all, the weekend had gone rather well, and he felt relieved to know that, when Sally-Anne returned next Friday, he would be able to answer with entire honesty that it had been a success. Part of that was owed to Jilly, for the boy seemed to have had a great time with Benji and Tom. He stopped at the bottom of the stairs and rushed to the study as the phone rang.

"Hello?" he panted, relieved he had got to it after only one and a half rings and hoping it hadn't unsettled the boy upstairs. There was silence on the phone. "Hello?" he asked again. A faint whirring, like tiny pieces of metal being scraped together, sounded through the speaker at his ear. "Can I help?" he ventured.

The phone went dead. The long tone sounded, stretching as far ahead as it had come from behind. He returned the receiver to the cradle and frowned. There was something about that sound, something a little familiar, but he couldn't quite put his finger on it.

He found himself jumping at everything as he did the washing-up. If the house creaked or groaned, Alastair would draw in a sharp breath. If anything moved at the window, he would stumble backwards. On one occasion, he found himself clutching a small vegetable knife as the wind made one of the windows rattle slightly. He set it down firmly on the worktop and rebuked himself for his stupidity. Closing all the curtains, he walked up the stairs to his room.

It was a little after ten o'clock by the time he climbed into his own bed, subconsciously reaching his hand across to the empty side of the bed and letting go of a breath he had not realised he was holding.

Alastair jumped awake at the sound of crying. It was violent and interspersed with little panting screams. He climbed out of bed, snatching his dressing gown and moving along the landing to Kevin's room. He opened the door and looked in.

It was dark, but by the light on the landing he could see the boy squirming in the bed. Flicking the light switch, he walked over to the bed and took the sleeping boy's hand in his own.

"It's alright, Kevin," he said, his voice calm and his words a prayer. "You're safe here. It's alright."

Kevin whimpered slightly in his sleep before he sat upright and seized the man before him. Alastair, unsure by this behaviour, especially enveloped in sleep as the boy was, hugged Kevin to him and continued to make soothing noises without speaking any words at all. After a few minutes, without waking up, Kevin settled back to a peaceful sleep.

Alastair returned to his room, leaving the door open so that he could hear if Kevin needed him. Through curiosity, he checked the clock. It was half past twelve. He lay back on the bed, staring up at the ceiling and trying to dispel the sound of the child's tears. They merged into one as he tried to fall asleep, until all the tears he had heard coming from that room became overbearing and he dropped into sleep under the weight of them.

Part Two

The First Week of School

Monday mornings had never been Kevin's favourite time of the week. He had learnt that the most exciting things usually happened on Thursdays. Fridays had always been the day when he moved into his new families, and weekends were invariably the time when his foster carers struggled to find anything to talk to him about, or activities that he would enjoy. He didn't think it was difficult. He considered himself quite an easy-going individual, as happy in front of a TV as any other child, but his favourite thing was exploring the landscape. He loved to go walking, foraging or climbing in the woodlands. But he had only had this opportunity with his adopted family, as his foster homes had been in different towns. There were no trees there, except scraggly ones which lined roads, and were much too high to climb. Every year, the council would come and cut off the lower branches as they tried to grow, not wanting anyone to climb them.

But this Monday morning was even worse. He didn't want to go to school. Another school with other children who singled him out as different, or who would want to know all about the details of his past. He couldn't hide who he was, and he was tired of trying.

He trudged down the stairs and into the kitchen where Alastair was standing eagerly by the breakfast bar. He was wearing the strange collar on his shirt, but was once again dressed in his woolly jumper. He waited until Kevin climbed up on the stool, then he grinned across at him.

"Will it be cereal, or will it be toast?"

"I'm not hungry," Kevin mumbled. "I just want some juice."

Alastair pushed a glass of fresh orange juice towards him. "You told me breakfast was the most important meal of the day. What's happened?"

"I don't want to go to school."

"Why not?" Alastair asked, forcing a smile onto his face and trying to remember that he had to send Kevin to school. "Was that what you were worried about last night?"

"No," Kevin answered, wrinkling his forehead.

Alastair nodded, realising that Kevin did not remember his nightmare at all. "Toast it is, then," he continued. He slotted two slices of white bread into the toaster and, while he was waiting for the bread to toast, he came and sat beside Kevin. "Is there anything you want me to get from town for you, Kevin?"

The boy shook his head.

"Just shoes?"

Kevin nodded.

"Any message for Jilly's mum?"

"Not yet," Kevin answered. "I'll see how today goes."

This answer puzzled Alastair but, before he could address it, the toast leapt up from the toaster and he went to collect them. He spread them with jam and passed the plate over. Neither of them spoke until Kevin had finished eating, at which point they got ready to leave the house. He helped him into the shiny leather shoes and the anorak. He had only known Kevin for a handful of days, but he felt as anxious on his behalf as if he had known him all his life. They left the house with twenty minutes to walk to school, and Kevin looked wistfully at the car in the drive.

"Are we walking?" he mumbled.

"Yes," Alastair replied. "It's only just next door to the church."

Kevin made sure he was on the opposite side of the path to the dogs and looked at Alastair's hand for a moment before he accepted it. Alastair carried the boy's book bag and they walked down the wooded pathway. The rain had knocked several more of the leaves to the ground, making it slippery and Kevin clung tighter to the vicar's hand.

As they passed the house with the dogs, the animals threw themselves at the fence beyond the hedge. Kevin pressed himself against Alastair and hurried past them.

The walk to the end of the path seemed not to

last as long as it had done yesterday, and both Kevin and Alastair silently shared the thought that it was because neither one of them was in a rush to reach its conclusion. While Kevin desperately wanted to avoid another new school, Alastair was constantly reminded of treading the path in other circumstances. They circled the church and Alastair arrived at the school gates, almost dragging Kevin after him.

"Do you want me to come in with you?"

Kevin nodded.

"Okay," Alastair continued, the light-hearted tone doing nothing to comfort the child. He guided Kevin before him, walking through the playground under the eyes of a dozen parents. He felt their surprised gazes on him, but he painted his calm smile over his features and met each of their eyes. The door stood open and he and Kevin walked in.

Almost at once, Mrs Henderson appeared from the office, and Alastair suspected she had been watching their approach on the CCTV which hung down from the corner of the porch. She smiled across at Kevin and Alastair.

"Kevin, I'm so glad I caught you. Do you want to come with me to the classroom and we'll get you settled before the rest of the class arrive? I've made sure you're next to Benji," she continued, walking as she spoke so that Kevin felt obliged to follow her. Reluctant to relinquish his hold on Alastair's hand, he pulled the vicar along behind him. "Did you have a good day with the twins yesterday?"

Kevin nodded.

"I think I'll leave you here, Kevin," Alastair

began. "I'm going into town, Mrs Henderson, but if I'm needed for anything, just give my mobile a ring and I'll get back."

Kevin gripped his hand even tighter but remained silent.

"Mrs Henderson will look after you now, Kevin. And I promise I'll be here to collect you this afternoon."

Alastair squeezed his hand before prising the child's fingers from his own. He walked out of the classroom and along the corridor, feeling torn between guilt and responsibility at leaving Kevin.

"Vicar," a friendly voice called from behind him, and he turned to see a young woman walking forward. "It's not an assembly day, is it?"

"No, Kathryn," he replied. "I was just dropping Kevin off."

"First day." She smiled, her voice becoming overly sensitive and gentle. "That must bring back memories."

"Yes," Alastair returned. He did not volunteer any further words but continued down the corridor and out into the playground. The sky was grey and overcast. The dismal light and the promise of rain matched his mood, and he walked to the gates with a purposeful stride.

"Gosh, it's been a while since I've seen you here, Vicar," cooed an older lady as she approached the gate, shepherding four children before her. "It's got to be three years since."

"Two and a half," Alastair replied, the smile once more affixed to his features. "Doesn't time just fly by, though, Mrs Tannart? Hardly seems a month since." He turned to the children and smiled with greater sincerity. "Last week, Molly! What are your plans for half term?"

"We're going to Wales, Vicar," one of the young girls answered. Her brother nodded in agreement.

"How about you, Coby?"

"I'm off to Grandma's," the boy replied. "Dad's still working, so it'll just be at the end of the week."

"I'm staying at home," the final child replied. "I've got a new game."

Alastair smiled at the childminders flock and watched as they hurried into the school building. "What are your plans for the holiday, Mrs Tannart?"

"My job never stops, just like yours, Vicar." She looked thoughtfully across at him before she added, "That young lad, is it? Finally got him?"

"Yes, Mrs Tannart. It's his first day. I've got to dash, though, I'm going into town." He did not wait to hear her reply, if she even made one, but walked back towards The Vicarage. He stamped his feet along the path, staring down at his shoes. He was lost in his own thoughts, not noticing the people who walked past him. He walked into the house and snatched the car keys, leaving at once and making the drive into town.

Having made his promise to find new shoes for Kevin, he decided he would not eat lunch until he had achieved it. The woman at the shoe shop reluctantly sold him a pair of shoes but pointed out that children's feet were better measured. Alastair nodded and agreed but explained that

Kevin was at school and couldn't miss a day for the sake of new shoes.

"Well, a good fit is very important, sir," she had explained. "You want your son to be comfortable, don't you?"

Her words were still echoing in his head as he travelled across town to the hospital. Parking was always a nightmare there, despite the car park signs announcing more than eight hundred spaces. He could remember that. There was usually a spare chaplain space and today he managed to park there, going to visit the hospital chaplain first, feeling duty bound after taking his space.

The chaplain, Father Levosky, was Catholic. He had taken the role because no one else would, although he was past retirement age but could not leave the sick in a position of spiritual destitution. He had tufts of grey hair and a neatly trimmed grey beard, while the top of his pale head was completely bald. He was capable of putting both patients and families at their ease, regardless of creed. He was something of a rock to Alastair, and the young vicar was grateful of this opportunity to visit him.

"Alastair," he announced, throwing his arms open. "Sneaked into that bay again?"

"I'm afraid so, Father." Alastair smiled. "I'm just visiting one of my parishioners."

"Nurse Macaulay's mother?"

"Yes."

"I saw her yesterday," he went on. "Here with that sister of hers, and three boys. I thought she only had two."

There was something about the inflection in

the man's voice which made Alastair realise he was being led. He nodded slightly but offered no words.

"She's a sweet lady, that Gillian. But I didn't know she had children. Strangest thing is, I'm sure I heard her mention that it was your boy."

"Yes," Alastair began. "I've adopted him."

"Alastair, that is wonderful news," the priest replied, with such conviction that Alastair found his genuine smile returning. "I'm sure you're a great reverend, but you were born to be a father. Of that much, I'm certain."

"I'm not sure God shares your view."

"How many times can we go over this? It's a great thing you've done for this boy."

"I hope so. It seems so strange having a child in the house again."

He and Father Levosky shared a meal of bakery-bought food which Alastair provided, before they parted company. As he reached the door, the father's voice halted him.

"I miss these chats, Alastair. I know it must be a relief to you, but we had some good talks, didn't we? Come and visit again some time."

Alastair nodded and walked out into the hospital, asking at the first ward desk where he might find the old lady he had travelled out to see. He followed the yellow line as it wove along the wall, guiding him ever closer to that place he had sought to forget. Every beep, every click of all the machinery, filled him with a sickened feeling and he forced his steps onward, reminding himself it was not a child who awaited, but an old lady. He continued to the end of the yellow line and opened one of the doors onto the ward.

A nurse sat at the desk and she smiled across at him.

"I'm looking for Hilary Franks," Alastair announced, the faultless smile returning to his face as she smiled back.

"Of course," she replied. "She's just here," she continued, walking around the desk and guiding him through a doorway in the glass walls. "There at the end."

"Thank you," he said, watching as she smiled before returning to her post, which he realised she had not let out of her sight. He walked along the rows of beds, some concealed behind drawn curtains, others empty. At the end, the room opened out into a wide space and in the bed to the right lay the woman he had travelled to see. She turned to him and offered him a smile.

"Vicar," she announced in a voice which, though tired, was clearly articulated. "Reverend Roberts, you didn't have to come all the way out here."

"To see a friend, Mrs Franks, I wanted to."

"Well, I appreciate it," she beamed, watching as he pulled up the chair which sat a small distance away.

"It's quite a room you've got," he said, looking about them before he turned his gaze out of the window and to the trees in the parkland.

"Trish pulled some strings, I think. Wanted to make it so there was plenty of room for her to bring the boys." She looked at the young man through eyes which seemed to stare right through him. "It must have seemed strange to you coming up here. I really appreciate it."

"You've said that already, Mrs Franks,"

Alastair replied, slipping his arms from the coat he wore. "Benji seems to be doing very well at school. Mrs Henderson mentioned him in the report she put into the church magazine."

"Ah," Hilary laughed. "He's a bright little thing, but a rascal with it. Poor Tommy can't keep up with that. I met their new classmate yesterday."

"Stop trying to skate around what you want to say," Alastair laughed.

"I'm so glad you've taken that little one in, Vicar. He needs love, same as us all."

"Same as me, you mean?"

"Two years, Alastair. You deserve to have a little one. And for all an old woman's view might count to you, I'm proud of you for taking little Kevin in."

Alastair smiled and took her hand in both of his own. "It's worth a great deal, Mrs Franks. But that's enough of me. How are you feeling?"

"You know better than to ask me that," she laughed.

"Jilly thought you'd be home for Christmas."

"Dear little Jilly," Hilary smiled. "She doesn't think that at all, Vicar. She hopes it. I do too, but I expect I'll be back in the home for a while."

"She wants to look after you, Mrs Franks."

"She's enough on," came the short reply. "I don't want her constantly worrying over me, sneaking into the room to check I'm still breathing. I did all that for my husband, as you did for Leonard. It's exhausting."

"But would either of us have swapped it?" he asked. "I know I wouldn't."

"No, Vicar. My mind is made up." She turned away from him for a moment, and Alastair sat silently, waiting for her to face him once more. "She's a little dreamer, Vicar. My little Jilly. She sees the best in all people and all situations. I'm worried she won't cope when I'm gone. Will you look after her?"

"As much as I can." Alastair smiled across at her. "But don't be going anywhere yet, Mrs Franks."

"I want to see Jilly happy, Vicar. And know that Benji and Tommy have their paths before them. I don't want them in the Forces like their dad."

"Did you have a good time yesterday?"

"Yes," Hilary said, smiling. "Benji's taken a bit of a shine to Kevin, I think. He always loved Leonard, you know."

"I remember," Alastair whispered.

Hilary smiled at him. "When you came, I was surprised by how young you were. Everything that happened since just made me realise you were too young to suffer it. But I've never questioned you as my priest."

"Any age is too young to lose a child." Alastair looked around the room and let his eyes settle on the toys Benji and Tom had left the day before. "I've got to get back to school," he said, returning the smile to his face. "But is there anything I can do or get for you, Mrs Franks?"

"No, Vicar. I'm just so pleased for you."

Alastair smiled across at her and tried to summon up the strength she believed he had. "I'll be back to see you soon."

"No, Vicar," she repeated. "You don't want to be visiting here. Wait until I'm home again."

"We'll see."

He arrived back at the school gates with two minutes to spare before the bell sounded. It was an old-fashioned system, one of the eldest children walking through the corridor ringing the old hand bell, and the secretary unlocked the door and stood back to allow the children out. Alastair's shoes were caked in mud from having run up the small path, and the bottom of his trouser legs were splattered. The car drive home had given him all the time he needed to order his thoughts and shelve the memories his visit to the hospital had brought him. There was no place in his outward existence for the sorrow which existed in his heart.

The other parents at the gate turned to watch him as he ran up, but by the time he arrived he didn't care what they thought. Jilly was there, waiting to collect Benji and Tom, and she smiled across at him. He leaned against the brick column and tried to get his breath back. It had been a long time since he had done any running. Jilly waved him over to her.

"Hello Vicar," she began as Alastair walked over. She was standing with Kate Humphries and Leona Johnson. Both of them smiled across at him and Leona laughed.

"You're looking a little out of shape, Vicar," she began, folding her arms under her chest. "Time to make the most of that gym membership."

"I'd love to," Alastair laughed. "But I suspect the shock of walking into the building would be enough to exhaust me."

He was cautious of Leona. She had just divorced her third husband and had collected something of a reputation in the village of taking on any single man under the age of forty. Alastair was never sure whether she hoped he was going to be the next one.

"I heard you've taken in a little boy, Vicar," Kate said, her smile deep and sincere. "That's wonderful."

"I think so," agreed Jilly.

"Thank you," Alastair said, looking down at his feet and noticing for the first time the state of his footwear.

All of them turned as the door to the school opened and a dozen children poured out. There was a moment that he was unsure who he had arrived at the school to collect. He stood staring at the children and waiting for one to claim him. At the end of this happy rabble came Kevin. He kicked his feet along the ground but was being pulled forward by Benji. Leona was already leaving with her two children, while Kate waited for her youngest to leave. Kevin looked sideways at her as he walked past and spared a noncommittal wave for Benji as he went to greet Jilly.

"Hello," Alastair beamed, trying to counter the look of tiredness on Kevin's face. "How was school?"

"Long," Kevin mumbled. "Can we go back to the house, now?"

Alastair nodded and parted company with Kate and Jilly, trudging round the church and onto the muddy lane beyond. There had been flagstones laid several years earlier, but they were almost all covered over now. Kevin didn't talk. He refused to take Alastair's offered hand and only walked beside him as they passed the noisy dogs. Alastair continued to try and make conversation, but Kevin only shrugged his shoulders or murmured inaudible words. He walked two paces behind Alastair almost all the way, and when they reached The Vicarage he trudged in and kicked off the shiny leather shoes without untying them. Alastair reached down to pick them up, watching as Kevin flopped onto the sofa and stared out of the French windows. The soles of the shoes were caked in mud, but he cradled them in his left hand, carefully unfastening the laces with his right. Each knot he teased out pulled at his heart. He marched through to the living room, determined to confront the boy, but the words melted from his lips as his gaze focused on the child.

Kevin was leaning forward. He had abandoned staring out of the window and instead gripped his hair tightly in his little hands. Alastair dropped the shoes and brushed the mud from his hand down the front of his trousers before he reached over and eased the boy's hands free from his hair.

"Do you want to help make some dinner, Kevin?" he asked, choosing to ignore the child's beetroot face. "What do you fancy?"

Kevin looked up and felt his angry frustration subside a little as Alastair patiently smiled down at him. He nodded slightly and took Alastair's offered hand. The vicar pulled him to his feet and let the boy lean against him, all the while feeling torn between whatever was upsetting Kevin and the boy's disregard for the sanctity of the shoes he had discarded. He guided Kevin into the kitchen and pulled open the fridge.

"We've got mince, and we can mash some potatoes. Or we've got sausages, and we can heat up some baked beans. Or, if you really want it, I can brave the fryer and we'll just have a plate of chips each."

Kevin nodded and the corners of his mouth twitched slightly.

"Chips, then?" Alastair asked, trying to coax the boy to talk to him.

"Yes, please."

"And you know what?" Alastair continued, feeling relieved giddiness strike him so hard that he found himself laughing. "Cheese is amazing on chips."

"Cheese?" Kevin repeated, the twisted corners of his mouth turning into a smile.

Alastair nodded and closed the fridge before reaching into the freezer and pulling out the packet of chips. He looked at the label in the pretence of reading it, but he was only using it as a way of steadying his thoughts.

"Can you reach into that cupboard, Kevin? There's a big circular tub. That's the fryer. Would you get it out for me, please?"

Kevin did as he asked and carefully lifted the fryer onto the worktop. "Why do you keep it in a cupboard?" he asked after a moment.

"I don't really like using it," Alastair conceded, pushing the chips back into the freezer and turning to face the boy. "But I'm happy to make an exception today. It's been an exceptional day, after all."

They sat down together, Kevin drinking orange juice and Alastair hugging a mug of tea, before Alastair began broaching the topic of school once more.

"Did you get any homework?"

Kevin shook his head.

"So what were you learning about today?"

His question was met with shrugged shoulders.

"When I was your age," he continued, attempting another approach. "My favourite lessons were art and music."

"I like music," Kevin muttered. "And science. I love science."

"Science?" Alastair repeated, trying not to sound surprised. "Did you do any science today?"

"No. No one wants to learn there. They just want to talk."

"You must have learnt something, Kevin."

"Numeracy."

Alastair gave up on the subject of school, walking into his study and picking up the ringing phone. Kevin listened to the murmur of Alastair's voice, unable to hear anything of what was being said beyond his gentle tone. Alastair was tireless in his patience. It was something Kevin appreciated, but it confused him. None of his foster carers had ever been like that. There was a hope in him which was beginning to rise to the surface. If Alastair was so different, perhaps he would break the curse Kevin seemed to carry. Perhaps the last person had died at his hands.

Alastair walked back into the living room several minutes later, collecting the shoes and cleaning the dirt from them before tucking them once more into the cupboard. Kevin had fallen asleep on the sofa, curled in on himself and clutching the little wooden horse. He looked so peaceful, Alastair simply stood and watched him, before the onset of evening inspired him to light the open fire. It would be the first blaze of the season. It had always been a special time to him, marking the march towards Christmas.

He struck the match in his hand and reached forward to catch the crumpled newspaper. The flames leapt beneath the coals as Alastair watched them, thinking about the words Sally-Anne had shared about the boy behind him. Flames caressed the black coals, smoke slipping upward around them. He pushed himself to his feet and collected the small mesh fireguard, placing it in front of the fireplace.

The sun was setting when Kevin woke up, but it wasn't that which first struck him. Tall orange flames were roaring up the chimney in front of him and he cried out, leaping to his feet and running into the kitchen to find Alastair pouring sunflower oil into the fryer.

"What is it?" Alastair asked, setting the bottle down and wrapping his arm around the boy while Kevin gripped a handful of Alastair's jumper.

"Fire," he whispered.

"It's okay," came the soothing reply. "It's our fire, and we're in control of it."

"Are you in control of everything here, Alastair?" Kevin asked in a small voice.

"Not everything. But I put my trust in God that He'll make all things right."

After a few minutes Kevin released his hold on the priest and sat at the breakfast bar, watching as Alastair tipped a generous portion of chips into the fryer's basket. Next, Alastair collected a block of cheese and began grating it into a small bowl.

"I didn't like school," Kevin said after a time. "All the kids are strange."

"All of them?" Alastair asked, trying to decide whether or not he was pleased Kevin was opening up about his day.

"Not Benji. But there's a boy who just kept calling me a name all day, and everyone else laughed as though it was funny."

"What sort of name?"

"Leonard."

Alastair felt his hand meet with the razor-sharp grater and he looked down at the blood on the side of his thumb. Walking to the sink, he felt the cold water bring him back to his senses, but it was so sharp his head spun.

"Who laughed?" he whispered.

Kevin turned to look at him. The calm smile had gone, and the vicar's eyes flashed and flared as much as the fire in the living room. Kevin shrugged his shoulders, frightened by this change. Seeing this expression, Alastair tried to steady his thoughts and gave a weak laugh.

"I hope that's enough cheese. I've made a bit of a mess of my hand."

Kevin nodded and watched as Alastair wrapped a wide plaster across his hand, moving over to the fryer and retrieving the chips as the light changed colour.

"Well, you're not a lot like Leonard," Alastair said, setting a plate full of chips in front of the boy. "He would have chosen sausages every day of the week, for a start."

"Who is he?" Kevin asked. "Why was everyone comparing me to him?"

"He was the little boy whose shoes you

were wearing," Alastair continued, seizing the opportunity to turn the conversation away from Leonard. "But I've got you some new shoes now. Shoes of your own."

"Thank you," Kevin replied with a smile.

The sharing of this conversation seemed to have set Kevin's mind at rest and, although every time school was mentioned he grimaced, the boy seemed content simply to imagine the school didn't exist.

Alastair, on the other hand, lay awake on the sofa, reluctant to go to the bed where no one waited for him, and considered all Kevin had told him. Looking at the glowing embers, he repeatedly sighed as a way of keeping his eyes dry. He stared up at the ceiling, begging and pleading silently with God. Why would anyone compare Kevin to Leonard? Surely he was the sole similarity. Leonard hadn't been to school in two and a half years, and everyone knew why. How could anyone think it was funny? And then afterwards…

Alastair sat up and looked across to the French windows. Did it all boil down to what Mrs Franks had said? Was he too young for the job? It was true that nothing had tested his faith so greatly as the past twenty-four months. And if there was a God, why didn't He care?

The hollow feeling seized him once more and he shook his head. It was late, and all he really needed was to sleep. To sleep and forget the past. Kevin was his future, and the boy was suffering because of Alastair's own past. He wouldn't let that happen.

The next morning, Kevin trudged down the

stairs to find Alastair in the kitchen again. The toast was already spread with jam and there was fresh orange juice sitting next to the plate. The man's irrepressible smile was on his face once more, but the plaster on his hand was a reminder of his slip yesterday. Kevin was intrigued about Leonard, determined to discover who he was. If he was going to be given the boy's name, he wanted to know why.

"I've got a service at nine," Alastair said, his cheerful tone raising the slightest smile on Kevin's face. "But Jilly will be here in a minute, and I asked her to walk you to school. Do you mind?"

"No," Kevin replied, brushing crumbs from his sky-blue uniform. "Thank you for the shoes."

"You're welcome," Alastair answered. "Today at school, talk to everyone once, and then you'll know who you want to stay with. I think Benji quite likes you."

"He's nice. And he's funny."

"And remember, you'll be home again by four. I'll make sure I'm there to pick you up."

Kevin nodded and turned as the doorbell sounded, watching as Alastair walked over, a positive spring in his step, to open the door. Jilly smiled across, her own expression as enthusiastic as the vicar's, while Kevin made hurried goodbyes as Alastair dashed out the door.

"Benji loved having you at school yesterday," she began, helping Kevin into his anorak. "He and Tom usually get defined by each other."

"What do you mean?"

"Most people just see them as one half of the

twins. In fact, most people can't tell them apart."

"I can," Kevin beamed. "Tom has a thinner nose than Benji, and Benji smiles a lot more."

"Right on both counts," Jilly laughed. "Benji was so proud to be able to show off his new friend yesterday."

"Who was that?"

"You," she chuckled. "Did you enjoy yesterday?"

"Not really," he answered honestly, and watched as her smile fell. "But I know today will be much better. Alastair told me what to do."

"Ah," Jilly replied, a different smile on her face. "The vicar is a very smart man."

She guided Kevin out and they walked together, talking about everything they saw to interest them. Kevin found a conker someone had dropped, and Jilly promised to take him hunting for conkers if Alastair would let him. She always called him Vicar, as though it was his name and not his job. Kevin continued to call him Alastair, but discovered it was much easier to address him as Vicar at school, or even Reverend Roberts, otherwise none of the class knew who he meant.

The morning was better. At lunchtime, however, three of the boys began tormenting him, laughing at him and telling him he was only a replacement for Leonard.

"I think the vicar's just traded in Leonard," one laughed.

"I'm not sure he got a good bargain," another replied. "This one might last a bit longer, though."

"I'm not Leonard," Kevin snapped, staring at the three of them. One was his own age, but the other two were the year older. "But I can curse people," he continued, his eyes burning. "Everyone I know says so."

"Is that why no one wants you," chimed the third boy.

"I want him," Benji snapped back. Clenching his little fist, he hit out at one of the older boys.

The fight escalated in seconds. Within moments, the entire upper school were either fighting or watching. One of the dinner ladies blew a whistle, and the crowd divided, but the three other boys continued to beat Benji and Kevin. Mrs Henderson stepped in, marching between them and silencing the hall with a glare.

Kevin hugged Benji, whose lip was bleeding and who shook with tears. All five of them were marched to the headteacher's office and parents were immediately called.

Alastair was sitting at the chair in his study, knowing what he should be doing but reading through the file about Kevin instead. He stared at the forms and tried to make sense of all the deaths which stared back at him. Kevin had been terrified of the fire yesterday. He couldn't have been the cause of them. The boy still jumped when Alastair lit the gas hob or struck a match.

He looked up as Jilly knocked on the open door and walked in carrying a cup. She had her hair covered in a scarf as she always did when she was cleaning. He couldn't understand why. The house really wasn't that dirty. She set the cup down, positioning the saucer so it wasn't sitting on top of any of the papers.

"How was the service this morning?"

"Good," Alastair replied, thanking her for the tea.

"I didn't hear you coming back in," she giggled. "I would have made you a drink earlier."

"I just had things to get on with." He scooped up the pages of Kevin's file and slotted them all away. "I love Tuesday services. They're uncomplicated."

"And unsung," she whispered.

"That's not what it is, Jilly," he replied, sitting back on the chair and rubbing his hands over his face. "No," he continued from behind his hands. "Of course that's what it is. I had an awful dream last night."

"What happened?"

"I was a child, but I was here. Out in the garden. I was trying to reach one of the apples on the tree." He lowered his hands to find her sympathetic eyes watching him. "Oh, it's stupid," he muttered.

"It wasn't your fault, Vicar," Jilly said. "Is it so bad that we make someone's final moments full of something they want more than anything?"

Alastair took in a deep breath which released over several seconds. "I shouldn't have taken in Kevin."

"Adopted," Jilly corrected him. "Of course you should. Benji loves him. Besides, little Kevin deserves a chance at life, doesn't he? And he'll get one here."

Alastair looked across at Jilly and reminded himself of the promise he had made her mother. This was exactly the thing he had tried to avoid, and for almost two years he had succeeded. He was meant to be a rock for her and for all his congregation, but he had slipped into his own despondency, bitter and sorrowful. The smile returned to his face and, though he tasted it as a lie, Jilly seemed convinced.

"Kevin loves Benji, too. I think he's the only thing which made yesterday bearable." He reached for the phone as it rang and Jilly quickly hurried from the room, not wanting to pry, and certainly not wanting to look like she was.

"Mrs Henderson," Alastair began cheerfully as the woman announced who she was.

"I wonder if you could come into school, Vicar," her clipped voice echoed. "There's been a little altercation."

"Altercation?" Alastair repeated, having to work on making his voice sound. Mrs Henderson was usually full of smiles and friendliness, but she sounded decidedly cold today. "Kevin?"

"Yes. He and some other boys were involved in a fight. I'm sure I don't need to tell you that we won't tolerate that here."

"I'm on my way," he said, rising to his feet as he set the phone down. He rushed out of the study and snatched his coat. Jilly watched through wide eyes as she stepped out of the unused dining room, but she remained silent as she watched him leave the house.

He rushed along the footpath, smiling at the dog-walkers he passed, but offering no words. He walked around the church and through the school gates beyond. Ringing the buzzer, he waited as the secretary, Kathryn, opened the door. She looked embarrassed as she stepped back to let him in.

"What happened?" he asked.

"Mrs Henderson is waiting in her office. She knows more about it than me, Vicar. But I don't think it was Kevin's fault."

"It never occurred to me that it would be," he answered honestly. "Thanks, Mrs Wood."

He walked to the little office which had a child's scrawled writing on a sign saying "Headteacher Mrs Henderson" on the door. Knocking three times, he pushed open the door and looked at the faces which met him. Mrs Henderson's was angry, but the five children all looked nervous or guilty. Kevin lowered his gaze while Benji's eyes brimmed with tears and he began to cry.

"Thank you for coming down here, Vicar," Mrs Henderson began. "Kevin, tell Reverend Roberts what happened."

"They said no one wanted me," Kevin mumbled. "That I was a replacement for Leonard."

Alastair bit his lips together in an expression the children all seemed to believe was anger, but Alastair was focusing all his efforts on dismissing the feeling of guilt which sprang in him. He had just shared almost this exact conversation with Jilly.

"Benji stuck up for me." Kevin looked across at the teary boy.

"I see," Alastair whispered. "Mrs Henderson, are the children going back to class?"

Mrs Henderson looked at him, seeing what he was hinting at. "They will all be having their lunches in the classroom for the remainder of the week, and each one will write a letter of apology to the others." She walked to the door and ushered the children out. "Get along," she commanded, and Alastair was unsure if it was a request for them to move or to resolve their differences. He waited until she shut the door before he sat down, waiting for her to do the same.

"What really happened, Mrs Henderson?" he asked.

"What Kevin told you. They all agree."

"Why were they allowed to say those things?" Alastair heard the disbelief in his own voice.

"Kevin told them he would curse them, Vicar. That's not the sort of thing I think children should be saying."

"Why were they talking about Leonard?" Alastair demanded, feeling the woman was coming at the problem with a heavy bias towards the other side of the argument. "And how could they say no one wanted Kevin?"

"They all remember Leonard," came the reply. "We shouldn't forget him."

"No," Alastair agreed, his face dropping into disgust. "But I'd rather you didn't use him as a weapon."

Mrs Henderson's expression altered, and she suddenly seemed to see the man before her as a human instead of a title. "I'm sorry, Vicar," she said with utter contrition. "I hadn't seen it like that." She paused for a moment before she asked, "Have you told Kevin about Leonard?"

"Not really," he replied.

"Perhaps you should. Then, what was felt as a weapon might become a badge of honour."

Alastair rose to his feet. "I'll see you on Friday, Mrs Henderson."

"Thank you, Vicar. The children love your assemblies."

He smiled, his shield against the world returning to his face, and walked to the door. He turned as he opened it. "I didn't notice any other parents coming in."

"I rang them, Vicar," came the self-assured reply.

Alastair nodded, the gesture hiding all manner of thoughts which flashed through his head. He left the school and walked through to the graveyard at the back of the church, sighing as he looked across at one of the headstones, reaching forward to trace his hand across the letters which formed the name Leonard. The indentation on the stone felt rough beneath his fingertips, but he could almost imagine the little hand taking his own. He smiled slightly, shaking his head, before he moved back to the path and walked slowly back to The Vicarage.

Jilly rushed downstairs as she heard the front door open, and she smiled across in relief to find him.

"I'm just on with the bathroom," she said jovially, seeing only the eternal smile on his face. "You wouldn't believe what a mess boys can make of bathrooms."

"Jilly," he said, causing her to turn as she began climbing the stairs again. "Do you want some lunch?"

"I've had mine," she replied, walking over and staring thoughtfully at him. "Are you alright, Vicar?"

"Fine," he replied. "Kevin got into a fight."

"Is he okay?" Jilly asked. "What was it about?"

"He's fine. Benji -"

"Benji?" Her voice became frantic. "What

happened?"

"They told him no one wanted him," Alastair chewed his lower lip thoughtfully. "And that he was a substitute for Leonard."

"Benji said that?" she demanded.

"No. Benji stuck up for Kevin. Anyway, Jilly, Mrs Henderson will sort it."

Alastair met Kevin from school that afternoon and walked back in silence. He oversaw the boy writing his letters of apology to the other children and made sure he read all of the other children's letters to him the following day. There was no reference in them to the curse, but every night Alastair sat at the desk in the study and read through the boy's file, cover to cover, trying to put some sense back into Kevin's tumultuous existence. All the fires, all the deaths, they all began with his father when Kevin had been a baby.

There was very little in the file, but Alastair had found a news report online about the incident. The van which was transferring Harry Alderman had caught fire and the driver had lost control, veering from the road and into a ravine below. There was a picture of the burnt-out shell of the van. Only one body had ever been recovered, the others being carried away by the river. After that, Melanie Alderman had died ensuring her young son's safety, and then Kevin had been adopted by Liam and Stacy Fletcher, and the file began in earnest.

On Wednesday and Thursday, Kevin settled into school and the fight drifted to the back of the children's memories. Alastair had returned to the usual duties of his vocation, travelling around the parishes, visiting people. He took Kevin with him to the church Youth Club in Little Golforth on the Thursday evening and watched with a growing affection as one of the teenagers tried teaching Kevin how to play pool. The cue was almost as tall as he was, but Alastair and he teamed up to beat the two boys.

Kevin loved the Youth Club. All the children were older than him and, barring one girl who spent the whole evening chomping gum, all of them loved teaching him how to play the games, or mix the non-alcoholic cocktails behind the bar. Alastair found himself enjoying the Youth Club far more than he usually did, watching as Kevin went from one to another of the young people, each pleased to have his company.

On the journey back, though, Kevin fell asleep in the passenger seat. He was still asleep when they reached The Vicarage and, reluctant to wake the boy, Alastair opened the house door before collecting Kevin in his arms and carrying him indoors.

As Kevin sleepily wrapped his arms about Alastair's neck, the priest hugged the child to him. He could remember Leonard doing the same thing, instinctively clinging to him while Alastair had carried him up the stairs to bed. But Leonard had been a lot thinner than Kevin was, so Alastair opted to place the sleeping boy on the sofa and fetch the astronaut bedding from the room upstairs, wrapping it over Kevin. He lit the fire and sat on the rug, leaning back on the sofa.

His eyes continued to travel to the large window and, concerned by the reason for this, he rose to his feet and walked over to pull the curtains closed. The apple tree stared back at him as he shut it out, reminding him of life's cycle, with all its hope and all its cruelty. He turned back as Kevin made a sleepy noise, snuggling further into the covers. Alastair walked through to the kitchen area and placed the kettle on the hob, turning the gas and clicking for the spark. The smell of gas seeped into the room and the flame refused to light. He turned the ring off and opened the window, dispelling the fumes. The story of Kevin's third foster carers came back to him, the gas explosion which had torn out the back of the house with the force of it, and he looked at the fire in the hearth.

"I don't believe in curses." He was repeating the words as though they were his mantra as he walked through to the front door and locked it.

He spent the evening in the deep chesterfield armchair. When he had been Kevin's age, he had never been able to sleep sitting up, but in his line of work, on call every hour of the day, he had learnt to seize sleep whenever and wherever he could. He always dreamed, though. Bad dreams, bleaker even than the events of two years ago, for in them he had no hope and had given in to utter despair. He was surprised to find that he was woken up by a gentle hand on his arm, and as he reached across to take it, he felt little fingers beneath his own.

It was still dark outside beyond the curtain, and he forced his eyes to try and focus on the boy beside him. He was surprised to find, although it was Leonard who had occupied his dreams, it was Kevin who stood there.

"Is it bedtime?" he asked sleepily.

"Past bedtime," Alastair replied. "Do you want to go upstairs?"

Kevin shook his head and, instead of returning to the sofa, he curled up on Alastair's knee and pulled the blanket about them both.

Friday arrived with great excitement for Kevin. It was the last day of school before the week off. He and Alastair walked along the path, and Kevin chatted away as they went. There was rain, but it was light enough so that the canopy of bronzed leaves overhead kept them both fairly dry. They arrived at the school with one minute to spare, and Alastair watched as Kevin ran over to where Benji was in the corner of the playground. He walked into the school with a renewed spring in his step, feeling relieved by the image of Kevin so happy.

He poked his head around the office door and smiled across at Kathryn.

"Vicar," she began, rising to her feet and walking over. "We've had a bit of chaos with the school hall, so will you be alright going into each class separately?"

"Oh dear," he said, unable to hide his jovial tone behind the mask of concern. "What happened?"

"The roof's leaking. We got in this morning to find we'd got a paddling pool rather than an assembly hall. It's okay, though," she continued, smiling up at him. "The council's found us an interim caretaker who's going to oversee the workers over the holiday."

"What happened to Billy?"

"He broke his leg on Wednesday night,"

Kathryn explained, handing over a visitor badge to the priest. "Outside The Green Man, so we're keeping it a bit quiet from the children."

Alastair nodded, feeling the smile could not be shaken from his features. He followed Kathryn to the infant classroom, the secretary making sure he had everything he needed. He only ran assemblies at the end of each half term, with occasional extra ones as and when he was needed. When he first arrived he had done one every fortnight, but with frequent travelling in and out of town to visit the hospital, the assemblies had been the first thing to go. The school had been very understanding of this, but the assemblies had never resumed their regular spots. There was no singing either. He used to start and finish with little hymns for little singers, but that had gone now. Instead, Jilly went in on a Friday afternoon and played piano for them to sing their praise songs.

Both assemblies went well, and Alastair gained a particular satisfaction in how pleased Kevin was to share his class with him. It was not until lunchtime that he made his way along the path, smiling with genuine sincerity at everyone he passed, but having to remind himself that Sally-Anne was visiting at two o'clock. He stepped into The Vicarage, hung up the scarf he had been wearing and walked into the study to check the phone messages. The automatic voice on the answer machine announced there was one new message and he clicked through to hear it.

He had hoped it might be Sally-Anne telling him she couldn't make their meeting. After all, she had a fifty-minute drive to get there. Instead, it sounded like a call centre, with chattering in the background. He was about to hang up when he heard a soft grinding sound. He had already committed to pressing the delete button, but there was something familiar about the sound which he wished he could listen to again. Dismissing these sombre thoughts, he walked through to the kitchen. He paused to watch as Ysolde scampered across the long arm of the apple tree, gathering the nuts from the feeder which hung there.

After watching her for several minutes, he moved over to the electric kettle and flicked the switch. He hadn't used the hob since last night, reluctant to meet the same fate as Foster Family Three.

Sally-Anne arrived at twenty-three seconds after two o'clock. Her punctuality was both exhausting and welcome, as he couldn't face the prospect of continuing to pace the carpet for much longer. He pulled open the door and smiled across at the woman. She returned the gesture and reached her hand forward.

"Reverend Roberts," she announced, and Alastair nodded as though he was answering a question. "How are we doing?"

"Fine, thank you," he beamed, letting her into the house. "Come on through, I've got the kettle on."

She walked into the living room and took a seat on the sofa, raising her eyebrow slightly at the folded quilt on the armchair. Her bright red lips, painted on in a greasy gloss, refused to smile as she glanced across at the stack of books which Kevin had been reading a few nights earlier, and

Alastair felt judged by each expression she gave or made.

"Two sugars wasn't it?" he called across.

"Good memory, Reverend Roberts," she said in an impressed tone. He brought through a tray with two mugs of tea and a plate of biscuits.

"If there's one thing the church is very good at, it's tea and biscuits," he said, trying to prepare himself for whatever the woman was about to throw at him.

"I didn't expect to find that in a clergyman," she answered with a smile. "More the wife, I suppose."

"Yes," Alastair replied. "Dawn was very good at it. She knew exactly which mugs would go with which plate, and exactly which biscuits fitted which saucer. Not bad for an American."

"How have you and Kevin been getting on?" Sally-Anne asked, realising that Dawn was a topic she was not welcome to discuss at this time.

"Brilliantly," Alastair said. "Not perfectly, but brilliantly. He's a lovely boy, in spite of his shaky start."

"Sleeping downstairs?" she muttered, pointing to the quilt.

"Not normally. I took him out to an event last night and I couldn't carry him upstairs." He paused and frowned slightly. "Is it bad to sleep downstairs?"

"We often find that children in Kevin's situation feel safer if they have their own room. And they tend to respond better to maintaining a normality to their routine."

"There's nothing normal about my routine,"

Alastair said, his smile returning. "But Kevin wasn't unsettled this morning."

"And what about school?" she asked, ignoring the way he challenged her. "How's he getting on there? All his other schools have been much bigger."

"He had a little disagreement," Alastair conceded, convinced that the woman already knew. "But he's settled in now. He's made friends, he loves the area. Everything is going really well."

Sally-Anne produced a notebook and began making a few notes, before she smiled back. "And the fire?"

"What fire?"

"Have you had any incidents with fire?"

"Well, that's just the thing," he began. "He's terrified of fire. It's like he really believes in this curse you've told him he has. And he's told the children at school too, which got him into a bit of trouble. He's not responsible for the fires. He can't be."

Sally-Anne sighed and shook her head. "I've heard others, more experienced carers than you, plead this about Kevin Alderman. But they're dead now or lost someone close to them. Just keep him away from fire."

Alastair had never spent a more uncomfortable afternoon. He was grateful for the reprieve of collecting Kevin from school. He invited Sally-Anne to remain in the house but locked the study door. Being out in the open air allowed him to regain the feeling of contentment he had lost during Sally-Anne's visit, and the smile he felt on his face was now one of relief. Kevin, he was pleased to find, was in high spirits, at least by the boy's standards. Alastair had still not observed the deep smile he was hoping to conjure, but he felt he was getting closer every day.

On their return to The Vicarage, Alastair hung back in the kitchen listening as Kevin told Sally-Anne everything he had done since arriving last Friday. Kevin missed nothing, even going into the incident on Tuesday lunchtime. This raised a new conversation for them, and Sally-Anne asked him about Leonard, while Kevin answered honestly that he didn't know who the boy was. Sally-Anne knew, of course. Alastair had been forced to relive every aspect of Leonard's story before he had been allowed to adopt Kevin.

"Well," Sally-Anne said as the clock chimed quarter past four. "I'd better be making tracks. Is that your squirrel there, Kevin?"

Kevin ran to the French windows and smiled. "She's called Ysolde," he announced, watching as the squirrel darted, with a curved back, up and down the tree.

"Reverend Roberts," Sally-Anne continued, walking out of the room and waiting for Alastair to catch her up. "Thank you," she said with utter gratitude. "I've been working with Kevin Alderman for six years, and I've never seen him so sharp, so engaged."

"He's a lovely kid," Alastair replied. "He just needs love, like I said."

"When are you going to tell him about your son?"

The bluntness of this question struck him, and the smile slid into disbelief. "Why is everyone in such a rush for me to tell him? There isn't a happy ending there."

"Not for me," Sally-Anne pointed out. "I'm an atheist. But I thought you believed in life after death. He respects you, Reverend Roberts. Respect him enough to tell him."

Alastair felt like he was being derided and belittled in this chiding, but there was a hint of truth to the inference Sally-Anne was making. Kevin did deserve to know why the children at school compared him to a child called Leonard. He saw her to the door, his usual smile resting on his face to mask those thoughts. As soon as the door was closed, however, he gave a heavy sigh and walked back through to where Kevin stood, his hand resting on the glass of the window and his face lit up.

"I thought she'd forgotten us."

Alastair wasn't sure whether Kevin meant Sally-Anne or Ysolde, but he nodded. "Holidays now, Kevin."

Kevin nodded and held Alastair's hand as they both watched through the window to where Ysolde leapt along the branches of the apple tree. Both of them had their heads full of thoughts, both excited and bleak, but while they held one another's hand they each found a certain amount of strength in the gesture. The holidays had arrived and they commended themselves for surviving their first week together.

Part Three

The October holiday

There was a lazy start to the Saturday morning which marked the first day of the holiday. At least, it was lazy for Kevin. After sleeping fully clothed and shod under the quilt the night before, Alastair had changed the bedding for him. It was still space themed, but instead of blue with astronauts, this was red and orange with planets on. There was always something especially comfortable about sleeping in a newly changed bed and, perhaps because of this, it took Kevin until nine o'clock to slot his feet into his slippers and plod downstairs.

He shuffled through to the kitchen, expecting to find Alastair there, but he was alone. There was a sheet of A4 paper with notes in the priest's handwriting. Kevin picked it up as he saw his name on the top.

"Good morning, Kevin," he mumbled, following the excessive curves of the penmanship with his finger. "I left toast in the toaster, and a glass of juice in the fridge. I've gone to find-" Kevin paused as he tried to form the word, but it looked unlike any he had ever seen. At the bottom of the page was a big X.

Kevin felt dropped. He had been left. He slumped over to the toaster and pulled down the controls, before sliding across the kitchen tiles to the fridge. Opening it, he lifted the tumbler and looked down at the red squirrel on it as he shuffled back to the breakfast bar. He climbed up onto the stool and rested his head on his hands.

"Just me, Vicar," a cheerful voice called from the front door, and Kevin walked around to see Jilly's mass of red hair. She was taking her shoes off, leaning over to do so, so that her hair was all he could see of her.

"He's gone," Kevin replied.

"Hello, Kevin," she continued, sounding as pleased to see him as she would have been to see Alastair. "What do you mean, gone? The car's still here, and there was no one in the church. I've only just come past it."

"Look," Kevin continued, guiding Jilly into the kitchen where his toast had popped, and showing her the note. "He left me."

"Ysolde?" Jilly asked. "Who's Ysolde?"

"Oh," Kevin continued, his face brightening at the sound of this name. "She's the squirrel who lives in the garden."

"There you are, then," Jilly replied, smiling across. "He'll be waiting for you out in the garden. But don't go out without getting dressed first. It's pretty chilly out there."

"Do you want some toast?"

"No, thank you, Kevin. I'm here to tidy the study, really. That's why I come on every second Saturday. I do the rest of the house on a Tuesday, but the vicar has Saturdays off, so I clean and tidy the study then."

"He's very lucky to have you," Kevin said.

"We're lucky to have him."

Kevin nodded. He collected his toast and spread it with more raspberry jam than Alastair usually put on.

"It's locked," Jilly called back through from the hall. "He never normally locks it."

"Will you read me a story?" Kevin asked, looking across at Jilly, ignoring her confusion.

"Don't you want to go out in the garden?"

Kevin gave a neutral grunt and trudged back up the stairs. He listened as the washing machine in the utility room began purring, and the smell of detergent drifted up to him. He made his bed and pulled open the curtains to his room. The window stared out across the expansive garden and, through the tangle of branches, he could make out the church on the high ground at the end of the path. He could see Alastair too. He was raking up the fallen leaves, shovelling them across to the compost heap against the garden wall.

A few minutes later, Kevin appeared downstairs to find Jilly washing his breakfast pots and wiping down the crumbs from the breakfast bar.

"Why do you do all this for Alastair?" he asked.

"He does pay me," she laughed. "It's not exactly slave labour."

"But he can cook and clean for himself."

"I needed some money when Mum got ill. So he said I could help him out around the house, and he'd pay me."

"How long ago was that?"

"More than a year and less than two," she replied. "I can't really remember now. But it was after-" she stopped and looked sideways at Kevin. "Well, less than two years ago." She smiled across, her face cheerful and laughing again. "But what do you think of The Vicarage, Kevin? Have you explored the rooms?"

"Alastair doesn't want me to go into the study. But I've been in here, and upstairs in my room, and the bathroom is my own."

"Have you been in the dining room?" she asked.

Kevin shook his head.

"There is the most stunning tea service," Jilly continued. "It belonged to the vicar's mother. Come and see it."

She held her hand out to him and he took it, while she guided him to the door opposite the stairs. She pushed open the door and stood back to let him in. The room was as different to the living room as he could imagine. There was nothing modern here, except the light fitting overhead. There were tall silver candlesticks akin to those he had seen in scary films, and all the furniture was so dark it was almost black. He reached out to the enormous table and ran his hand along it. Jilly pointed back to the wall.

"Isn't it beautiful?"

It was beautiful. Every piece of porcelain was painted with animals. There were all sorts of animals and birds, and no two were the same. Around the edge of each of them were hand-painted bows which looked so real, he could almost feel the knot as he reached out his fingers. He smiled slightly, but his gaze shifted to the photographs on the worktop of the huge dresser. There were old ones, and newer ones. On the newer ones, Kevin spotted a familiar face and he picked up the frame. It was the boy whose picture was in the alcove, below the horse which looked like a zebra. But on these pictures he looked younger, and the plastic tube wasn't there.

"Who's this?" Kevin asked, and he was surprised to see Jilly's cheeks redden.

"That's Leonard," she whispered.

"This is who they named me after?" Kevin asked, surprise in his voice for he looked entirely different.

"Well, you do have something in common."

"I don't think so," Kevin scoffed.

"You have Alastair."

Kevin felt surprised to hear Jilly use his guardian's name. He used it all the time, but somehow it seemed odd hearing Jilly use it.

"Leonard was the vicar's son."

"Where is he now?" Kevin asked. "Was he adopted like me?"

"Kevin," she whispered, lowering her voice to such an extent that he had to lean towards her to hear her words. "You're better asking-" she stopped abruptly as Alastair appeared at the window, smiling and waving indoors to them.

Jilly turned and smiled across. "Ask the vicar," she finished.

They left the dining room as Alastair was coming in through the front door. He stamped his muddy feet, scrubbing his Wellingtons on a rubber mat before stepping inside. Jilly grinned across at him.

"Good morning, Vicar," she chimed in exactly the same voice she had used when she had first arrived.

"Hello Jilly," Alastair said, pulling the leather gloves from his hands and unzipping his coat. "I thought you might come out and join me, Kevin."

Kevin smiled across, all feelings of neglect and loneliness fading away, although he couldn't help but feel slight concern that the priest's last child seemed to have disappeared completely. Alastair remained unaware of the conversation Kevin and Jilly had shared and the thoughts inside the boy's head, but Kevin wasn't sure what words to offer the man.

"You locked the study," Jilly said. Her interjection and the look on her face seemed to suggest that she knew the thoughts both of them were having. "But I've set the laundry going and cleaned up a bit in the kitchen. Not that there was much to do."

"Sorry, Jilly," Alastair said, hanging up his coat on the hallstand and pulling the bobble hat from his head. "I locked it yesterday." He left the statement short and without qualification, not wanting Kevin to know he didn't trust Sally-Anne. "Let's have a drink before you start the study," he continued. "It's so cold out there! Winter is definitely on the horizon."

"I'll get the kettle on," Jilly said, rushing through to the kitchen.

"Thank you for breakfast," Kevin muttered.

"You got my note," Alastair said. "I thought you'd come out."

"I couldn't read her name. Jilly read it for me."

"Oh," Alastair whispered with a smile. "I hadn't thought about that."

The three of them sat down around the empty hearth, Jilly and Kevin sharing the sofa, while Alastair slouched into the armchair. Each gripped their mugs, letting the tea warm them inside and out. Jilly leaned forward after a while.

"This is ridiculous," she laughed. "We're all staring at the fireplace and shivering. I'll make us a fire."

Alastair glanced across at Kevin whose eyes opened wide.

"I don't have to," Jilly continued, confused by the expression on their faces.

"The fire won't hurt us," Alastair said, before he turned to Jilly. "Kevin has had some bad experiences with fire."

Jilly nodded and sat back. She was obviously uncomfortable with the situation she had unwittingly stumbled across. She finished her tea and leapt to her feet, asking Alastair for the key to the study. Kevin watched her go back to work before he turned to Alastair.

"Will you read me a story?" Kevin asked.

Alastair's smile faltered, but he nodded. "Which one would you like?"

Kevin got to his feet and walked over to the alcove which was filled with books. He ran his hand along the colourful spines before his finger settled on one and he teased it out. It was not a large book, but had bold illustrations which he wanted to follow, so he sat back on the sofa and waited for Alastair to join him. He leaned against the priest as he opened the book. The same name he had found in the other books was written on the front page, but this time it was in an adult's handwriting, the same handwriting he had read on the note that morning. Alastair read the title, his fingers obscuring the name Leo beneath them, before he turned the page and read on. Kevin had found a loose thread on Alastair's jumper and he twisted it in his small fingers as Alastair read the story.

Alastair was a wonderful storyteller. He put in all the voices, and made the words come alive from the page, so that the bright, adventurous illustrations were nothing compared to the world his voice built around Kevin. He got to the final page and Kevin felt the man tense. The last page was ripped out, as it had been in the other book.

"How does it end?" Kevin asked as Alastair fell silent.

"As it should," Alastair finished, closing the book as his voice became somewhat pathetic. "They all lived happily ever after."

"Why did Leo tear out the last page of his books?" Kevin demanded, disappointed by the anticlimactic ending. "He ruined it for everyone else."

"Leo didn't tear out the pages," Alastair said, hearing the words of Mrs Henderson and Sally-Anne revisiting him.

"I don't like him." Kevin slid from the sofa and stomped out of the room.

His heavy footsteps on the stairs caused Jilly to poke her head out of the study, and she looked across to see Alastair sitting alone in the living room. His head was turned slightly, so she couldn't see his face, but the light shone on his streaked cheek. Staring from the study doorway Jilly was torn about what to do. She wanted to comfort him, but she couldn't bear for him to know she had seen him like this. It wasn't that he was crying, Jilly had seen him cry several times over the events of two years ago, but she didn't want him to think she was spying of him.

"Sounds like elephants on the stairs," she called, stepping just inside the study door.

Her voice pulled Alastair from his thoughts and he rose to his feet, returning the book to the shelf, and scrubbing his cheeks dry.

"Just an angry little boy," Alastair explained, appearing at the study doorway. He smiled across at her, none the wiser about her observation.

"What happened?" she ventured.

"I can't tell him about Leonard. I can't relive it yet." Alastair slouched against the door frame, needing the support.

"It wasn't your fault," Jilly said.

"Then why did he die in my arms?"

"Because he felt safe there," she said. She set the paperweight she held down on the table and walked to stand in front of him. "He was going to die anyway. You gave him the strength to go."

"It was a foolish idea to think I could do this." Alastair let go of a breath he had been holding. "But it is what it is."

"Do-?" Jilly paused as she watched the smile slowly return to his face, where he had trained it to remain. "Do you want me to tell him about Leonard? I don't want to be pushy," she stammered, trying to explain her motives. "But I don't want this to drive a wedge between the two of you, either. You need him as much as he needs you, Vicar."

Alastair gave a slight laugh, driven by surprise more than amusement. Jilly's eyes never strayed from his own and they were both anxious and intent.

"Thank you," he breathed. "Thank you, Jilly."

"Is that a yes?"

"That's a please."

"Okay," she said, her smile deepening.

"I think I'm going to do a bit more gardening," he muttered, snatching his hat and pulling it on. "I'll be outside."

She nodded and watched as he collected and pulled on his boots, before he walked out, still pulling the coat on as he left.

Kevin watched through his window as Alastair began collecting the windfall from the base of the apple tree below. He hadn't meant to lose his temper about the books, but the unfairness of a child, who had so much, destroying their possessions so no one else could use them, burnt at his jealous heart. He watched as Alastair stood at the tree, his hand resting on the trunk, and looking as though he was drunk. Kevin knew about people getting drunk. His first foster carer had been familiar with alcohol, and he had learnt all about its effects from him.

He turned as there was a knock on the door.

"Kevin?" Jilly's voice asked. "Are you in there?"

Kevin watched as the door opened.

"Can I come in?"

"Did Alastair send you?"

"Not exactly. But I remembered that I told you we could find some conkers. And, well, they're pretty much past their best now, but I'll show you where I used to get all my winners from. Do you want to come?"

"No."

"What did you think to your story? The vicar is great at reading, isn't he?"

"It didn't have an end. Leo tore it out."

"I don't think Leo did," Jilly said, pointing to the chair. When Kevin nodded, she sat down. "Leo was what the vicar called Leonard, like his pet name. Like Benji is really Benjamin, and Tom is Thomas."

Kevin lowered his head slightly.

"The picture in the alcove, that's Leonard with his mum." She rose to her feet and reached out her hand. "Come on, let's go get conkers."

Kevin took her hand and they left the room. Both of them spared a glance for the priest through the French windows before Jilly told Kevin to leave Alastair a note. He wrote, in the neatest handwriting he could, "I have gone with Jilly to find conkers". There was no kiss as Alastair had left for him, just a statement of fact.

They walked together down the path. Jilly pointed out who owned each house, only one was owned by someone Kevin knew, everyone else was a stranger to him. When they reached the house where the dogs were, Kevin crept to the other side of Jilly.

"It's okay," she said. "They're only saying hello. And they can't get out anyway."

"Whose are they?"

"The school caretaker, Mr Sinter. He has had an accident and broken his leg."

"Who walks the dogs now?"

"His wife." Jilly laughed as she opened the gate into the churchyard. "But they're much too big for her. I saw her walking them the other day, one went one way, the other went the other, and they tied poor Mrs Sinter up in knots. They're softies really, but you're smart to be wary."

"Do you have a dog?"

"I did when I was your age, but not now."

Kevin followed her around the church to the only corner the path did not cover. There were a number of gravestones, some new, some frighteningly old, but in the corner stood a huge horse chestnut. Its leaves were speckled with the rain, but at its base were hundreds of conkers and their shells.

"No one but me ever dared come here. But this tree always gave me winners."

She guided him down the slight slope and they collected all the conkers Kevin could fit in his coat pocket, because neither of them had thought to bring a bag. Kevin was particularly proud of one he found peeking out of its case, and he took the prickly case with it still inside. Once he had gathered them all, he and Jilly walked up towards the church. Jilly stopped at one of the gravestones and smiled slightly.

"This is my dad," she whispered. "Cecil Franks."

Kevin placed his hand on the headstone and read the words. "Do you have a brother? Who is John?"

"Yes," Jilly said, smiling across. "He's my brother. He's in the navy, in the same part of the navy as Benji's dad. That's how he and Trish met."

"Why aren't you married?"

"I don't want to be," Jilly laughed. "I haven't got the time to have a husband. I always seem to be dashing all over the place." She walked over to another grave and waited for Kevin to follow her.

"Leonard Peter Roberts," he whispered. "He's dead?"

"Yes," Jilly said placing her arm around the boy as he leaned against her. "Sacred to the memory of Leonard Peter Roberts. 'For the Lord is my resting place, and in Him shall I know peace'. This is where Leo is now."

"Why did he die?" Kevin asked, leaning back to look up at Jilly.

"He was very ill. He had leukaemia, like a form of cancer. He died when he was about your age."

"Is that why everyone at school calls me Leonard?"

"I suppose. And for what it's worth, I know it's not nice to be compared to other people, but it's the highest compliment. Leo was the sweetest boy I've ever known. Even sweeter than Tom."

"Was he really Alastair's son, or was he like me?"

"He was really his son," Jilly replied. "But you're his son, too, Kevin."

"No," Kevin replied stoically. "I haven't had a dad since Liam, and I don't want the same thing to happen to Alastair that happened to him."

"What did happen?" Jilly asked, holding the

child to her as they both looked at the grave.

"He burnt to death in his car." Kevin gripped Jilly's coat and his voice became little more than a whisper. "I'm cursed, Jilly. Everyone who looks after me dies in a fire, or someone they love does. I don't know how to stop it."

"Well," she said firmly, trying not to let her fear at his words show. "I don't believe in curses, only bad luck. It sounds to me that you've had your share of that. But then, so has the vicar. Shall we go back home and try out some of those conkers?"

Kevin smiled slightly and nodded. "Who is Dawn Louise Roberts?" he asked as they turned away.

"That was Leonard's mum. She's in the picture with him."

"Her name was on the stone too," he pointed out as Jilly opened the gate and began walking down the path. "Is she buried there too?"

"No," Jilly replied.

She clearly did not want to talk about Leonard's mum. Kevin let her change the subject, pointing out some of the shelves of fungus which jutted out of the trees, or the snuffled tracks of hedgehogs through the banked-up leaves. Kevin was distracted by this discovery, keen to learn more about the hedgehogs, and he watched the sides of the path as though he expected one to leap out at him.

By the time they reached The Vicarage, thoughts of Leonard's mother had gone from Kevin's head, and he ran around the side of the building to tell Alastair what he had seen. Jilly hung back, watching as the vicar held one of the apples, which was still attached to the tree, in his hand. He turned as Kevin's voice sounded and the smile returned once more to his features.

"Did you find a hedgehog, then?" he asked later, looking over Kevin's shoulder at the children's encyclopaedia which was open on a page about hedgehogs. Jilly had gone home, and the evening was closing in around The Vicarage.

"No, but I will." Kevin closed the book and looked up at Alastair as he walked around to sit on the sofa beside him. "It says they hibernate, though, so I'll have to be quick. Jilly showed me the best tree for conkers, too. I've collected loads, but she said most of them are past their best. Next year, I'll know exactly where to get them from, though."

Alastair felt his smile deepen. Kevin was planning on being here next year.

"Have you ever seen a hedgehog?"

"Yes," Alastair replied. "Sometimes they're in the garden."

"Your garden is like a zoo," Kevin said, impressed. This reminded him of what Alastair had said about going to the zoo in the spring and he looked across at the alcove where the wooden animals were. He slipped from the sofa and walked to collect the photo. "Jilly said this is Leonard."

"Yes," Alastair said smiling at the picture in his hand. "That's Leo."

"Leonard Peter Roberts," Kevin continued, remembering the writing on the headstone. "She told me he died."

"Yes. Two years ago. But he was poorly for a long time before that. I couldn't keep him forever."

"Is she your wife?" Kevin asked, pointing to the woman.

"Yes, she is," Alastair replied, drawing up all his courage to stare into her eyes. "I've had this picture up for so long, I think I'd forgotten to look at it."

"Am I sleeping in his bed?"

"Well, it's your bed now," Alastair said, unsure where the boy was going with this. "Leonard doesn't need it anymore."

"Did he die in the bed?"

"No," Alastair replied. "He died in my arms, out there," he pointed to the garden. "He didn't sleep in your bed for a long time before he died."

"What was his favourite animal?" Kevin asked, looking through the encyclopaedia.

"He loved the squirrels. He wanted to climb the trees and go hunting for Tristan and Ysolde, just like you. But I haven't seen Tristan since Leo died."

"And did he want to be an astronaut?" Kevin asked.

"Yes," Alastair replied, letting Kevin lean against him. They both stared at the picture with different thoughts. "He knew the names of all the stars you can see from your window. We would imagine that chair in your room was a rocket. It goes up and down, you know."

"I didn't," Kevin replied, excited. "Will you teach me the names of all the stars?"

Alastair nodded, kissing the boy's hair. They sat together for the rest of the evening except for when they made dinner. Leonard was scarcely mentioned, but Alastair felt relieved that Kevin knew about his son, while Kevin was pleased to better understand the man he was living with. He went to bed that night imagining he shared the room with Leo, and his dreams were that they were both piloting a rocket into space. They weren't alone in the rocket. Hedgehogs and squirrels were moving freely throughout it, and Leonard passed the time by telling amazing stories, just as his father had done that morning.

The next day, Kevin joined Alastair at church again. Alastair had told him he could stay at home and he would find a babysitter, but Kevin was keen to join him. There was something about the building which fascinated him, and the service was intriguing. He sat with Tom and Benji at the back this week, but he missed sitting with Jilly and decided, next week, he would go and sit in the empty pews next to the organist.

At the end of the service, he rushed into the vestry and helped tidy away all the ceremonial ware into the safe. There was a little map on the door which showed him where each thing should go. While he was there, Mrs Henderson came into the vestry.

"Vicar," she began, sparing a smile but no words for Kevin. "The school hall is being mended tomorrow, but I'm taking Paul down to London to see his brother. Kathryn's in Spain somewhere. Do you think you could let them in and lock up afterwards? I should be back on Wednesday, so if you could just do Monday and Tuesday, that would be perfect."

"That's fine, Mrs Henderson. We didn't have long distance plans, did we, Kevin?"

"Nope," Kevin chirped from the safe. "I'm going

to find Tristan, though, and look for a hedgehog."

Alastair smiled broadly while Mrs Henderson replied.

"That sounds very exciting, Kevin." She turned back to Alastair. "Thank you so much, Vicar. The interim caretaker will be around, I hope. His name is Samuels. Ken, I think."

"Have a nice trip to London, Mrs Henderson," Kevin said. He watched as Mrs Henderson smiled and left the room at the same time as the final chord on the organ faded away. Alastair was squeezing his vestments into the cupboard, but he turned around as Jilly poked her head around the door.

"I'm off, Vicar. Is there anything you want from town?"

"No, thanks, Jilly. But, about yesterday." Kevin watched as Alastair tried to find words which were cryptic enough to hide his thoughts from the boy but have them still clear to Jilly. "Just, thank you."

"You're very welcome. See you on Tuesday. You too, Kevin."

"Pass on my love to your mum," Alastair said as she smiled and backed out of the doorway.

Kevin accompanied Alastair to Little Golforth in the afternoon. He was amazed by how different the services were here. There was no organist, but younger members of the congregation, some of whom he remembered from Thursday's youth club, played guitars and keyboards. For the most part, the congregation was much younger too. Kevin enjoyed the service, but he shared in Alastair's exhaustion and, when they got back to The Vicarage in the late afternoon, both of them fell asleep.

Alastair woke with a start as the telephone rang. It took him a moment to remember where he was, his deep sleep distorting all his senses. Kevin squirmed slightly as Alastair stumbled through to the study and, leaning on the desk while he tried to wake up, picked up the phone.

"Hello?" he asked sleepily.

"Vicar?" a trembling voice asked. "I didn't know who else to call."

"That's fine," he said. "You were right to call." He tried to work out who the voice belonged to, but it was contorted by hysteria, and the blaring tannoy in the background.

"It's Billy," the voice continued. "He's had a stroke, I think."

"Mrs Sinter," he began with absolute certainty. "Is there anything I can do?"

"I don't know," she sobbed down the phone.

"I'll come out there. Are you at the hospital?"

She made a snuffly affirmative noise.

"Okay," he replied. "I'll be there as fast as I can."

Alastair set down the phone and rushed into the hall, pulling on his smart coat and snatching up his car keys. He turned at the sound of a voice behind him.

"Why are you going?"

He looked back at Kevin, feeling unforgivably guilty that, in that moment, he had completely forgotten about the boy. "To the hospital, Kevin. Grab your coat."

"What happened?" the boy asked, pulling his coat on while Alastair knelt down to fasten his shoelaces, wincing each time the cord passed through his hands.

"Mr Sinter has had a stroke, and his poor wife has no one else to ring. But you won't have to see him. There's someone at the hospital who will be very pleased to meet you."

Alastair didn't expand on this, but ushered Kevin out of the door. Their journey was done in silence. There was hardly anyone else on the road, and Alastair drove them at a speed which pressed Kevin back firmly into the seat. They reached the hospital in thirty-seven minutes, in what Kevin was sure would be a new record.

He shakily followed Alastair through the halls until they reached the A&E ward, where Mrs Sinter was sitting. She was leaning forward in her chair but, when Alastair stepped over, she leapt to her feet. She was much smaller than Alastair, not a lot taller than Kevin, but her high grey hair seemed to add inches to her height. She sobbed and gripped Alastair's hand, thanking him repeatedly for coming out. Alastair sat beside her and talked softly, reassuring her, coaxing her not to fear the worst. Kevin watched as, little by little, her features lifted in smiles and, although she remained frightened, she had found a comforter in the man beside her.

"I'm just going to go and find somewhere for Kevin to wait a while, Mrs Sinter. I'll just be a few minutes. Why don't you get a coffee from the machine? Here," he continued, dipping his hand into his pocket and handing her some money. "I think you deserve something to warm you up."

Kevin got to his feet and took Alastair's outstretched hand. He tried to smile at Mrs Sinter, but the caretaker's wife was beside herself and could hardly acknowledge anything around her. Alastair guided him from the ward and on through the maze of corridors. Neither spoke. Both were remembering their own past experiences of hospitals, both with horrible recollections.

Kevin was so enveloped in these memories, he continued walking as Alastair stopped at a door. He stumbled backwards while Alastair gave a slight smile.

"There's someone in here I think you should meet. I think he should meet you too."

Alastair pushed open the door and smiled across at the coated back of the man who occupied the room.

"You're leaving," he stated. Father Levosky turned to them and smiled at the image before him, remembering Alastair arriving there with another little boy.

"If I'm needed to stay, Alastair, I shall stay."

"No, I won't ask you to," Alastair replied. "But at least you can meet Kevin. Kevin, this is Father Levosky."

"Hello," Kevin whispered, unsure how he should correctly greet a man of this position.

"Hello, Kevin," boomed back the other man. "Can you keep a secret?"

"Yes," Kevin replied, leaning forward as the Catholic priest did the same.

"I have a stash of sweets in my drawer with a chess set. Can you play chess?"

Kevin shook his head.

"Would you like to learn, while you eat the sweets?"

Kevin nodded excitedly, and Alastair was

unsure whether the excitement was more at the prospect of the sweets, or at the new game Father Levosky was about to teach him.

"Can I stay?" Kevin asked, turning back to Alastair.

"Yes. I have to get back to Mrs Sinter." He turned to his friend and smiled. "Thank you. I don't think I'll be long."

"Take as long as she needs, Alastair," the man said. "I have the bed set up in the office. Kevin can sleep here if needs be."

Alastair thanked him again, and Kevin watched as Reverend Roberts left the room.

"Why don't you call Alastair 'Vicar'?" Kevin asked as Father Levosky hung his coat up on a hook once more.

"That is a question with a very complicated answer, full of church history and reformation splits, young man. But let it suffice to say, I did not come to know your vicar through his church but through his time here. Not ministering, but caring and then grieving."

"Leonard?" Kevin took the chair Father Levosky offered him and stared across the table intently.

"Yes. He used to sit for hours in the chapel, just through there," he motioned to a door. "And I would sit and talk with him. And, although we are very different, we have a lot in common."

Kevin considered these words throughout the evening as Father Levosky tried to teach him to play chess while plying him with sweets. He learnt a lot about the time Alastair had spent in the hospital with his son, but Kevin couldn't connect the broken man of Father Levosky's stories to the perpetually smiling and positive man who had opened up his home to him. The Catholic priest was both guarded and open simultaneously so that, as Kevin found himself falling asleep on a sofa in the man's office, he realised that he knew nothing more of Leonard than when he had arrived, and all he had discovered of Alastair was the man's engagement with the priest.

He didn't remember the drive back to the village, nor getting ready for bed, but the next thing he knew was that he was waking up in Leonard's space themed bedroom, staring up at Jupiter as it twirled in the heat from the radiator. There was a grey light seeping around the edge of the curtains, not enough to have woken him up, and he turned to look across at the door as Alastair pushed it open.

"I know it's the first real day of our holiday," he began, sounding apologetic although the smile remained on his face. "But we have to go down to the school, remember."

"Jilly said Saturday was your day off," Kevin muttered. "But you don't really get a day off, do you?"

"No," Alastair said, stepping into the room. "But I knew that when I signed up. Are you wishing you'd stayed with a teacher or an accountant?"

Kevin shook his head as he sat up. "I like it here."

Alastair smiled as though he had won a great victory, and the two of them met downstairs, breakfasted and hurried along the little path.

Kevin was beginning to learn that everything

Reverend Roberts did was last minute. He arrived at the school with only one and a half minutes to spare. Everyone else Kevin had ever known would always arrive early at a place, sitting outside as the minutes rolled by. Alastair made timekeeping an art. He unlocked the school and latched the door open, guiding Kevin through to the hall. The floor was still damp and slippery, the leak in the roof obvious as a sliver of daylight shone through.

"I'm glad there's someone coming in to sort it," Alastair conceded. "I don't like heights."

"Hello?" asked a voice behind them, deep and gravelly. "Oh, sorry," it continued as the owner's gaze took in Alastair's collar. "Mrs Henderson told me you'd be coming along. I'm Kenneth Samuels," he announced, pulling his woollen hat from his head and offering his other hand to Alastair.

"Alastair Roberts," he announced, shaking the man's hand. "You must be our caretaker. Thank you so much for stepping in like this."

"Not at all," his low voice growled. "Coming up Christmas, I'm glad to have the work." He made no attempt to engage Kevin, seeming almost determined not to, but turned back to the door. "The builders were just pulling up. I'll go get them. I've got this covered, Vicar. You go and enjoy the first day of your boy's holiday."

"Thank you, Mr Samuels. I'll pop back at about five and see how it's going."

Alastair and Kevin left the school and walked back to The Vicarage along the road instead of the path. Alastair had assured Mrs Sinter that he would check on the dogs and make sure they were walked, something which made Kevin uneasy. He watched as Alastair slotted the key Mrs Sinter had given him into the lock and angry barking sounded from inside the house.

"I don't want to go in," Kevin snapped, his fear resulting in anger.

"You don't have to," Alastair's eternally calm voice replied. "I can let them out in the back garden. Jilly will come and walk them later. She used to walk them sometimes when the Sinters were away."

"She works all the time, too. Like you."

After seeing to the dogs, the pair returned to the house, had lunch, and went into town to do some shopping. Alastair gave Kevin ten pounds to spend, but Kevin was so in awe of the note he was handed, that he could find nothing he thought merited it. Every shop they explored was like an adventure, and they laughed and chatted about everything and nothing.

As they were driving home, Alastair called in at the school, two minutes before five. Mr Samuels had locked up and all the lights were out. Assuming this meant the roof had been successfully fixed, Alastair ducked back into the car and drove the remainder of the distance to The Vicarage.

On Tuesday morning, however, they walked down to the school again. The builders' ladders were still in place, and Mr Samuels once more appeared behind them. Alastair smiled across.

"I came by last night, but the school was locked up," Alastair began.

"The builders left at three," Mr Samuels replied. "I did a few bits and pieces, but I headed home about four."

"That's fine," Alastair said, realising the caretaker had assumed the vicar had being berating him. "Well, we'll be heading off."

"Actually, Vicar, there's some post marked urgent came through yesterday. I had to sign for it."

"I don't think Kathryn would like me opening the school's post."

"Fair enough." Mr Samuels nodded. "I just thought I'd mention it." He turned to Kevin and smiled. "Are you enjoying your holidays, young man?"

Kevin was thrown by this question, not the words, but the fact he was asked at all. "Yes, Alastair is going to open a bank account for me. And today Jilly and I are going to look for hedgehogs."

"Alastair?" Mr Samuels whispered, clearly confused by Kevin's use of this name.

"He's not my real dad," Kevin explained, wishing suddenly he hadn't spoken, as Alastair's expression fell. "But he's the only one who wants me."

"No, Kevin," Alastair said. "That's not true."

Mr Samuels looked uncomfortable to be suddenly caught up in this discussion, but Kevin couldn't stop the words from coming.

"I'm cursed, Mr Samuels. Everyone who tries to help me burns to death."

"Good Lord," the caretaker muttered, but there was a curious look to his face. He didn't look scared, or even especially shocked. He just looked sad.

"Come on, Kevin," Alastair said, offering

his hand to the child. When Kevin didn't take it, he reached out and took his hand, pulling him gently from the school. "You're not cursed, Kevin," Alastair said as they walk past the church. "No more than I am, or Jilly is."

"You haven't seen them," Kevin muttered. "I've killed so many people, Alastair."

"That wasn't you."

The man would hear nothing else on the subject, but changed the conversation to talking about Mr Sinter, whose wife had rung that morning to tell Alastair the doctors thought he would be able to go home the next day.

When they got back to The Vicarage, Jilly was already there. Eager to speed up the opportunity to go hedgehog hunting with her, Kevin offered to help clean the house. He folded laundry, pairing socks. Sometimes, Jilly would ask if a pair of socks was Alastair's or Kevin's, which resulted in hysterical laughter from Kevin as she suggested the small socks covered in superheroes were Alastair's.

"Well, I'll have to keep an eye on the vicar's feet from now on," she laughed.

He also helped strip the beds and dust some of the surfaces, although he gave up on this when he got a splinter in his hand from the balustrade. Jilly fetched some tweezers from the bathroom cabinet and eased the wooden dagger out. Kevin watched with fascination but as his palm began to bleed after she had pulled the splinter free, his eyes welled with tears.

"Come here," Jilly said, pulling the boy towards her and hugging him close. "It's had me on one or two occasions too."

Later that afternoon, after he and Jilly had returned from looking for hedgehogs, Kevin went upstairs and looked at the wood of the balustrade. There was only one spot where it was coarse, and he frowned at it, rubbing his wounded hand. Alastair had found him a little plaster and rubbed antiseptic cream on it.

While Kevin and Jilly had been doing the housework, Alastair had been working downstairs in the study. He usually closed his door, knowing he would work better when he was in his enclosed little space, but today he left it open. The sound of Kevin's laughter was too rare and precious not to listen to. A house needed a child's voice, especially a house which had borne so many tears. He placed his hand on a small photo frame which held a picture of Leonard, imagining his own son's laughter. Had God sent him Kevin as a cure for the absence in his heart? If He had, Alastair was not sure it was working for, since Kevin had arrived, Alastair had thought more and more of little Leo.

That night, when Kevin had gone to bed and Alastair had tried to teach him some of the stars in the clear night sky, he pulled out Kevin's file once more. He knew almost every word off by heart, now. Each detail was etched on his mind with the horribly graphic images to join them. The boy's words to the caretaker that morning continued to swirl in his head, and the fear in his voice. The worst part was that Alastair couldn't protect him from this fear. He could shield the boy from the Sinters' dogs or protect him from anybody who might hurt him. But this fear was of himself. The thing which frightened

Kevin most was Kevin.

He read through the notes once more, but despite all the death and heartbreak the ink on the page spoke of, Alastair would not believe Kevin was cursed. There were things in common with the deaths, it was true. They all involved fire. They all spared Kevin, in some cases miraculously. He spread the sheets across his desk, along with some news articles he had printed which told of the accidents. They didn't add up. There was something missing from each one of them. It was as though the corner piece of the jigsaw was missing, but it was peripheral, so no one had thought to look for it.

"I'm no detective," he muttered, but the sound of his own voice only made him feel more anxious. The silence of the house was closing in on him, pressing down. He gathered up the papers and shut them in the drawer. Every noise seemed out of place and, as he walked to the study door, he felt an unbearable fear course through him. His blood was pounding in his head as his heart rate seemed to double with each second. What was waiting outside? Was the gas hob pumping out flammable fumes? Had a coal rolled free from the fire? Would those eyes be there to stare into his own?

He shook himself awake. Images he had sought to forget had been forced to the forefront of his mind. He snatched the door and pulled it open. There was nothing untoward there, neither sight, sound nor smell.

Throughout the week of holiday, Kevin shadowed Alastair in all he did. Mr Sinter returned home on Wednesday afternoon, and

Alastair and Kevin visited that evening. The dogs were shut in the couple's spare room to appease Kevin. As they were leaving, Mrs Sinter asked Kevin if he would like to meet the dogs one at a time.

"On their own," she explained, "they're quiet as mice. It's when they're together that they bark."

Kevin was nervous of this plan, gripping Alastair's hand in both of his own. Alastair offered no answer, but was a reassuring pillar as Kevin whispered,

"Okay."

He changed his mind the moment Mrs Sinter's hand was on the door handle, but it was too late to say anything, as one of the dogs shot into the hall. Kevin hid behind Alastair, who kept a reassuring hand on the boy. Kevin pressed his face into Alastair's jacket, clinging onto the man.

"Look, Kevin," Alastair said, easing the boy to face what he was talking about. The dog sat in front of him, its tail wagging and its paw occasionally lifting as though it wanted to shake his hand. Kevin gave a nervous laugh as he looked at it. It stared back at him through dark, eager eyes. Mrs Sinter put a small dog treat in his hand and he offered it to the dog, which took it gently.

"Thank you, Mrs Sinter," Alastair said, feeling relieved by how well this encounter had gone.

"Boys and dogs," she laughed. "They're two creatures born to get on with one another, Vicar."

Kevin felt delighted with himself, and he chattered away excitedly as he and Alastair left the house.

On Thursday, Kevin went over to Benji's and Tom's house for the day, allowing Alastair the chance to go and visit one of his parishioners who was in prison. He didn't want to take Kevin there. He was unsure how much the boy knew of his father, but Alastair saw no need in unsettling him if he knew Harry Alderman had died in the hands of the prison service.

As he was driving back through town, he decided to call in at the hospital and visit Mrs Franks. The afternoon was wearing on, and there was a thin veil of rain from the steely blue sky. Feeling he needed something to brighten the day, and imagining Hilary needed that even more so, he called at a florist shop in the High Street and bought a collection of five sunflowers. He arrived at the hospital with a spring in his step and walked through the sterile corridors with a determination not to allow the past to haunt him.

Hilary was sleeping when he arrived. Her eyes seemed to have sunk within her skull and the muscle which had supported her skin was wasting away, making her skin wrinkled and heavy on her face and arms. He set the flowers in the window ledge and sighed. Was he only imagining it, or did he feel a weightless hand, small and childlike, in his own? He swallowed back his tears, spluttering over them, and turned around. There was no one there.

He walked out of the ward, feeling this had been a mistake. He had noticed Father Levosky's car had not been parked outside, so he walked into the hospital chapel and sat on the back pew. The room was modern and unromantic, with no soul of its own, but so many souls had been comforted and soothed here, his own included. There was a stained-glass panel at the east side. It was supposed to be a window, but it faced onto another ward, so the hospital had just backlit it. On the positive side, it meant the sun always seemed to be shining there. There was no iconography, something he always found strange, but he pulled a cypress cross from where it hung beneath his jumper and ran his thumb over the smooth surface.

No one else came in while he sat there, never looking at his watch and losing all track of time. He wasn't praying exactly, just thinking, trying to make sense of things. Occasionally, he dared to form a thought into a question, not expecting an answer, just content to know there was one. He closed his eyes, shutting out the haze of pastel hues which the glass panel filled the room with. His vision filled with a sacred memory, as painful as it was beautiful. A little hand, marked with the scars of drips, reached towards an apple hanging from the branch. He watched the weak fingers clutch the fruit, tugging at it. Finally it came free, but the apple simply fell to the ground. The hand dropped and the soul fled from the child in his arms.

He let go of his cross and buried his head in his hands.

"Blessed are those who mourn, for they shall be comforted."

Alastair jumped at the voice, surprised to find he was no longer alone. He felt disconcerted, unsure how long he had spent in his meditation and grief. Father Levosky sat down beside him but his eyes were turned to the glass panel.

"He's a smart little one, your boy. He admires you already, loves you perhaps."

"Do you think I was wrong to take him?" Alastair asked, feeling he needed approval for his own actions. "I thought he was a Godsend. A way of helping a child in need at the same time as filling the need I've always had to care for a child. Was I just being selfish?"

"The only person who thinks you are selfish is yourself, Alastair. If God sent the boy to you, He did so because you need one another." He turned to face Alastair and smiled. "You've done a great thing, taking in Kevin."

"Then why do I feel guilty?" Alastair asked, staring into Father Levosky's eyes. There was something strangely comforting about not having to smile. This man would know any feign of joviality was a lie. "I keep remembering that moment Leo left me. Kevin believes he's cursed, but-"

"Stop." Father Levosky frowned across at Alastair. "Think about what you're about to say. You don't believe in any of that, you're just looking for an excuse for what happened. There isn't one. Sometimes bad things happen to good people, I don't need to tell you that." The Catholic priest rested his hand on Alastair's shoulder, his tone softening as he realised his words had found their mark. "Come on. I put the coffee machine on when I saw your car outside, it will be done by now."

The man's words, brutal and precise, were nonetheless appreciated by Alastair. He hated self-pity, but was becoming increasingly subjected to it. He promised himself he would stop the next time he fell into that trap.

He made sure Kevin never witnessed his doubts, and they began to fade as the week drew to a close. The following day, he and Kevin returned to town and Alastair opened up a bank account for the boy. Kevin was reluctant to hand over his ten-pound note, but Alastair promised he could have another one the next time they came shopping together. Kevin was pleased to have his own account, feeling very grown-up, but he was delighted that Alastair had believed he was ready for this. They wandered around the shops together, but neither bought anything, just enjoying one another's company.

The weekend had arrived before either of them noticed. Saturday was a dismal day, the rain falling so hard each drop bounced out of the puddles. Alastair had decided to take the day away from The Vicarage, feeling unable to turn off his phone, but wishing to escape its constant ringing on his day off.

They went to the cinema together, driving through the pouring rain to reach the town. Kevin was grateful of the rain, for it slowed down Alastair's driving. They reached the cinema with five minutes to spare. Kevin loved the film, but Alastair found he was forcing his eyes to stay open by the end of it.

"I've never been to the cinema," Kevin exclaimed as they left the screen. "It's so big."

"Well," Alastair said, rubbing his eyes as they stepped out into the rain. "We can try and go once a month if you like. There's always loads of great films in the build up to Christmas."

"Christmas?" Kevin asked excitedly. "Helen wouldn't let us talk about Christmas until November."

"It's my favourite time of the year, even though my workload goes through the roof."

The two of them talked about Christmas as they walked over to the priest's car, the topic keeping them warm despite the rain. They went for a meal together at the pizzeria, Kevin deliberating over his topping for several minutes. The waitress waited patiently, giving suggestions of what other people put on theirs and what went well together. After a while she lowered her notepad and smiled slightly.

"Why don't you just have what your dad's having?"

"I don't know if I like olives," Kevin said.

"You can take off anything you don't like, and you know your dad will happily eat them for you," she added, smiling across at Alastair, who was already grinning uncontrollably.

"Okay," Kevin conceded, sighing slightly as though he was disappointed that the choosing was over. "And can I have chips, please?"

"Chips *and* pizza?" Alastair laughed. "I had no idea watching a film could build such an appetite. Of course you can, if you want them. Today's a treat. For me, too, so I'll have chips as well, please."

The waitress nodded, but her smile dropped as Alastair took off his coat and placed it on the chair next to him. "Reverend Roberts isn't it?" she whispered. "But I thought," she faltered as she looked across at Kevin. "That's not Leonard."

"No," Alastair replied, the smile on his own

face trembling slightly. He tried to recall her face, but he couldn't bring her name to mind. "This is Kevin."

She smiled across with an acidity which burnt at his soul, before she turned away, with no further comments. Kevin watched this in confusion, amazed by how quickly someone could change. He didn't question what had caused this change to appear, but this was the only thought which ran through Alastair's mind as he stared at the cutlery on the table, lining them up with the checks of the gingham tablecloth.

"You don't remember me, do you?" the waitress asked as Alastair paid at the end of the meal. "I was one of Dawn's friends." She spoke in a clipped tone, all but snatching the card out of Alastair's hand and shoving it into the card reader. "I still think of her every single day. But you've clearly moved on, Reverend Roberts."

"What do you mean?" Alastair asked, taking back his card. "Because of Kevin?"

She didn't answer but walked away. Alastair forced the smile back onto his face as Kevin wandered over to him.

"That was really good," the boy said.

He continued to talk about the film all the way back to The Vicarage, giddy about the experience of the whole day. Alastair was grateful of his words, feeling he needed some distraction from the waitress's comments.

As Alastair switched out the light in Kevin's room that night, he was met by the boy's thin voice.

"I had a great day today."

"Me too," Alastair replied, willing the short statement to be true.

"I'm glad people keep thinking you're my dad. I wish you had been my dad."

Alastair gave a slightly strangled sound, choking back the appreciation he felt in these few words. "Thank you, Kevin," he whispered. "Goodnight."

"Goodnight Alastair."

The darkness in the room was complete but for the glow-in-the-dark stars on the ceiling, a comforting night light to Kevin as he drifted to sleep. Alastair closed the door and walked downstairs to his study. The waitress' words still stung him. A part of him, a part which was rising increasingly to the surface, wanted to challenge her on what she had said and implied. But he knew it was wrong. Still, Leonard's death was his own loss, not hers. And while it might also have been his wife's, she had chosen her own path. He looked through the papers on his desk, calming his thoughts with plans for tomorrow's service, until he fell asleep with his head resting on the desk.

Alastair had managed to make it to bed in the small hours of the morning, but by the time he and Kevin embarked along the muddy path to walk to church, he was wide awake and fully smiling once more.

They went into the vestry together, Alastair lighting the taper, before walking up to the altar. The taper was on a long-handled snuffer which he handed to Kevin. The boy tried not to take it, but Alastair held Kevin's hands in his own, gently forcing him to take the handle.

"You're not cursed, Kevin. You wouldn't be here if you were. Now, look. You have to catch the wick of the candle with the taper."

Alastair guided the taper towards the candle and gradually lessened his hold on it. When they came to the second candle, Kevin lit it alone. His hands shook and it took several seconds for the flame to take but, as he handed the taper back to Alastair, he felt overwhelmingly proud of himself. This feeling was only enhanced as Alastair beamed across.

"Why does no one sit in the pews near Jilly?" Kevin asked as he blew out the taper.

"They're the choir stalls. We haven't had a choir for quite a while."

"I think there should be a choir again," Kevin continued, smiling across at Jilly as she walked in with a cheery hello.

"You boys look deep in conversation," she said, laughing.

"I think there should be people in the choir pews," Kevin said, turning to Jilly. "Don't you get lonely sitting up at the front?"

"Not if you'll sit next to me," she said, shooting a sideways glance at Alastair, whose face never shifted. "But the choir takes lots of practise, so we'll maybe just leave it at me and you for now. Are you looking forward to Halloween next week?"

"Next week?" Kevin asked. "I've lost track of time."

"That always happens during the holidays," she smiled, pulling on the blue robe she wore to play the organ. "It's next Saturday. Benji and Tom are going Trick-or-Treating. If you talk nicely to the vicar, he might let you go with them."

Alastair smiled across. "Let's see how we do with school this week."

Kevin watched the service unfold around him, still unsure where his own beliefs fitted around the events. Despite how much he had enjoyed the service at Little Golforth last Sunday, he was pleased to have the afternoon free for hedgehog and squirrel hunting in the garden. There was no service in Little Golforth on the last Sunday of the month. Instead, they had a shared brunch, which clashed in time with the morning church service. But their brunch was more a social gathering than a spiritual affair, so Alastair felt no responsibility to attend.

That evening, Kevin sat in front of the fire and watched as Alastair put a match to the newspaper in the grate. He waited as the vicar stepped back and took the seat beside Kevin. After a moment, the boy shuffled along the sofa and leaned against Alastair, who wrapped his arm around him.

"This holiday went too quickly," Kevin sighed.

"Yes," Alastair agreed. "Are you ready for school again?"

"Yes. And the first thing I'm going to do is find Mr Samuels."

"The caretaker? Why?"

"I want to tell him that I do want you to be my dad. Can I call you Dad, Alastair?"

"I wish you would, Kevin," he answered honestly.

They sat together, watching the flames as they seeped around and through the coals, thinking over the events of the holiday. Both were happy to have found a family, small though it may be. And, for Alastair's part, he smiled at the truth both Jilly and Father Levosky had tried to tell him. He needed Kevin as greatly as Kevin needed him.

halloween and Remembrance

There was rain on that Monday morning, a fitting start to the new term. But for all the worry Kevin had over his return to school, he need not have wasted his energy. That day he was beginning as an equal to the other children. He was not the new boy anymore, he was just a member of the class, equally as excited about the upcoming Halloween events, and the promise of Christmas at the end of the term.

He sat with Benji, talking excitedly about his plans for a costume to wear while they went trick-or-treating, and the houses they would be allowed to call at. Benji's mum knew most people in the village, and Benji and Tom had a list of people they were allowed to visit. They had planned their route during the holiday, and the only house Benji was unsure about was Mr Sinter's.

Mrs Henderson was delighted to have order restored to her class, and she paid particular attention to Kevin's social development. Not that Kevin could have noticed, but she had moved the seats of her classroom around, trying to maintain a supportive network around the young boy. It may have been whispered that she had done this because of who had adopted the child, but this was not Mrs Henderson's real reason. She was growing fond of Kevin. He was a boy who tried consistently and, where knowledge may have been missing, he more than made up for it in enthusiasm.

By the end of the first week, Kevin felt he was as much a part of the school as Benji. He would skip along the path back to The Vicarage, and rise earlier in the morning, keen to find out what the day had in store.

Alastair was both proud and impressed by this change. Everyone he visited asked after the boy, and it was a topic he was happy to discuss. He had filled his week, dashing around the village and into town, feeling The Vicarage had suddenly become very empty while Kevin was at school. Eager to avoid the empty house as much as possible, he visited his parishioners, and attended the Monday coffee morning. He even travelled out to the big house in the woods beside the village, the home of Lord Dalton, although this was to find the man absent.

"You've let all those apples go to ruin again,

Vicar," Jilly said, as she presented him with a cup of tea on Tuesday morning. "Next year, I bet Kevin would love to help you pick them."

"And I'll let him," Alastair said with determination. "He says the sweetest things, Jilly," he added. "I just wish I could convince him he's not responsible for all the deaths around him. How much bad luck can one person have?"

"Well, it won't happen here. We're all rooting for you both." She returned his smile with an enormous grin, pulling the scarf back over her voluminous hair. "Everyone in the village. Did you want me to take Kevin out on Saturday with Benji and Tom?"

"I'll come with you," Alastair replied, bringing a surprised laugh from Jilly. "What?" he asked. "I won't if you don't want me to."

"I'd love you to," she chuckled. "You'd make a great wizard. You'll have to dress up too. I always do."

"I thought a vampire, actually."

"Okay." Her cheeks burning to the same colour as her hidden hair.

"No, its fine," Alastair said quickly. "I'll let you take the boys alone."

"No," Jilly protested, the smile on her face being replaced by an anxious expression. "Kevin would love you to come. We all would."

Alastair was not entirely convinced by the truth of this but, when he mentioned the possibility to Kevin, the boy was delighted.

"What will we dress up as?" Kevin asked, tossing his book bag into the cupboard. "Benji's been asking me all week. He's going as Frankenstein and Tom is going as a ghost."

"What would you like to go as?" Alastair asked, considering the alarming array of disturbing characters Kevin might choose.

"I'd like to be a bat."

"A bat?" Alastair repeated. "That's perfect."

They sat together at the breakfast bar in the kitchen, hugging the mugs of tea Alastair had made. He had spent the afternoon collecting up bits and pieces for the bonfire next week, so the door into the garden had been open most of the day. The house was suffering the effects of that. Not wanting to mention the possibility of a bonfire to Kevin, unsure how he would respond, he chose instead to continue the topic of Halloween.

Until last year he had always held a bonfire in the garden of The Vicarage for everyone to attend. Even after Leonard's death, he had shared the event with his parishioners. But last year, by himself and feeling overwhelmed by the conflict between his vocation and loneliness, he had abandoned it. No one had minded. They were only grateful that he wanted to withdraw in his grief. His congregation were caring, but not pushy, and his private sorrow gave them the chance to support him without feeling obliged to visit him.

"I haven't seen Ysolde all week," Kevin remarked after a period of silence. "Is she getting ready to sleep?"

"She might be," Alastair replied, looking out at the garden. "She sometimes comes out in the snow, though. Maybe she's just slowing down for winter." He looked across at Kevin and smiled as he nodded sagely.

Neither of them spoke for a time until Alastair suggested they made dinner together. This was met with great excitement from Kevin. The child loved all practical activities, whether it was cooking dinner or making Halloween decorations. Alastair noticed, however, that he was reluctant to light the gas hob. During the week, Alastair had called out the servicemen to check the gas, but Kevin was not entirely convinced they had spoken the truth in confirming its safety. Alastair lit the hob and set Kevin cutting up the rashers of bacon, using scissors rather than a knife.

They shared the meal they had cooked together and talked, once again, of Halloween.

"I've got a little cauldron somewhere," Alastair said after a moment. "It's made of wood, not metal, so it's not too heavy."

"Why do you have a cauldron?" Kevin asked. "You're not a wizard."

"No, it was for trick-or-treating, but it only ever got one outing."

"With Leonard?"

"Yes, with Leonard. It was when he was five, every other Halloween since then he was too ill to go."

"Maybe his ghost will go out with us tomorrow," Kevin said, in what was supposed to be a comforting gesture, but Alastair felt a chill seize him at the boy's words. He tried to hide the shiver he gave, and hurriedly collected the pots.

"How about pudding?" he asked, hiding his thoughts beneath a tone of enthusiasm.

It was a clear, cold night. There were hosts of stars to be seen, so Alastair suggested they went outside to look at them. Kevin, not wanting to appear scared, agreed but when they had pulled on their hats, coats, scarves and gloves, he gripped Alastair's hand tightly in his own.

"I don't really like the dark," he admitted, as they stood a short distance beyond the apple tree. "Not when I'm outside in it."

"But you're safe here, Kevin," Alastair said, hugging the boy to him. "This is our little corner of the world, and you'll always be safe in it. The dark can't hurt you."

"But what's inside it might."

"No, not here. Any little scrambling you hear is just Ysolde. You might hear the owl out hunting mice. If you hear a scream, it will only be him flying home."

"How do you know so much?" Kevin asked, feeling comforted in the priest's explanation.

"I've lived a lot longer than you, Kevin. You'll know even more than me when you're my age. Just keep learning."

Kevin leaned against Alastair and smiled up at the stars overhead. There were so many in the heavens, shining with a twinkling glow which made them dance and move. But, when he lay in bed later that evening, listening to the sound of Alastair whistling downstairs, he felt his forehead furrow. He was afraid. He was afraid of the curse which followed him. It had seemed like the most natural thing in the world to have told Alastair that he wanted him to be his dad. But this was how it always began.

He had lived with Helen four months before she had started getting strange phone calls. It had only been when he had settled in at the house that the trouble had started. And he remembered with a stomach-clenching sickness how it had ended. And now he had told Alastair how he wanted to call him dad. Kevin felt sure something bad was going to happen. Since then, every time Alastair sparked the hob, or lit a match for the fire, Kevin recoiled.

His dreams were filled with fire and ghosts. Not sweet ghosts with sheets over their heads like Tom would be when he was Trick-or-Treating, but the real people he had known. All of them were like wax, melting away in the fire. Liam and Helen, and the three families in between. Kevin tried to save them. He tried to extinguish the fire, to pull them to safety, but nothing worked. He clutched his head in his hands, tightening his fingers in his hair and screaming. And then a hand took his own, leading him through the fire, out into the darkness of the night sky. He looked up, expecting to see Alastair, but instead it was a faceless figure whose features had disintegrated in the flames.

Kevin screamed. He screamed so loudly he woke himself up. Immediately the dream, which had seemed so real, began to fade. Alastair was already at his side, holding the boy close to him and rocking him gently as though Kevin were only a baby. Kevin didn't care, he was just so relieved to be back in The Vicarage, safe from the flames and the monsters it had caused.

Alastair stayed until the boy had fallen back to sleep. Then he laid him back on the bed and walked out the room. The clock on the landing showed it was a little after half twelve. He walked along the landing, imagining he could hear Kevin's frightened scream again, but the house was silent. His hand skated across the balustrade, instinctively rising to avoid the splinters part way along. He didn't even notice he was doing it, now. It was a part of the house. He stepped into his room and walked to the window, staring out towards the church. Only the illuminated Norman tower was visible beyond the skeletal fingers of the trees. Winter seemed to have come early this year.

He walked over to the bed and lay down, leaning up on his elbow and looking thoughtfully at the empty half of the bed. Dawn loved Halloween. He'd never really done it until they got together. Resting his hand on her pillow, he lay back and fell asleep.

Halloween dawned much the same as any other day. Jilly arrived while Kevin was still in his pyjamas, and Alastair made her a drink while the boy went to get dressed. Jilly insisted that, if Kevin wanted to help her, he would have to be dressed and ready to start.

"Don't worry about the study today," Alastair said. "It's not that bad."

"I'm not worried about it," she chuckled, thanking him as he passed her a large mug of tea. "It's freezing out there now, it will be bitter this evening. What did you want me to do instead?"

"I'd like you to help make Kevin a costume. I know you make Tom's and Benji's every year."

"Tom's always a ghost. All I have to do for that is cut two circles in raggy sheets."

"He wants to be a bat," Alastair went on, his eyes looking pleadingly across at her, while his mouth wore its eternal smile. "There's an old cassock in the vestry which is a perfect size."

"That's not yours," she laughed. "That belongs to the church."

"It will never fit me. Are you planning to oust me in favour of someone a foot shorter?"

"No," she whispered, setting the mug down on the coffee table and hurriedly sorting the scarf over her hair.

"I'll go fetch it, then," he returned, his smile turning impish as he grinned across.

Jilly spent the day trying to turn the cassock into a bat costume for Kevin and, when she had finished, she felt quietly pleased with the result. Kevin was beyond excited, rushing around the house collecting all the things Jilly needed. His nightmare was a distant memory.

Alastair found the wooden cauldron and dressed himself in a long black cape and a red bowtie. Jilly had gone to collect Benji and Tom, and they were to meet at The Vicarage at five o'clock before heading out around the village. He set the glow-in-the-dark teeth into his mouth and looked at his reflection in the full-length mirror. He looked ridiculous.

"It's almost time," an eager voice announced. "Can we go outside and wait?"

It took Alastair a moment to realise it wasn't Leonard. He walked out onto the landing and was met by an excited squeak. Kevin lifted his hands to his mouth and jumped up and down as he looked across.

"You look really scary," he began, grabbing Alastair's hand and pulling him towards the stairs.

"I'm not sure, Kevin. I think I look a bit silly."

Kevin stopped and looked critically at the man, before he shook his head. "You look scary," he said again.

"You, too," Alastair said, hugging the boy to him. "Come on, then, let's go and wait for them."

They walked down the stairs and waited in the large hall. They didn't talk, but not for any reason other than the fact they had nothing to say. Jilly arrived with ten minutes to spare. She was always early, Kevin had realised, while Alastair was always on time. No one in the village ever appeared to be running late. Perhaps that sort of thing happened to the people who went to the other school, but everyone in his own community of Saint Hubertus was prompt, keen, and prepared.

"All set?" Jilly asked, grinning beneath her witch's hat. Her mass of hair burnt its natural red and matched the red stripes on her white socks. She wore a long, pointed nose which looked as out of place on her round face, as Alastair's fangs were on his placid features.

Kevin nodded, and he, Benji and Tom ran off, brandishing their torches like weapons as they ran down the path towards the church. Jilly and Alastair followed, careful never to let the three boys out of their sights. They didn't need to worry, though, for all three of them stopped at the end of the path, reluctant to walk around the church and past the graves.

Jilly had a strict itinerary which she wanted to make sure they kept to. They had planned out a route for them, and they joined the handful of other Trick-or-Treaters as they wandered around the village. She had decided against calling on

Virginia Crow

Mr and Mrs Sinter. The couple's house was in darkness, and they took this as a hint that they wouldn't be opening the door to anyone tonight. But they called on Mrs Henderson and Mr Samuels, as well as the houses of all their friends. For the most part, they were well received, except at Mrs Humphries' house. On opening the door, she scowled at them all.

"Well," she began, her tone as cold as the ground. "I can overlook this heathen event in the children, but the organist and the vicar..?"

Alastair felt the full weight of this open-ended statement and swallowed back the words he was about to offer.

"It would be wrong to let the boys walk around alone," Jilly said sweetly. She knew Mrs Humphries' two eldest boys were doing exactly that. "And it would be a shame if we didn't make that extra effort."

"Trick-or-Treat," Tom's little voice sang out, and he lifted his little bucket up towards Mrs Humphries.

"I thought you were overlooking it in the children, Mrs Humphries," Alastair said, smiling across at her so that the fangs in his mouth were clearly visible. "Dawn used to love Halloween," he continued. "She taught half the village to love it too. It's not entirely heathen, after all. So I'll see you for the All Hallows Day service tomorrow."

Mrs Humphries scowled once more but dropped sweets into the tubs of the three children. They called their thank yous as they ran back down the path.

"You should be ashamed of yourselves," she muttered, slamming the door closed before either Alastair or Jilly could offer a response. They followed the boys in silence for a moment before Jilly burst out laughing.

"It's not funny," Alastair whispered, pulling the fangs from his mouth. "Maybe she's right."

"Come on, Vicar. She's just riled because she's full of Victorian temperance." She rushed around to stand in front of him at the gates. "Just because Dawn taught you to love it, you don't have to hate it now she's gone. Put your teeth back in, Dracula," she laughed. "You really do look silly in that outfit without them."

The three boys seemed to think nothing of this altercation but were talking to two skeletons on the opposite pavement, comparing their hoard of sweets and gifts. Alastair and Jilly walked across the road to them, but all of them turned towards the church as it chimed half past six.

"That's home time," Jilly announced. "I think we've done all the houses on the list."

"We're one short of last year," Benji said.

"We didn't go to Mr Sinter's," Tom replied.

"But we did go to Mr Samuels' house."

"We didn't go to The Vicarage," Jilly pointed out. "But wasn't it great having Kevin and the vicar with us?"

"Yes," Benji said, squeezing Kevin's hand, while the ghostly Tom nodded and looked up at Alastair, the vicar imagining his thin, smiling face. But for a moment, the ghost became Leonard. Alastair rubbed his eyes and forced a smile.

"It's been great. Thank you for letting us tag along."

He held his hand out to Kevin, and the boy

took it, saying goodnight to his friends and following Alastair as he guided him towards the church. There was a slight wind picking up, and it carried a host of smells, enhanced by the frozen air. Kevin felt overwhelmingly giddy but, as they reached the churchyard, he fell quiet.

"What's the matter?" Alastair asked.

"Graves are scary," Kevin whispered.

"No, they're lovely."

"Lovely?" the boy hissed, reluctant to make too much noise.

"They remind people how much we loved those who have gone before. They're markers of love, not death."

"You make me feel so safe," Kevin said, his wide eyes staring up at the man beside him. "Who taught you all these things?"

"I found that out myself," Alastair said, opening the gate onto the path. "You could say it was the hard way."

Alastair flicked on his torch and they walked together along the path. It was strange how different it looked, with the torches lighting up the underside of the trees. The branches looked pale against the dark sky, like white, bony fingers. The leaves were slippery where the damp ground was turning to ice. No Trick-or-Treaters used this path. It was much too spooky.

But Kevin barely noticed. He was admiring his cauldron of treats and wondering what they would have done if someone had opted for a trick. They had never thought of that. He felt sure Jilly would have planned something. He turned as Alastair stopped on The Vicarage drive, watching as the priest paled so quickly it was visible even in the strange orange glow of the security lamps.

Alastair had enjoyed the walk home, watching Kevin as he studied his swinging pot of treats, but the moment he crossed the threshold of The Vicarage he could tell something was wrong. There was nothing to see which stood out as being different. The security light flicked on as soon as they stepped towards the house, the car was exactly as he had left it, and the light on the first floor was on, as he always left it on. He took a step forward, repeatedly telling himself he was being foolish. Kevin looked up at him, his eyes widening.

"I've just got to find the key," Alastair whispered, looking for an excuse for his erratic behaviour, one which wouldn't frighten the boy. "Wait a moment, Kevin."

He looked up at the house again and realised what was wrong. The study window showed a flash of light pushing around the blinds. It only showed up as the security light switched off. Alastair clutched the keys in his hand, unsure what he should do. Was it better to go into the house? Would it be wiser to leave? It would certainly be safer. He clicked his torch on once more and ran it across the study window. The security light returned, but the light in the study remained the same.

"I think I've frightened myself," he laughed, looking down at Kevin. But he wasn't convinced, even now. He walked to the door and slotted the key in. Twisting it took all the courage he had, so that none was left to give him the strength to open it. Kevin pushed it back and Alastair braced himself for what lay within. The first thought was that he would find Dawn staring across at him, as she had done almost two years ago, her eyes challenging him to confront the bitterness of their son's death. It had troubled her how Alastair had found any form of comfort when she could find none. Her dismissal of God and faith had been instinctive, but it had wounded him.

But the hall was empty. The vast space lit up as Alastair flicked the switch. Everything was as it should be. Kevin pulled off his costume and collected his cauldron, rushing through to the living room.

"I'm going to see what I got," he called excitedly.

"Okay," Alastair replied, trying to pretend everything was normal. He reached for the handle to the study and swung the door open. The lamp on the table was switched on. He swallowed hard. He knew he hadn't left it switched on. He hadn't even worked at the desk today. Perhaps it had been Jilly earlier. But she never used the desk lamp, she would use the centre light. He reached across the table and checked the messages. There were two. Snatching a pen and notepad, both of which were exactly where he had left them, he began writing them down. Normality and rational facts were returning.

He felt the telephone slip from his shoulder, while his numb fingers spilt the pen and paper.

The picture of Leonard had a large cross covering his face. Alastair stumbled out of the room and rushed through to the living room.

"Kevin," he began, his voice trembling. "I think you should give Benji a ring and you can compare your Halloween takings."

"Why?" Kevin asked.

"I'll give Jilly a ring."

Alastair turned towards the hall once more but gasped as he saw the picture in the alcove, which had a matching cross over the boy's face.

"What is it?" Kevin sobbed, leaning against Alastair. "What's happened?"

"I think someone's been in the house, Kevin," Alastair whispered. "So, as soon as I've called Jilly, I'm going to ring the police."

"It's happening all over again," the boy stammered. "Why is it happening so soon?"

"It's okay," Alastair reassured him, but guided the boy out of the room and into the study. "We'll be fine and safe. That's what the police do, they keep people safe."

Kevin did not seem convinced by this but, as the pair barricaded themselves into the study, Alastair realised he had to be the pillar Kevin needed him to be. He called Jilly, her home number going to an answer machine so that he had to rummage around his desk to find her mobile number. She came at once, appearing at the door within minutes.

"Are you sure you're okay, Vicar?" she asked. "Maybe you shouldn't wait on your own. He could still be in the house."

"No, I don't think so," Alastair said with a smile, but it was marred by nervousness. "I think she came with a specific aim in mind."

"She?" Jilly breathed.

"He; she; it. Will you just look after Kevin tonight?"

"Of course I will," Jilly said, smiling across at

the boy. "Just take care, Vicar."

"Be good for Jilly, Kevin," Alastair said. "We'll get this sorted."

"It's because of me," Kevin cried. "It's the curse!"

"No," Alastair said firmly. "This is about me, not you."

He waved to them both and walked back purposefully to his study, calling the police the moment his hands were steady enough to dial the number. He didn't ring the emergency line, just the local station, and he stood in the hall waiting for them to arrive. After fifteen minutes, he realised how ridiculous it was to stand there, and he untied the cloak from his neck, carrying it upstairs. He walked along the landing and into his room. Everything was exactly as he had left it, except for the picture of Leonard on the drawers, which had a cross through his face.

He couldn't understand why anyone would go to so much trouble to do something which only wounded him. There had been money in the study, and his wallet on the kitchen worktop, but the intruder hadn't taken them.

He walked into the dining room and flicked on the lights. A sea of black crosses stared across at him from the dresser. His little boy's face obscured on every single one of the pictures. He leaned on the back of one of the chairs and let go of a long breath, trying to steady his rapid heartbeat.

He jumped as the doorbell rang.

The police stayed for a little over an hour, going through the house with him and checking for any sign of a forced entry. There was none.

Whoever had been in The Vicarage had arrived and left in invisibility. Alastair tried to explain to the officers that he had no idea who might have done such a thing, and that anyone in the village would have known he was out. By the time they left, he felt no closer to knowing who had done this.

The moment the police left, he opened the frame on each of the photographs, relieved to find it was only the glass which had been defaced. He felt lonely in the big house on his own, and he picked up the phone repeatedly, willing himself to call Jilly and ask her to drop Kevin back at the house, but the boy was safer where he was. Alastair sat in the armchair and stared at the fire. He felt like a trespasser in his own home. The question of who had gained access to his house had been shelved in favour of another question: how?

He didn't stop considering this as he fell asleep. He didn't want to go to bed, he couldn't bear to sleep in his bedroom when a stranger had been in it. But he could no longer remain awake, and he drifted to sleep, haunted by dreams in which he was trying to save Leonard and Kevin, while the three of them were being hunted. The figure of threat in the dream never revealed themselves, and this only made the chase more frightening.

The next day began with a shower, and at once the world began to settle into its normal routine. When Jilly and Kevin came rushing into the vestry, he assured them there was nothing to worry about. The church service was concluded with his normal calm, measured tone, and only

Mrs Humphries' refusal to talk to him at the end of the service marked it as unusual. Jilly had not told anyone but Trish about the intruder, and neither sister was the type to gossip. At the end of the service, as the weekly notices were being read, Alastair announced to the congregation that he intended to hold his bonfire party on Thursday night.

This announcement was met with surprise and delight from most of the congregation, but Kevin felt only fear. The curse had begun to take effect, sooner than it ever had before. Was it that he was happier with Alastair than he had been at any of his houses since Liam's death? Or was it just that the curse was gaining a terrible momentum, which swept him and those around him along in its storm? Kevin remained silent as they walked back to The Vicarage. He couldn't believe Alastair wasn't taking this threat seriously, and yet there was nothing more that Kevin could do to persuade him of it.

The only thing which was able to distract Kevin, was Mrs Henderson's announcement on Monday morning that they would be beginning their rehearsals for the school play. Kevin was cast as the star, a role he intended to make his own, and he already had plans concerning his costume. Initially, he had wanted to be a king, but when he had gone back to The Vicarage on Monday evening and told Alastair he was going to be the star, the man was so excited that Kevin decided he should be, too.

Thursday loomed like an insurmountable obstacle in the boy's mind. There was so much which could go wrong. He considered hiding all the matches, but Alastair probably had them tucked all around the house. He hoped it rained, prayed that it would, but when Thursday morning arrived it was to brilliant sun and a frost on the dewy ground. Kevin was silent as he walked downstairs and sat at the breakfast bar. He spread the raspberry jam across his toast and stared at the speckles of the seeds. Alastair talked happily about his plan for today, going to visit Mrs Franks in the hospital, calling in to the sweetshop in town to collect cinder toffee, but Kevin could only imagine tomorrow's breakfast with the desperate hope he would still be sitting beside Alastair.

"Look," Alastair whispered, pointing out of the window. Ysolde sat on one of the steppingstones in the lawn, twisting a nut in her tiny hands and nibbling at it. "She's excited too."

"I want to be here tomorrow," Kevin whispered, sniffing back tears.

"We'll both be here tomorrow, Kevin." Alastair smiled across at him. "We're going to have a wonderful night, gathering with friends around the bonfire, and you'll see that you had nothing to worry about. I promise."

Kevin scrubbed the back of his hand across his face and nodded. He tried to tell himself that Alastair would never promise something unless he knew it would come true, but he always came back to the thought that the priest would not take his curse seriously. They walked to school in silence, but when they reached the playground, Kevin hugged Alastair's arm, refusing to let go.

"It's nearly nine o'clock," Alastair coaxed. "You've got to go in."

"I don't want to," the boy stammered. "You're going to leave me tonight. You're going to die. I know you are."

Alastair knelt down on the cold ground and looked up at Kevin. "I'm not going to leave you, Kevin. We're going to have a great party, surrounded by friends. Now, come on. I'll take you into the school."

He rose to his feet and led Kevin into the building. Other pupils and their parents watched, and some remarked on their behaviour, but Kevin ignored them all, reluctantly letting go of Alastair's hand as Mrs Henderson guided the boy through to the classroom. The vicar left, constantly looking back over his shoulder and, every time, Kevin was looking back at him.

Kevin didn't talk to anyone that day, even Benji. He sat and hugged his hands about his head, blocking out the sounds of the classroom and trying to block out the world around him. Mrs Henderson spent the whole day attempting to engage him, but Kevin had no interest in school. Several of the other children found his behaviour amusing and, after many snide remarks, Mrs Henderson chose to lead Kevin out of the class and down to her office. She was at a loss, unable to guide, or even reach, the child. She asked Kathryn to come and sit with him as she went to dismiss the class for lunch.

By the time she returned, it was to find Kevin, Kathryn and Ken Samuels all sipping cups of tea in the suddenly crowded office. Kevin hugged his mug and sniffed, trying to hold back his tears, but the streaks on his cheek which caught the light proved he had failed. Being a Thursday, the art teacher was in that afternoon, so Mrs Henderson invited Kevin to stay in her office, keen to try and find out what was so upsetting the boy.

After several minutes of gentle prying, and some more obvious questions, Kevin spilt out the full extent of his fears. He detailed each of the horrific deaths he felt responsible for as well as the one he feared would come tonight.

"Not this curse again," Mrs Henderson said. "It's all nonsense, sweetheart. There's no such things."

"That's what Alastair says," Kevin wailed. "But he hasn't seen what I've done, and neither have you."

This statement unsettled Mrs Henderson, suddenly unsure what he had done, but she didn't allow her fears to show. Instead, she and Kevin stayed in her office for the afternoon and, when the bell rang, she returned the boy to Alastair. She handed over his hand as though he was little more than a toddler, but Kevin was eager to stand beside the priest.

They didn't speak as they walked back to The Vicarage, Alastair carrying Kevin's book bag in one hand, while his other arm was around the boy's shoulder. They walked into the house and Kevin kicked off his shoes without untying them. Alastair frowned across at this regression.

"What do I have to do to prove you're not cursed?" he asked, breaking the silence as he picked up Kevin's shoes and untied the laces, wincing as he tugged at the cords.

"Be here tomorrow, unharmed. All of you." Kevin hugged one of the cushions to him.

"And then you'll believe me?" Alastair asked.

In reply, Kevin nodded. He could find no words to speak, but curled up, burying himself in the corner of the sofa. He jumped as Alastair sat next to him.

"Good," Alastair said. "Now, will you help me get everything onto the table?"

Kevin had never used the table in the dining room before, but now he helped Alastair lay the tablecloth and put out stacks of paper plates. There was an enormous spread of buffet food, as though Alastair was expecting not only the churchgoers, but the whole village to attend. All the pictures of Leonard had been re-framed, and the young boy stared down on them from every shelf of the dresser, overseeing their progress. Stacks of bakery pies and cocktail sticks arranged to make giant hedgehogs filled the table, but the centre was a mass of toffee. It was intentionally placed so that little ones couldn't reach it without the help of longer arms. Kevin collected a few pieces and stood back, trying to break into the rock hard sweet.

The bonfire was going to be lit at six o'clock, and ten minutes beforehand the first of their visitors arrived. Everyone gathered at the side of the drive, waiting for Alastair to lead them around to the bonfire. Kevin trudged out and met Benji, grunting to him rather than speaking. Alastair appeared, running out to meet everyone and smiling across at each one of them in turn.

"Come on, everyone," Alastair called, guiding the gathered congregation round to the garden. "Let's get the bonfire lit."

Kevin was surprised by how small the bonfire

was. It was a pyramid about his height and was wide enough so that Alastair could poke his head in, checking the structure for little hedgehogs. He lit the fire, and Kevin realised there was another pile of wood a little further away, which Alastair began carrying across to the fire. Kevin hung back from the flames, wincing each time sparks flew up as Alastair threw the next piece of wood on. One of the parishioners had donated four pallets which Alastair had dismantled.

The boy walked off a short distance and leaned against the apple tree. He watched the gathering for a while, hidden in the darkness. He could watch the people without them seeing him, and he amused himself by collecting some of the fallen nuts from the squirrel feeder. There were quite a few, and he followed the trail, hoping it would lead to the squirrel's home, or at least her hoard. He wandered off into the darkness, lost in his thoughts.

He wished he hadn't opened his heart to Alastair. That was when trouble started. He wished Alastair would believe him, he had seen so many people he cared about losing someone they loved or dying themselves. Instead, the priest seemed determined to play with fire, the very tool the curse used to kill people.

Alastair threw the final piece of wood onto the bonfire forty minutes after he had lit it and looked at the sea of happy faces. Last time he had hosted this event, Dawn had been by his side, silent and sad. The loss of his son had been raw, but somehow it seemed far more present this year. Leonard loved the fire. He would lean against Alastair's side, holding his hands out, his thin face red with the cold, his hands toasting by the fire. Alastair coughed, hiding his sudden burst of emotion.

"Vicar," Tom asked, his thin hand slotting into Alastair's. "Can we go and eat now?"

"Yes," Alastair said. He walked over to the French windows and pulled it open, guiding the visitors through to the dining room. Most of them had been in his house before and knew where they were going, but Alastair realised he had missed this aspect of his vocation. He handed out the plates and looked around the crowd, concern causing his smile to slip.

"Where's Kevin?" He looked around the room, panic seeping into him, but he forced himself to keep smiling. "Tuck in," he continued. "I'll just go find him."

He squeezed past the gathered people, but Trish stopped him at the door.

"Are you alright, Vicar?" she asked, her voice clipped but her tone caring.

"I'm just going to find Kevin," he explained.

"Did he do it?"

"Do what?" Alastair asked, confusion on his face.

"That," she said, pointing at the dresser.

"No," Alastair whispered, staring at the array of crossed out photographs. He didn't know whether the word was in answer to Trish's question or a statement of disbelief. Perhaps it was both. He took the door handle and put all his weight onto it.

"Do you want me to go find him?" she asked. "He'll just be outside."

"No, I'll go. But would you do something for

me?" he asked, looking over his shoulder at the other people.

"Yes. What is it?"

"Don't make a fuss, just take them down."

Trish placed her hand on his arm and nodded across at him. Alastair stepped out of the room and back over to the French windows, then out into the garden. The sudden change from clear electric lights into the darkness took his eyes a moment to adjust, and he stood still for a time, waiting for them to focus.

"Kevin?" he called softly. There were one or two people still standing by the bonfire, smokers mainly, but Kevin wasn't with them. "Kevin?" he called a little bit louder, and listened as leaves moved in the furthest corner of the garden, and Kevin rushed towards him. "What is it?"

The boy's face was so pale it shone. His wide eyes brimmed with tears, and he pressed himself against Alastair, breathing in his smoky scent.

"I thought you would be dead," he sniffed.

"What have you been doing?" Alastair asked. "Everyone's in the dining room."

"I followed Ysolde's trail," he replied.

"Have you been inside?"

Kevin shook his head. "I didn't want to be trapped. The fire is only deadly when you're trapped."

"I told you it would be fine," Alastair said, mustering the strength he needed to reassure the boy. "And the bonfire's burning away now. It'll just be ash, soon."

Kevin gripped him tighter, but gave a little laugh. "Do you think the curse is broken?"

"I don't think you're cursed, Kevin," he

said, leaning down and kissing the boy's hair. "Unlucky, not cursed."

He didn't mention the photographs, but they both walked back to the house and ladened their plates with food, walking through to the living room and talking with their guests. Trish had quietly collected up the photos and piled them in the corner of the dining room, taking them one or two at a time so as not to raise too much attention. No one mentioned it to Alastair as he moved among them, smiling and laughing with them.

After a while, people began to leave, and by eight o'clock only Trish, Jilly and the boys remained. Jilly was pulling Tom's coat closed about him, the boy laughing so naturally as she kept missing the zip. It was such a beautiful sound, Alastair found himself laughing too.

"Thank you for going to see Mum today, Vicar," Trish said, pulling his attention from her son and younger sister. "I called in on her at the end of shift."

"It's my pleasure, Trish. Your mum is a lovely lady."

"She's dying, Vicar," Trish said bluntly. "Jilly won't accept it, but the chemotherapy isn't working."

"Isn't it a bit early to tell?" Alastair asked, guiding Trish back to the dining room.

"Maybe," she said, shrugging her shoulders. "But Jilly respects you. If Mum doesn't get better, will you help me break it to her?"

"If that's what you want me to do," Alastair said.

"Thank you, Vicar. I'm sorry about your

pictures. Was it Kevin?"

"No," Alastair replied with absolute certainty. "It's not the first time, either. Someone broke in when we were Trick-or-Treating and did the same thing."

"That's awful."

Alastair nodded. "Do you know what really hurt tonight?" he whispered, surprised to find he wanted to open up to the brusque woman before him. "Everyone who was here tonight was part of my congregation. That means, one of my congregation did this."

Trish took his hand and squeezed it gently, both turning as Jilly appeared in the doorway. Her smile never slipped as she observed this moment of tender support between her sister and the priest, but her eyes widened slightly.

"Ready to go?" she chimed.

"Yes," Trish replied, turning away from Alastair and following her sister through to the hall.

Tidying up the house took a long time into the evening. Kevin fell asleep on the sofa, while Alastair carried the remaining food through to the kitchen, bagging it up and putting it into the fridge, while he tipped all the cinder toffee into a tin. The carpet was muddy and stained but, as he pulled the vacuum out of the cupboard, his gaze fell on Kevin, sound asleep. He didn't want to wake the boy. Instead, he walked into the dining room and carried the pile of frames over to the table, removing Leonard's photographs from each of the marked frames.

Confident he would hear if Kevin woke up, he allowed the smile to fall from his face. Every clasp he undid from every frame felt like a blow against his heart, and he found himself sobbing like a child. It was cruel enough that anyone would do such a thing, but that one of his own congregation could do it was beyond belief.

He lifted one of the pictures, a school photograph from when Leonard had been seven, and ran his finger down his son's face. How could anyone obscure and damage something so beautiful? Defiantly, he stood the photos up on the dresser again, propping them wherever they would stand. He would not stop looking at his boy simply because someone's warped mind wished to destroy the happy memories. They were all that was left of him.

He switched off the lights, deciding to leave the cleaning until the next day, and unlocked the door to the study. He carried the frames through, not wanting Kevin to stumble across them and discover any trace of negativity at the party. He set them down and looked at the picture of Leonard on the desk. Written across it in the same permanent marker as the others had been graffitied with, he read aloud,

"Remember, Remember."

"Gunpowder, treason and plot," a sleepy voice added from the doorway.

Alastair set the photo face down on the desk as he looked across at Kevin, smiling at him. He could not let the boy know anything was amiss. These messages were Alastair's curse, and had nothing to do with Kevin.

"Mrs Henderson taught us that today," Kevin said. "Did someone really try to blow up parliament?"

"Yes," Alastair replied, walking around the desk and guiding Kevin towards the stairs. "But that was a long time ago."

Alastair stayed with Kevin until the boy fell asleep. He looked so calm as he slept, so safe, a far cry from how Alastair felt as he slipped silently from the boy's room, switching off the light as he went. All the shadows instantly disappeared, before new moon-shadows began to appear. He walked along the landing, pausing to stare down over the hall below. He stepped into his own room, checking the picture of Leonard there. It was unmarked, his own little boy smiling up at him. He gave a heavy sigh as he smiled back.

Finally, he returned to the study and lifted the picture of Leonard out of its frame. But it wasn't the picture he stared at, but the writing on the glass. Gunpowder. The word Kevin had spoken in innocence played in his head, until he could imagine every one of tonight's guest saying it.

"Treason and plot," snapped another voice, and he looked up from the desk. The sound of an American accent should have told him at once who he would find standing there, but he still felt his heart pound as he saw her.

"Dawn?" he whispered, rising from the chair and looking across at her.

Her eyes were wide, bulging almost, and filled with as much despair and loathing as the last time he had looked into them. But it wasn't just him she hated. She hated the world, she hated God, she hated anything she could blame for the death of her son.

"You betrayed me, Ally," she continued. "You let him die. I trusted you. You let my boy die and

I wasn't even there."

"That's not my fault, Dawn," he replied, questioning for the briefest of moments that he had not heard her come in. Perhaps she still had her key? No, it made no sense. Dawn couldn't be here.

"And you left me," she continued, ignoring his attempt at pacifying her.

"You left me," Alastair pointed out, trying to maintain a hold on his racing thoughts. Something was wrong. Dawn looked different. She was more angry now than sad. She had always been sad before.

"You provided the treason and plot," she continued. "You and Hilary Franks."

"What?" Alastair whispered, utterly confused by the twist in the conversation.

"I'll provide the gunpowder."

"No!" Alastair tried to stop her as she struck a match. None of this made sense. But as he tried to step forward the air round him lit up in a brilliant white, like a firework as it soars into the sky, before it bursts into an array of coloured explosions. There was no colour here, only a light explosion, the force of which sent him backward.

He crashed to the floor in the darkened room of the study. His chair, which he must have been sitting on when he fell asleep, was still moving backwards with such force, it bounced forward as it hit the bookcases on the wall. He clutched his chest, repeatedly reminding himself it had been a dream. Dawn had not returned, neither angry nor sad. There was no gunpowder, and no explosion. He climbed to his feet, leaning down on the desk, trying to support himself.

After a moment, he walked through the house, switching off lights and closing doors. Mundane routines to conquer his shaken thoughts. He got ready for bed and lay down, staring at the empty space beside him. It hadn't been Dawn. She would never harm him. It had only been a dream, a nightmare, brought on by all these thoughts of curses and fires. Despite knowing this to be true, Alastair struggled to fall asleep.

Kevin was woken up by the whirring sound of a vacuum cleaner downstairs. It took him a moment to remember where he was. He had been so sure that last night would be the end of his stay in The Vicarage that he could not believe he was lying here now, listening to the sounds of normality. He got out of bed and looked at the neatly folded school uniform on the chair. His face fell. He had forgotten it was Friday, hoping instead that it was weekend. But this disappointment was short lived as he crossed the landing to the bathroom. This was new territory for him. The next day had arrived, full of life and happiness. Perhaps the curse had really been broken. He dressed and brushed his hair before rushing down the stairs, imagining he was driving a car and pulling on the invisible steering wheel so that he could turn into the living room where Alastair was still vacuuming.

Kevin leapt on him, hugging him more tightly than he had ever held anyone before. Alastair stumbled forward, not having heard Kevin come downstairs, before he held him just as close.

"I didn't think you'd be here today," Kevin muttered into Alastair's side.

"I told you, curses don't exist. Do you believe me now?" Alastair's face held his usual smile, but it deepened as Kevin smiled back at him. The boy's expression plastered every inch of his face and Alastair felt victorious. Kevin chuckled at Alastair's expression, and the two of them sat down for breakfast.

"Next year you can actually enjoy the bonfire party," Alastair said, pouring a glass of orange juice and setting it in front of Kevin.

"Do I have to go to school today?"

"Yes," Alastair replied. "I have to do work. It's not fair if you don't."

"But school-" Kevin hung onto the last word, stretching out the vowel as though he was waiting for Alastair to complete his sentence.

"Mrs Henderson will have to be at school today. It's only right you go, too." He set the raspberry jam on the breakfast bar and smiled. "She said you're doing really well."

"I didn't yesterday."

"That's just because you were worried. Can you remember all your words for the spelling test?"

Kevin watched as Alastair stood the toast up on the metal toast rack and offered it to the boy, sucking his fingers to emphasise how hot it was. There was nothing which seemed to dampen the priest's spirits.

"I think so," Kevin laughed.

"I think you know them better than I do, anyway. Spelling has never been my strong suit."

The morning's conversation, ordinarily tedious, was only a bolster to Kevin's excited response to the second chance the world had given him. There was nothing which could dissuade him from his happiness and relief.

As the days passed, his mood never altered, except perhaps to increase his relief. Alastair maintained his silence over the events of bonfire night. He compartmentalised them in his mind, turning them into rational or foolish thoughts. Someone had played a game, a cruel game, but it was nothing more than that.

The following Wednesday, Kevin's school joined with the other primary school in the village to remember Armistice Day. There was a large turnout at the memorial, the road was blocked, with police diverting traffic through the twisty back streets instead of along the main road. Kevin watched this with greater interest. It was not that he didn't care about the service, but Benji and Tom were taking the event so seriously, they would not even smile at him. He fidgeted with the zip on his coat pocket and watched the steam billow every time he breathed. He watched as the flags were lowered and tried to imagine what war was like. Was it as frightening as his curse had been? Was there a way to end it, as Alastair had somehow ended the curse?

The cold was biting at his cheeks and he lifted his hand to brush away the tear which had fallen there. It was the product of the cold weather, not grief, but Mrs Henderson must have thought he was deeply moved by the respectful silence, for she placed her arm about his shoulders. Trish was crying too, silent tears which her boys didn't notice as they stared at the elaborate white cross with a sword engraved down the centre of it.

Kevin jumped as a trumpet player, a little to

the side, began playing a tune. This seemed to mark the end of the service, except for everyone joining in with a song Kevin had only ever heard being sung at the start of football matches. He joined the rest of the children in returning to school. Benji walked along beside him, quieter than usual.

There was a damp feeling in the air and, by the time they had reached the school, the first drops of rain were beginning to fall. This resulted in an indoor lunchtime, during which Kevin found a chess set in the games cupboard and began teaching Benji how to play.

Alastair thanked the Salvation Army band for attending, and shook hands with the head of the Royal British Legion's local branch, before he began walking back to The Vicarage. He paused as he heard Jilly's voice behind him.

"Have you got a moment, Vicar?"

"Of course," he replied, turning to face her. His face became gentle as he looked into her teary eyes. "Do you want to come back to the house?"

"No," she said, wiping the tears away. "It's Trish. I'm worried about her."

"Why?"

"She was crying just now, during the service. That's why I'm crying," Jilly laughed. "I'm a terrible sympathetic crier."

"What's the matter?"

"I'm sorry about yesterday, too," Jilly stammered. "Not turning up without letting you know."

"I assumed you had your reasons."

"Did Trish tell you?" She watched as Alastair

shook his head. "Her husband's boat has gone missing."

"A whole navy ship?" Alastair asked in disbelief.

"He wasn't on the big ship. He was out on a little surveillance boat." Jilly looked across at him. "She hasn't told the boys. I only found out by accident, because Mum mentioned it when I went to see her on Monday. What should I do?"

"Just be there for her, Jilly," he said. "She'll need someone to talk to. Make sure you're there when she does."

"Will you talk to her?"

"Not unless she wants me to. But my door's always open. To both of you."

"Thank you, Vicar," she replied, smiling slightly across at him. "I'll work twice as hard on Saturday to make up for yesterday."

"Jilly," he said, snatching her hand as she turned. Her eyes burnt as she looked up at him, her cheeks reddening as she smiled nervously. "You can't carry all these things on your shoulders. Take Saturday off. Have a break. Do something you want to do."

"I want to be a good sister, a good daughter, and a good aunt. That's all. See you Saturday, Vicar."

Alastair watched her walk back over to Trish, who was crouching down in front of the memorial, pushing a little wooden cross with a poppy on into the soft ground to the side. Their family was seeped in military tradition. Jilly's uncle had died in conflict overseas. It seemed too cruel that Benji's and Tom's dad might have died in the same way. Placing the Franks family at the forefront of his prayers, Alastair walked back to The Vicarage.

Part Five

The School Play

Once the Remembrance Day parade was over, the school began looking forward to Christmas. This had been met with great excitement by the children, while parents invariably began trying to make last year's costumes look fresh and different for this year's play. As the star, Kevin expected his costume to be the most exciting. Alastair already had plans for it, but he wouldn't give anything away to the boy. Kevin didn't mind. It all felt as though Christmas was coming early this year, and he was sure it was going to be the most amazing Christmas he had ever had.

Mrs Henderson was running the school show. She had written the script herself, giving a new approach to the nativity, and incorporating several traditional carols. Kevin loved singing, and was immensely proud to be given the chorus of We Three Kings to sing by himself. As he felt more and more secure in his situation, his diligence and determination in school grew. Mrs Henderson had awarded him the Star Pupil badge two weeks in a row, and at the parents' evening the week following Remembrance Day, she gave a glowing report to Alastair.

Since Bonfire Night, Alastair was relieved to find that The Vicarage had remained unvisited by the unwelcome guest. But, as the month wore on, he frequently felt as though eyes were watching him as he moved around the house. The worst sensation had been after returning from Little Golforth youth club on Thursday night. He had been unable to open the door, haunted by an image in his memory, afraid of what would be waiting inside. Kevin had taken this pause as a demonstration of how tired the vicar was, and had taken the keys from him, opening the door and showing him in. This had given Alastair cause to smile at the boy, and the moment of dark fear passed.

The curse had not been mentioned, either. Although both of them began to feel quietly anxious about the visit of Sally-Anne at the end of the week, this was what they hoped would be the last of her visits, at least until the new year.

On the morning of the day she was due to visit, Jilly called round at The Vicarage. Alastair had only just got back from taking Kevin to school. He was rushing around the house, trying to arrange everything exactly as he believed the social worker would want. He loved having Kevin, and he felt afraid Sally-Anne might take the child away from him.

"Just me, Vicar," came the cheerful announcement as Alastair opened the door. "I just wondered if you wanted me to help out. It is the big day, isn't it?"

"What do you mean?" Alastair asked, stepping back to let Jilly in.

"Isn't it today that you get to find out whether Kevin will be staying?"

"Oh," Alastair returned, unsure how she knew. She must have seen this, as she gave a slight laugh.

"Kevin told Benji. Look," she added as Alastair shut the door. "I'd like to talk to you, Vicar, if you've got time."

Alastair listened to the door latch and willed himself to speak candidly to her, but she had been his concern longer than Kevin had. Swallowing back his words, he smiled across at her.

"Of course, Jilly. Why don't you come through? I'll put the kettle on."

"I'm not sure it will fit you," she laughed.

When they were sitting together, Alastair in his armchair and Jilly in the furthest corner of the sofa, he cleared his throat in an obvious attempt to ignite conversation. Jilly hugged the mug in her hands, studying it intently. It was the last one of a set which Dawn and he had been given for their wedding. It was rounded and had hand painted flowers on it, but he couldn't see what required such determined staring.

"Trish says Mum's going to die," Jilly whispered.

Alastair wasn't sure what he had expected her to say, but it certainly hadn't been this. He sat forward in the chair and stared at her as she slipped her feet out of her shoes and pulled her knees up to her chin.

"How did her chemo go? Was it no help?"

"The doctor said it's too early to tell." She stared at the mug, tracing the flowers with one finger. "But Trish says it doesn't look good." Her shoulders shuddered, the effort of withholding tears becoming too much for her. "But she wouldn't leave me, would she?"

"I'm sure it's not her intention to leave you, Jilly. Your Mum's crazy about you and Trish, she'd do anything for you."

"Why won't she stay?" Jilly asked, her words childish, but her drive desperate. "I'm sorry, Vicar," she continued. "I feel so selfish. You lost Leo and Dawn; Trish still hasn't heard from Daniel; poor Benji and Tom still don't know what's happened to their dad. But I'm-" She stopped and turned her teary eyes towards him. As her gaze met with his, she found she was unable to contain her tears and her cheeks were awash with them. "I'm so afraid."

"You'll never be left alone, Jilly," Alastair said. "You'll always have somewhere to go."

"So you think she's right? You think Mum will die?"

"I think Trish is a nurse," Alastair replied neutrally. "She knows more than me, but she doesn't know for sure. Can you take comfort in the knowledge God knows, and will stay with your mum?"

"I know I should," she sobbed. "But, no. Why can't God's plan be to let me go first?"

"Jilly," Alastair said, a slightly stern tone entering his voice. "That would kill your mum.

She loves you so much, she couldn't bear to lose you. Don't let grief drive you to do anything stupid." He stared across at her, waiting until she nodded. "Still no word of Daniel, then? When does it become an issue of national security?"

"I don't know," she muttered, her tone suggesting that she was beyond caring.

"And how's John?"

"I haven't heard from him."

"Was he with Daniel?"

Jilly shook her head and rose to her feet, taking her empty mug through to the kitchen and washing it. "I'm sure he's fine," she answered.

Alastair watched in confusion, and a certain amount of awe, at how readily she switched back to her normal, jolly self. The moment of uncertainty, the dip below the horizon of happiness, was fleeting and was now hidden. She proceeded to change the subject and actively sought against it returning once more to her mother. But there was a fear in Alastair, too, as he watched her. She was so fragile, so timid, and so vulnerable. There was a gnawing doubt in the back of his mind about what she might do when something did happen to Hilary Franks.

Jilly had not always been so fragile. A short while before he had arrived in the village, she had been an exuberant girl with the world before her. But ten years ago, under continued and intense pressure from her peers in college, she had suffered a nervous breakdown. She had been little more than a child at the time, and she hadn't dared leave the house. When Alastair arrived almost two years later, she had still confined herself to the house. He could remember going around to visit Mrs Franks, who had been churchwarden before Mrs Henderson, and being introduced to the young woman who would nervously smile across at him, beaten and berated by all the other people she had known, too timid to talk.

There was little wonder Jilly was afraid. Her mum had been a rock to her, while Trish and John did not really understand their younger sister. But over the years, Jilly had grown into a sensitive and caring young woman, stronger in dilemmas than most people. She had returned to the person she had always sought to be, someone who always had a smile going spare, or a hand to help in support. She had conquered her demons which the bullying had caused, but she had done so with the help of her mum. If anything were to happen to Hilary, Alastair was unsure what effect it would have on Jilly.

But her determination to continue this pretence of normality was complete, and she spent until lunchtime helping him clear and clean the house. Alastair was grateful for her help, but even more grateful of her company. The house looked spotless when she concluded her work and she beamed across at him.

"I wanted to thank you, Vicar," she said at last, as she pulled on her scarf. "You've always helped me out, and you've always been there for me. Mum said, the first day she met you, that you were one of a kind. I think she was right."

"What a lot has happened since then," Alastair laughed, helping her with her coat.

"I've no regrets. Have you?"

"Not at all," he replied. "Look after yourself,

Jilly. And remember, my door is always open to you."

"I know," she laughed. "I've got a key." She became sombre and shook her head. "I wouldn't ever do that, you know?"

Alastair nodded and laughed. "You're a rare one, Gillian Franks. Take care of yourself."

"Good luck this afternoon. I know it'll go well."

"Thanks."

He watched as she collected her bike and rode out of the drive, along the path and back towards the church. Alastair shut the door, and returned to the armchair, slouching down into it.

He only meant to sit there until he had calmed his thoughts, but he must have fallen asleep, for the next thing he knew was that someone was ringing the doorbell and pounding the door. He rose to his feet and rubbed his eyes, trying to remember what he had been doing. The calendar on the wall stared back at him, warning him of Sally-Anne's visit, and the clock on the mantelpiece pointed out that she was due at the door five minutes ago.

Alastair rushed to the door and pulled it open, smiling across at the lady who stood there. She was sheltered from the rain where she stood on the step, but her hair was windswept, and her face held a trace of anger as she looked across at him. Alastair stepped back and ushered her in.

"I'm so sorry," he began, taking her coat and hanging it up on the hall stand.

"Is parenthood exhausting, Reverend Roberts?" she asked, but as she looked across at him she shook her head. "Sorry. I've got to admit, I'm pleased to find you well. How's Kevin?"

"Fine. Great. He's just been cast in the school play." Alastair realised this wasn't what she meant, but he felt suddenly nervous. Being asleep when she arrived had put him on the back foot and he had no idea how to right himself.

"That's great."

"And he's learning all the constellations. And hunting for-" Alastair stopped abruptly as Sally-Anne took a seat, staring at him with an unimpressed expression. "Do you want a cup of tea?"

"Is this a bad time, Reverend Roberts? Only, I don't remember you being so distracted on the last few occasions."

"I'm sorry," he conceded. "Kevin's doing great. He's settled here. He seems to enjoy our routine. And we're combating his fear of fire."

Sally-Anne made an exasperated sound.

"He's not cursed," Alastair continued, before she had the chance to argue. "But so many people have told him it, he's started to believe it himself. But we had a bonfire party, and since then he's completely dropped this idea of a curse. No one was hurt and everyone had a great time."

"I'm pleased," she said, her tone suggesting more relief than pleasure. "But just keep your eyes open."

"I think you're trying to scare me," Alastair laughed, moving into the open plan kitchen, setting the kettle on the hob and listening to the whoosh of the gas flame igniting. "I've looked through every page of his history, and I can't see anything more than bad luck."

"Perhaps you're right," she said, shrugging her shoulders. "But it normally takes a bit longer than a month."

"Well, I'm not afraid," Alastair continued. "I'm still really pleased he's come to stay here."

"Did you tell him about your son?"

"Yes," Alastair replied flatly. "I've done everything you, and the paperwork, said I should."

"Reverend Roberts," Sally-Anne began, rising to her feet and smiling across. "I'm not here to take Kevin away from you. I can't believe he's settled so well, but I'm so pleased he has. I'm on your side here."

Alastair nodded as he took on board her words, and he found himself easing muscles he hadn't noticed were tense. The atmosphere in The Vicarage, which had been agitated since her arrival, relaxed, and they talked freely. When it reached the time for Alastair to go and collect Kevin, he did so with a spring to his step.

For her own part, Sally-Anne was pleased and relieved to see how settled both Alastair and Kevin were. She had spent so long, and lost so many lives, trying to find a home for the boy. This was perfect. A part of her considered the possibility that the others had failed in order to prepare the boy for this home, but she couldn't bring herself to believe that anyone's happiness was worth so much death, even someone as sweet as Kevin.

When Sally-Anne parted from them, both Kevin and Alastair felt they had crossed the final hurdle which had stood in their way. Now, Christmas suddenly became an imminent event, with nothing to fear or dread before it. Kevin was eagerly trying to learn his lines for the school play, and sang his solo at any opportunity. Alastair loved going through the lines with him, impressed by how many of the other characters' words Kevin knew. Sometimes, if he was doing something else at the same time, Alastair might have missed a cue line, and Kevin always knew how to correct him. But Alastair would never practise his song with him. Instead, he insisted Jilly should go through it with him.

"You can use the piano in the study," he began on Saturday morning as he and Kevin sat down with a cooked breakfast. "I guess it's still in tune."

"You've got a piano?" Kevin asked excitedly.

"Yes," Alastair replied. "Maybe Jilly will teach you to play it. She's a very good musician."

"Can you play it?"

"Not now," Alastair replied, laughing slightly. "But I did used to learn when I was your age."

"So why do you have a piano now?"

"Leonard's mum wanted him to learn. Now she," he said, with his customary smile deepening. "She was a great pianist."

There was no wonder Kevin had never noticed the piano, even on the rare occasions he had been in the study. With its lid down and the books piled on top of it, it looked just like a bookcase. It had books tucked under it, as well, and Kevin and Alastair spent some time excavating the instrument. As soon as they were able to lift up the lid, Kevin ran his small fingers over the keys, reluctant to press any of them down. Alastair smiled down at the boy and, resting his own hand over his, guided his fingers to the notes which would play We Three Kings. Kevin stood with his eyes wide and his mouth to match.

"How did you know?" he gasped.

They spent a lazy day, writing a Christmas card list and cooking dinner. In the evening, the pair walked out into the onset of dark, calling in on Mr and Mrs Sinter. Kevin was growing more confident with the dogs and was learning that, when he was less sure of them, the best thing to do was to ignore them. Mr Sinter was recovering well, although he still was not able to walk the dogs. Jilly had been going round to help Mrs Sinter with this, both women managing one dog far more easily than either could manage both. They walked on a short way to Mrs Henderson's house which was set in a picturesque garden. Even at this time of the year, it was well-kept, the fallen leaves having been raked away. There were tiny lamps lighting up the path to the door, while the indoors lights beckoned them in.

Kevin stopped a few paces from the door while Alastair walked forward and rang the bell. With excitement, he turned back. He had heard a shuffling sound and, desperate to try and find the cause in the hope it was a hedgehog, he tiptoed away. Alastair turned to him, but spun back to face Paul Henderson as he opened the door.

"Hello," Alastair said, smiling across at the man. "How are preparations going in London?"

"Ah," Paul said, standing back to let him in. "You know James, he's not letting his fiancée do any of the planning."

"Kevin!" Alastair called, and waited as Kevin rushed up to the house, before he turned back to Paul. "Is Mrs Henderson in? I just wanted to check something with her about tomorrow's service."

"Sure," Paul replied. "Bea!" He shut the door after Kevin and Alastair had walked in. "The vicar's here."

Kevin stared around him, his mouth dropping open. This house was unlike any he had ever been in before. There was a myriad of pictures, both paintings and photographs, on the walls of the thin hallway. Wherever there was a shelf, which occurred at irregular intervals and heights, they were filled with ornaments in fine china or brass. His fingers reached out towards one of a cat, but he stopped as Alastair shook his head quickly.

"Hello Kevin," Mrs Henderson began. "Is that one your favourite?"

Kevin felt confused, caught between different aspects of his life at having entered his teacher's house. "Yes, Mrs Henderson," he whispered.

"She's called Percy."

"But Percy is a boy's name."

"It's short for Persephone," she explained, guiding them into the living room. A huge fire was burning in the hearth and Kevin shied away from it, positioning Alastair between himself and the flames. "Here she is in real life," Mrs Henderson continued, pointing to one of three cats which were curled up in front of the fire.

Kevin sat cross-legged on the floor and watched as one of the cats walked over to him. As he began stroking it, from its head down to its tail, it gave a hollow, rasping purr, which seemed to rattle from its soul. Its little paws, tiny compared to those of the Sinters' dogs, pulsed out her claws.

He didn't listen as Alastair and Mrs Henderson spoke, but continued to stroke the cats who, one by one, added themselves to his lap. Paul had disappeared. When it was time to go, Kevin tried to shuffle the cats off him, realising the only way to remove the stubborn animals was just to stand up.

"It's funny," Mrs Henderson mused as she saw them to the door. "Normally they run off when visitors arrive. There must be something very special about you, Kevin."

Alastair nodded. "Without a doubt."

"Thank you," Kevin whispered, feeling his cheeks burning, but in the darkness they couldn't have seen him blushing. As they walked down the path, Kevin turned to Alastair. "Mrs Henderson has a house like a museum."

"Yes, she's a keen collector."

"Does she have any children?"

"She has three. They're all grown up now. And she has a grandson, too."

"Where do they live?"

"Her son, Philip, lives in Madrid, in Spain. He works at the British Embassy. Her daughter, Veronica, lives in London. She's the one who has a child, Harry. And her other son, Graham, lives in Little Golforth. He's the one who runs the youth club."

Kevin considered this as they walked back to The Vicarage. Because they had walked across the village to Mrs Henderson's house, they didn't go through the churchyard, but the tower was visible as they walked on. It looked black and foreboding, and Kevin slipped his hand into

Alastair's. The vicar made no comment on this, but waited until Kevin spoke.

"Is the church haunted?"

"Haunted?" Alastair mused. "Not that I know of."

"Do you believe in ghosts?" Kevin asked, unsure where Alastair's religious views left him in terms of such things.

"I don't not believe in them," came the honest reply. "I think I believe more in people's souls. I've never seen a ghost, but sometimes I feel like people are near me, people who have gone before. But I've never heard that Saint Hubertus is haunted."

"It looks scary, though," Kevin said, almost excusing his thoughts.

"I suppose. To me, it looks majestic. And maybe a bit mysterious. Two words which sum-up faith, I guess."

Perhaps it was Kevin's choice of conversation, but while the boy seemed comforted by Alastair's response, the priest became disquieted over the subject. He hadn't lied to Kevin. He really did believe in souls more than Hollywood-style ghosts. But he also believed hauntings happened to individuals, and he grew increasingly convinced that ghosts of his past were haunting him.

As they reached the house, he handed Kevin the key, not wanting to open the door as he had two years before to discover the scene before him. Kevin was delighted to be trusted with this job, and slotted the key into the lock. As he turned it, Alastair thought he could hear his own voice singing. It was Hills of the North, the first verse, his verse. Kevin pushed the door open and flicked on the light switch. Alastair looked up, expecting to find Dawn's eyes staring at him, challenging him to accept her decision. But there was no one there.

"Shall I put the kettle on?" Kevin asked, unaware of the churning thoughts in Alastair's head.

"No, I'll do that," Alastair replied with his usual smile. He felt the blood returning to his face and normality resumed.

November moved into its final week. The next Thursday, Alastair and Kevin ducked into the car, preparing to drive out to Little Golforth for the Youth Club. It was the first time Kevin had been since discovering it was Mrs Henderson's son who ran it. The ground had frozen, and the thin country roads were icy, so Alastair had decided to leave in extra time to reach the next village. They crawled along the road, which was single track in some places, and Kevin stared in amazement at the power of the almost full moon on the world below. Every time the hedges opened, the gap revealed fields of moonlight as it lit up the icy ground. He didn't watch the road, but pressed his hand on the window and gazed out through the glass. The world looked cold but beautiful.

There were fewer people at the Youth Club when they arrived, hardly surprising as the weather forecast had announced that drivers should only travel if their journeys were imperative. Kevin met the leader with a smile tugging at the corners of his mouth.

"I didn't know your last name was Henderson,"

he chirped. "Your mum's my teacher."

"I know," Graham laughed. "And how is being a star going, Kevin?"

Alastair watched them go, before he walked over to the kitchenette and put the kettle on. The drive over to Little Golforth had left him a little rattled and he felt he needed caffeine to help keep him awake. The kettle was boiling as Graham stepped over to him, smiling at one of the boys who called across, before turning to Alastair. His smile dropped a little and his forehead furrowed in concern.

"You didn't pass Mum on the way over, did you?"

"No," Alastair replied, pouring the water into two mugs and grabbing a teaspoon from a drawer under the worktop. "Was she meant to be here?"

"I'd asked Dad to drop off some stuff for tonight, but he's gone to see Uncle James, so she said she'd drive it over."

"Have you given her a ring?"

"Yes, on the house phone and her mobile, but I'm not getting anything on either."

Alastair handed him the mug of coffee and looked longingly at his mug of tea. Instead of lifting it, he dipped his hand into his coat pocket and pulled out his car keys.

"It's probably just that your dad's car won't start," Alastair said, tapping his hand on the younger man's arm. "I'll go find her. Keep an eye on Kevin."

Graham thanked him, and Alastair walked out into the frozen night. He loved the cold, how it sharpened everything, but he hated driving in icy conditions. He pressed the button which unlocked the car, and the lights sprang on, filling the moonlit carpark with an orange glow. He sank down into the seat and turned the ignition. At once, the noisy fan jetted warm air across the windscreen, which was already beginning to freeze over. He cautiously set the car in motion, and tried to tell himself how many times he had made this journey, even in the ice. This time, it was different. He had to make sure he was there for Kevin.

Every twist in the road, every open patch where the bitter wind had caused a flash of ice across the tarmac, seemed like a battle he had to win. When the village lights came into view, after twenty minutes of driving a stretch which normally only took eight, he muttered an appreciative prayer and drove across the village to Mrs Henderson's house. His smile was firmly on his face, and his relief even caused him to laugh.

His laughter faded as he turned the corner onto the quiet road where Mrs Henderson's cottage was. It wasn't quiet now. Blue lights filled the street, and Alastair stopped the car as a police officer appeared, lifting her hand to stop him. He turned off the ignition and climbed out of the car.

"What happened?" he whispered, looking at the fire engine which towered almost as high as the small cottage's eaves. The cottage windows closest to him were smashed, but the house was not where the fire had been. The burnt-out remnants of the car, still in the drive, told the story. "Is Mrs Henderson alright?"

"Are you family, sir?" the policewoman asked.

"No," Alastair replied. "I'm her priest. Her son sent me to find her. Is she okay?"

"She's been taken to hospital. She was unconscious when her neighbour found her. Looks like she forgot something and was going back to the house when the car set alight."

"This wasn't an accident, was it?" Alastair asked, feeling sick as he remembered the picture he had found online of Kevin's adopted father's car. Mrs Henderson's vehicle looked exactly like it.

"We'll have a team check out the vehicle," came the reply.

"I'll go tell Graham," Alastair muttered. "I'll go tell her son."

The drive back to Little Golforth was much shorter. Alastair's mind raced and the car matched its speed. He skidded once, as he was approaching the tiny village, and he saw it as God pointing out how reckless he was being. He crept along in a low gear after that.

As he walked to the door, he told himself repeatedly that he had been trained to deal with this but, as he watched Graham playing table football with some of the kids, he felt all his determination and self-belief fade away. He waved across, securing the smile on his face. None of the children had to know what was going on. Graham must have seen through the gesture, for his face dropped and he excused himself from the game.

"What is it, Vicar?"

"Your mum's going to be okay, Graham," he said, praying he had understood the police officer correctly. "But the car had a bit of an accident."

"Where is she? What happened?" Graham followed Alastair into the kitchenette, and the priest looked across at the transformation of the young man into the child he had been when Alastair first arrived.

"She's in hospital. I'll take you to her, Graham. Somehow the car caught fire, but she wasn't in it at the time, just caught up in the blast from it. She'll be fine," he repeated.

Graham nodded and seemed to relax slightly, but with this acceptance came a burst of tears in the man's eyes.

"Do you want me to ring Beth and ask her to take you?"

"She's gone to some show with her sister," Graham replied, his voice trembling.

Alastair felt at a loss. He couldn't let Graham drive in the state he was in, not when the roads were so bad, but he couldn't throw the children out of the youth club either. Their only option was to wait for the club to end.

Graham sat in the little office, while Alastair ran the club for the rest of the evening. He passed off Graham's absence with the cryptic announcement that he'd had some news, but he wouldn't answer any questions on the subject. He avoided any mention of fire, preparing himself for the inevitable discussion about curses with Kevin.

Once the last child had left the church hall, Alastair gently ushered Graham and Kevin to the car while he locked up. The roads were still treacherous, and the journey into town lasted twice as long as it should have done. No one spoke. After a while, Alastair flicked the radio on, looking for a way to fill the silence. Kevin observed all this, but remained silent. He was distracted by the beautiful landscape once more, storing questions in his head.

As they reached the hospital, however, Kevin's face began to pale. He climbed out of the car and gripped Alastair's arm, while Graham rushed in. Alastair assured Graham that he and Kevin would wait for him, and that he was to take as long as he needed, but the young man hardly seemed to hear the words. They sat in the front waiting room, watching as people came and went with their own worries and their own cares. Kevin fell asleep, leaning against him, but Alastair couldn't settle his mind enough to sleep.

It was someone, not something, which had caused the fire. He looked down at the sleeping child and felt suddenly angry. He wasn't angry with Kevin, he was angry at the people who had allowed him to believe he was cursed, and more so at whoever was following the boy around doing these things. Or perhaps it wasn't one person, perhaps it was several. The longer he sat there, ignored by everyone, the more confident he became in his ludicrous idea. But who would want to hurt the boy? Who could take such a gentle soul and torture it with the horrific deaths he had been witness to? But they had failed this time. Mrs Henderson had not died.

He rebuked himself as Graham walked towards him. This may have had nothing at all to do with Kevin.

"How's your mum?" Alastair asked quietly, not wanting to wake Kevin.

"You were right," he said, sniffing slightly.

"She's going to be okay. She broke her hip when she fell, and the doctors said she's got a concussion or something, but she'll be okay."

"Good," Alastair said, before adding, "thank God."

"Who did this?" Graham whispered, anger overtaking hurt in his voice. "Who would do it?"

"That's a question for the police, Graham. Let them chase it up."

They both turned as Paul came rushing in. Alastair watched as father and son talked and comforted one another. He woke Kevin and excused themselves from the hospital. The sun was rising, and the mystery of the moonlight gave way to the burning truth of a red sky. Kevin stayed silent until they reached The Vicarage.

"It was a fire, wasn't it?" he whispered, as Alastair closed the front door.

"Mrs Henderson fell," Alastair said truthfully. "She's broken her hip and bumped her head, but she's going to be fine. She'll probably not be able to do the play, though. She's never missed one all the time I've been here."

"I don't want to go to school," Kevin's voice trembled. "They'll all know. They'll all know it's my fault."

Kevin kicked off his shoes and dropped his coat to the floor, running up the stairs and into his room. Alastair stood, frozen in disbelief at the disarray which filled his hall. He collected the shoes, unfastening the laces with the same nauseous feeling cord always gave him, and returned them to the cupboard, beside Leonard's shiny shoes. Next, he hung up his own scarf and coat, before he collected Kevin's coat from the floor and his scarf from the stairs. He could hear the boy's crying drifting down from his room, and he walked up the stairs, along the landing, and paused at the bedroom door.

"Kevin?"

The crying stopped.

"Kevin? Can I come in?"

In reply, he heard only silence. He reached down and twisted the handle. A terrible image flashed before his eyes, imagining what the silence might mean. He sighed in relief to find the boy lying face-down on the bed, sobbing into his pillow.

"I know you think this is your fault, Kevin," Alastair said, perching on the side of the bed and resting his hand on the boy's back. "But I promise you, you're not responsible."

"How- how many cars burnt mysteriously before- before I came?" The broken sentence, choked by tears, was hardly audible.

"That's not the question you should be asking," Alastair said. "Someone set fire to that car. And it wasn't you."

"What question?" Kevin asked, lifting his head so that his tear-stained face looked up into Alastair's own.

Recognising the need for careful handling, Alastair modified what he knew the question should be. "Who would do such a terrible thing?"

Kevin twisted slightly so that his head rested on Alastair's lap, gripping the priest's arm tightly around him. "Are you sure it wasn't me?"

"I promise you," Alastair said. "But you don't have to go to school today. I'm exhausted, though, so let's have a day where we hardly do anything. Does that sound good?"

Kevin nodded as he sat up beside him. "I don't want anything bad to happen to you, Alastair," he whispered. "I'm going to make sure it doesn't."

"And I," Alastair replied, pausing to kiss the boy's head, "will make sure nothing bad happens to you. I'll go and put the kettle on."

The village was in shock with the news of what had happened to Mrs Henderson. Miss Downs, a retired teacher from the school, came back to teach the class, while Jilly volunteered to help out with the play. Despite the sadness at Mrs Henderson's incident, Alastair was grateful Jilly had the chance to think about something else.

He continued to visit Hilary Franks in hospital, and he had realised Trish had been right in her assessment of her mother. Mrs Franks was fading fast, and her request that Alastair should keep an eye on Jilly suddenly became more pressing.

During his visits to Mrs Franks and Mrs Henderson, Alastair had also made time to visit Father Levosky. The Catholic priest always had time for him and, while Alastair blinded himself to the fact, the chaplain saw his conversations with his friend as being as important as any he had with patients. For his own part, Alastair loved being able to talk to a man who understood his past, but offered only advice without judgement.

Alastair was pleased with how he had handled Mrs Henderson's situation with Kevin, and he felt he had finally managed to rid the boy of his fear over the curse.

All Kevin thought about was the school play. He took his role very seriously, and had even taken on the job of lighting, which Jilly was helping him with after school. They would call off at the church on a Tuesday afternoon, and she showed him how to dim and control the lights in the chancel from the back of the church. She also took him through his song with the organ as accompaniment. She sang the verses and he took over for the choruses.

"Alastair never sings," Kevin mused, as Jilly switched off all the lights on the first day of December, which had fallen on a Tuesday. "But I think he likes music, or he wouldn't have a piano."

"The vicar has an amazing voice," Jilly replied, pulling on her sheepskin mittens, and turning the enormous key in the lock.

"He bought me an Advent Calendar which has the verse of a Christmas carol on each door. But he won't sing them to me."

"I haven't heard him sing in two years," Jilly said, shaking her head in disappointment.

"Since Leonard died?"

"No," she said, and her voice and smile dropped as one. "It was a little after that. Last time I heard him sing was at a choir rehearsal. We used to have a choir, you know? Saint Hubertus was quite well-known for our choir, locally anyway."

"Did you used to sing in it?"

"Sometimes," she said, smiling again. "Usually, I played the organ, though. Ally's wife was in the choir too."

"Ally?" Kevin laughed.

"The vicar," Jilly corrected herself, her face matching her red hair. "Dawn was an amazing singer. She had such emotion in her voice. She used to say it was because she grew up with gospel choirs."

"What did they sing?" Kevin asked, holding back the little iron gate and waiting for Jilly to walk through, into the tree-lined avenue.

"We were practising for our Christmas concert. We used to go around the village singing carols, and into the nursing home up by the beck. I'd play guitar then."

"You play everything," Kevin said, his tone one of awe.

"Not quite everything," Jilly laughed. "The vicar and Dawn led Hills of the North. It was their song. He'd do the first verse, being from the north, and she did the fourth, being from the west. It was something special. But after Leo died, well, Dawn was devastated."

"Wasn't Alastair?"

"Yes, but-" Jilly said quickly, shaking her head. "Don't worry. It's just that the vicar hasn't sung in a long time. It's not a reflection on you, or your singing. It's just something he has to come back to in his own time."

"What happened to the choir?" Kevin asked as they reached The Vicarage gates.

"It just, sort of, dissolved." She walked him up to the house. "We'll get it up and going again soon."

The school play was set for the following Thursday. The tenth of December was always the play, unless it fell on a weekend, as it was considered close enough to Christmas to relinquish ordinary work. After the play, the school centred on Christmas crafts, carol singing in the community, parties and games for the children.

Alastair felt strangely nervous as the big day arrived. He had been to every Christmas play since he arrived, more as the vicar than a father, as Leonard had missed most of his. He loved them, with all their unpredictable, unscripted improvisations. But Kevin had put so much of himself into these practises, Alastair desperately hoped the boy wasn't disappointed. It was his first nativity play, and Alastair wanted it to be something special.

Mrs Henderson was coming to watch, and Jilly felt a certain amount of pressure to make the event live up to her high standard. Mr Samuels had offered to help set up the lights, arriving with a huge ladder to direct them as spots onto the stage area. Kevin was beside himself as he walked home after school, swinging off Alastair's hand and talking excitedly. The play started at half past six, giving them time to have some dinner and sort out Kevin's costume. But Kevin was too excited to eat.

The only time Alastair managed to have any conversation, other than the show, was when Kevin rushed to the kitchen window and planted his hand against it as the outdoor light flashed on. Ysolde bounded through the branches of the apple tree, searching for the larder of nuts she had stashed there during the milder weather. Every time she had searched a branch, she returned to the trunk and scurried up to the next one.

"I suppose if we had a dog, Ysolde wouldn't come anymore," Kevin said with a sigh, as the squirrel disappeared along the other side of the apple tree.

"A dog?" Alastair spluttered. "We can't have a dog."

"Why not?" Kevin asked.

"Well," Alastair began, trying to find a gentle way to dissuade the child. "Like you say, Ysolde wouldn't come anymore. And who would walk it? I'm never here, and you have school."

"You're always here when I am," Kevin replied, his childish honesty shaming Alastair's efforts. "We could walk him together."

"Oh, it's a him, is it?"

"Yes. Called Rover, like in Leonard's book. I want to have a best friend to conquer mountains with."

Alastair smiled across at him, wondering what had happened to the shy, jumpy boy who used to be terrified when Mr Sinter's dogs barked through the hedge. He made Kevin eat some food, although biscuits were all he could tempt him with and, at six o'clock, they walked out towards the church.

It was disappointingly mild. Kevin had wanted snow, and told Alastair this.

"It's so you're the only star to shine," Alastair replied. "Stars twinkle most when it's cold. They don't want to over-shadow you. Anyway," he continued as the two dogs beyond the hedge began barking as they walked past, "some of your audience are travelling a long way to come and see you. If it snowed, they'd never get through."

When they arrived at the church, Alastair took Kevin through to the vestry where Jilly was collecting the children and helping them on with their costumes. All the shepherds wore tea-towels on their heads, all the kings wore crowns, and the angels had halos of glittery tinsel. Nothing had changed since Alastair had been performing in his own nativities so many years ago.

He returned to the nave and took a seat on the front pew, feeling nervous and proud in equal measure. Mrs Sinter came in a little while later, pushing her husband in a wheelchair, and Alastair rushed over to help her. She was barely tall enough to be seen behind her husband, and struggled with the chair. Alastair positioned Mr Sinter close to the front of the church, determined he should have a good view, and pleased that he had been able to share the play. Mr Samuels was waiting at the back of the church. He was showing Kevin, who was now dressed as the star, where he had directed the lights. Trish came in, and Alastair felt his smile deepen as she entered beside her husband. He walked over to them.

"Daniel," he said, offering his hand to the man. "I didn't know you were back."

"Benji and Tom don't know," Trish said, her smile hiding relieved tears. "With all that's going on, I thought it would be a great thing to surprise them with. Jilly brought them along earlier."

"I'm so glad you're safe," Alastair said with heartfelt sincerity. "We were all really worried about you."

"Secrets of state, I'm afraid, Vicar. We had to go for a time."

Alastair smiled and nodded, before he returned to his seat at the front. He watched as the church filled up, with far more people than on any Sunday. Graham came in with his mum, Mrs Henderson smiling across at everything with gratitude and a certain amount of relief. Even Paul Henderson attended, something Alastair had never seen. Everything seemed so perfect. The only person missing was Hilary Franks, and Alastair found his thoughts and prayers turn to the matriarch of that family.

The play commenced, to excellent lighting Alastair proudly reported later, and he watched it with no small amount of pride in Kevin. His voice filled the church with beautiful music, perfectly projected and precisely pitched. He didn't know why, not fully at least, but he felt tears form in his eyes as he watched him. Memories of Leonard came back to him in abundance, and he felt guilty for every moment he had thought of Kevin without considering Leonard. He turned as he felt a little hand squeeze past his side to link arms with him. There was no one there, and the sensation faded away.

Alastair shook his head slightly and rubbed his eyes. Leonard would not have begrudged Kevin any of Alastair's affections.

Despite the star's shining performance, the night was ultimately stolen by Melchior, who rushed away from the star and flung himself on one of the audience members. Tom lost his cape and crown as he leapt at Daniel.

"Daddy!"

"I think you're meant to be finding Baby Jesus," Daniel replied, to much hilarity from the rest of the congregation.

The night was closing in when the play finally concluded with a heart-warming rendition of

Away in a Manger, with the audience being invited to join in. Alastair listened, smiling as the church filled with innocent music. He didn't join in, but closed his eyes and let the music wash over him. The song ended, and applause ensued, jolting Alastair to his senses. He smiled across at Kevin, who beamed back.

Children returned to their families, some changing their costumes first, others like Tom simply running into the arms which waited for them. Alastair spoke to everyone he could, each one congratulating Kevin, and Alastair felt more and more proud in this praise.

By the time Mr Samuels had helped Kevin switch off all the lights, and the boy had changed out of his costume, the church was almost empty. Jilly was still tidying up some of the props, but she was taking a break to talk to Mrs Henderson, who congratulated her on the success. Trish was waiting for her sister at the back of the church, but Daniel had already left with the two boys. Feeling content that the church was in good hands, Alastair and Kevin began the short walk home.

"You blazed up there," Alastair began as they walked out.

"I loved it," Kevin squeaked. "And now it really feels like Christmas."

"What was your favourite bit?"

"My solo," Kevin replied with certainty. "I've decided I love singing. Jilly said you were a very good singer, but that you haven't sung in years."

"Oh, did she?" Alastair muttered. "Did she tell you why?"

"Only that your wife lost interest in singing,"

Kevin continued, too enthralled with the evening to notice Alastair's reticence. "And that the last time you sang was at a choir rehearsal. Can we have a choir again? Can I be in it?"

"You used to have to be in secondary school first," Alastair replied, looking up at the branches above him and feeling choked by the clawing image. "But Jilly was right. I haven't sung in two years."

"She said you and your wife had a song. Something about hills."

"Yes," Alastair laughed, trying to recall the joy of the evening instead of the sorrows of two years ago. "That was the last song I sang."

"Why did you stop singing?" Kevin asked as they walked up the drive to The Vicarage.

"Dawn took the wind from my sails, and the breath from my lungs."

"What?" Kevin demanded, confused by Alastair's words. But before the priest could answer, he continued. "It was nice to see Mrs Henderson."

"Yes, it was," Alastair agreed, pleased the conversation had turned. "I think she was quite impressed by you. Perhaps it is time to start up the choir again."

Alastair lit the fire, and the pair of them sat together on the sofa, each clutching a mug of hot chocolate. For a long time, neither of them spoke. Alastair was recalling each of the times he had returned from a nativity play, while Kevin was already looking forward to next year's performance.

It was after nine o'clock when Kevin sleepily agreed to go to bed. He was in a daze, half blinded by contentment and half by tiredness. Alastair assured him he would come up soon to switch out the light and, as he heard Kevin's feet pattering above him, he washed the few pots, set up the fireguard, and began switching off all the lights and appliances. This might have been a late night by Kevin's standards, but Alastair was looking forward to getting to bed early. He walked up the stairs and peeped around the door to Kevin's room. The boy was not in bed, and Alastair looked across in surprise to see him standing at the window.

"It's too late and too cloudy for a stargazing lesson," Alastair began.

"Is there something happening at the church tonight?" Kevin asked as he rushed the few paces to bed and snuggled under the covers.

"Only your concert," Alastair replied, laughing slightly. "You haven't forgotten already, have you?"

"No," Kevin chuckled. "But why are there lights on in the church?" he asked, pointing back to the window.

Alastair walked over to the window and stared out in confusion. There was a little light coming from the church, but it was more than there should have been. He frowned and tried to steady his thoughts, but his mind raced. Had someone broken in? Should he go and find out? He couldn't leave Kevin, but surely he couldn't take the boy with him, could he? Not towards potential danger.

"I'll go have a look," Alastair whispered, more to himself than Kevin, but the boy walked over and held his hand.

"Aren't you scared?" Kevin asked, looking up.

"No," came the gentle reply. "That's my church, my home as much as this house. Do you want to come, too?"

Kevin nodded.

"Come on, put your wellingtons and coat over your pyjamas."

He glanced out at the muffled light which glimmered through the church window, before he rushed downstairs to where Kevin was pulling on his wellingtons. Alastair slipped on his boots and snatched his coat, holding Kevin's hand and rushing along the path. It was most likely someone had forgotten to switch out the lights, since they had all been moved for the play. But, as he and Kevin reached the church, without passing anyone or speaking any words, he felt as though he was trespassing. He had never felt this before, and it almost stopped him from walking in.

The door was locked, but he had at least the sense to bring the keys, and he heard the mechanism thud as he turned the immense key in the lock. Alastair opened the door and at once knew something was wrong. There was a strange smell which made him gag, and he lifted his hand to his mouth as he stepped in. His eyes took a moment to focus, but he held his hand out towards Kevin, halting his steps.

"Wait there," he commanded, passing the boy his phone. "Call an ambulance." He rushed forward, not checking whether Kevin was doing as he asked, pulling his coat from his shoulders as he ran the length of the church.

Someone was standing in front of the altar,

which was now a mass of white foam, but the figure's coat was burning down the right sleeve, and they thrashed as they tried to shrug out of the garment. They made a frantic sound, half crying and half screaming. The spent fire extinguisher was on the ground a short distance away, and the same white foam was like a carpet as he ran up. He wrapped his own coat about the person and, gripping them tightly to smother the flames, helped them down to the foamy ground.

It was only then, as Kevin ran in carrying Alastair's phone as though it were a dangerous animal, that Alastair looked down at the person in his arms. There was no fire now. The church was once more in darkness.

"I can't unlock your phone," Kevin called, skidding to a halt on the slippery surface.

"That's okay," Alastair said, hugging Kevin to him with his free hand, while his trembling fingers punched in his password. He was relieved Kevin had not seen the image of the writhing individual lit up in flames. The boy would never escape the horrors of that. He suspected he never would. As the phone lit up the church, Alastair looked at the mass of red hair which rested on his lap, and Kevin gasped.

"Jilly?" he whispered, reaching his hand forward to try and wake her.

"It's okay, Kevin," Alastair began, dialling the repeated nines as fast as he could. "Just sit here and hold - hello?" he interrupted himself as his call was answered. Somehow, through his racing mind and pounding heart, he managed to communicate to the operator that he needed an ambulance. Kevin stood, staring down at Jilly, his whole body shaking. Alastair hugged him tighter as he ended the call.

"It's okay, Kevin," he repeated, but the boy was beyond his words.

"Vicar?" Jilly's voice whispered and Alastair dropped his phone into the dissipating foam to nurse her head with his free hand.

"Help's on its way, Jilly."

None of them moved. Alastair was not sure Kevin *could* move. He clung to Alastair's head, his arms still trembling, and Alastair maintained his hold on the boy. Jilly lay unconscious on his knee and he held her head gently. After a time, blue lights throbbed through the windows and the green-clad paramedics arrived. One of them had the sense to switch on the lights, and Alastair suddenly felt he was on show as the spots shone down.

"Kevin," Alastair whispered. "Let's move back and let the paramedics help Jilly."

Kevin shuffled backwards, watching as the men in front of him talked to one another, one holding a mask to Jilly's face. He stared at the scene, feeling his muscles tense every time he acknowledged what he saw. Trying to block out Jilly's burnt skin, he closed his eyes, but the image was branded onto his eyelids and he felt his hands clench into fists as he tried to control his fear.

He opened his eyes as someone took his arms, and stared straight into Alastair's face. The man's smile was there, as it always was, and he was purposefully blocking Kevin's view of the events behind him.

"The doctor says Jilly's going to be alright,

Kevin," Alastair said. He felt the boy's arms relax slightly. "They want to take her to the hospital and look after her tonight, but we can go and visit her tomorrow. Only if you want to, though."

Kevin didn't answer, but as the paramedics took Jilly out to the ambulance, Kevin walked beside them, holding Jilly's left hand. Alastair watched this with a deep sorrow and, as the ambulance drove away, this feeling only grew. Kevin hugged his arm, unwilling to let go as they returned to The Vicarage.

There was no peace that night. The elation of the school play was gone, forgotten in the nightmare of what had happened since. Twice, Kevin woke screaming and, after the second time, Alastair sat beside him on the bed, letting the boy fall sleep against his side. The next thing Alastair knew was that Kevin was waking him up, shaking his arm.

"Is it morning?" Alastair moaned, which brought a slight smile from Kevin.

"I want to go to school. I don't want to see Jilly."

"I totally understand," Alastair said, smiling back.

"No, you don't." Kevin's hands curled into little fists once more. "This is because of me. I know it is. And Mrs Henderson. It's all because of me."

"Kevin," Alastair said, taking the boy's hands and straightening his fingers. "Someone is doing this. What happened to Mrs Henderson, what happened to Jilly, what happened to all those people you knew. Someone else is responsible. Not you."

"Aren't you worried you'll be next?" Kevin asked, directing his big eyes towards Alastair.

Alastair shook his head and rose to his feet. "I'm not scared, Kevin. And I'm going to prove to you that you're not responsible. Come on, let's go find some breakfast."

After dropping Kevin off at school, calling off to speak to Kathryn in the office and make her aware of what had happened last night, Alastair walked back to The Vicarage and climbed straight into his car.

For a while, minutes rather than seconds, he sat staring at the dashboard and thinking over the events of last night. The picture of the frenzied figure continued to haunt him, and the discovery of who it had been left him feeling sick. He had promised Mrs Franks he would look out for Jilly, and he had failed already.

He turned the keys in the ignition, almost surprised to find the vehicle didn't explode. Kevin's certainty about his curse, and his own idea that someone was behind this, was making him jumpy. He reversed out of the drive and set off for the hospital.

Father Levosky's car was there, and Alastair pulled up beside it, walking into the hospital and asking at the front desk where he could find Gillian Franks. He had got quite used to coming here to see her mother, it seemed strange to arrive searching for Jilly.

Despite the trouble in her college years, Jilly had taught herself to smile in all cases. She had a work ethic unlike anything Alastair had ever seen, giving her whole to every project she undertook. She had been tirelessly loyal to him, and a constant friend in advice and silence, during Leonard's illness and all which had happened since.

So, when he arrived at the ward, it seemed wrong to find her without her smile, and her face distorted by the burns across her jawline.

He pulled over a chair and sat at her right-hand side, resting his hand so that his fingertips almost touched hers. She woke with a start and looked up at the ceiling, confused and frightened as she tried to tense her hand to take his own.

"Hush," Alastair whispered, and waited until she tipped her head to face him. "You're safe now."

"Vicar?" she sobbed. "What happened?"

"You fought a fire in the church. You're a bit of a hero, really," he added, smiling across at her and taking her left hand as she reached it over to him. "If you hadn't been there, the whole church might have gone up in flames."

"No," she whispered. "I lit that match."

Alastair watched as she breathed in deeply. "Why?"

"Trish told me," she replied, pulling her hand free of his so she could hide her face from him. "She told me about Mum. The chemo didn't work. I just wanted to think about it," she continued, lowering her hand and struggling for breath. "I tidied up the church, and took everything back to the school, then I called back. I only wanted to have a quiet meditation, me and God. I didn't mean any harm, Vicar, I swear."

"Jilly," Alastair said, hoping his tone and words would be enough to calm her nerves. "There is never any harm in talking to God, and the day I think otherwise will be the day I know I've forgotten what He is."

"I lit the candle, just the same way as always. But this time, there was a snake of fire."

"What do you mean?" Alastair asked, knowing he shouldn't be pushing the woman, but feeling he had to hear her words. If this was to do with Kevin's insistence of a curse, he had to know.

"I was in the middle of it. It was like it was alive." She licked her lips nervously. "Have I done something wrong? Why did it happen? Why would He do that?"

"Jilly, this is man's work, not God's. Someone, some person, is trying to frighten Kevin."

"Kevin?" Jilly whispered. "Is he safe?"

"Yes. But he couldn't bear to see the hurt he feels he's done you."

"Tell him I don't blame him. He can't help it. It was someone," she gasped, trying to steady her breathing. "I had to put it out, but then I looked down and I was burning." Her voice became frantic, and Alastair tried to comfort her, but she was inconsolable. "I couldn't put it out. I couldn't get my coat off, and it was creeping up my arm. And then-" she looked up at him, her eyes surprised. "It was you," she whispered. "You. Whoever did it, Vicar," she continued, calming as she looked across at his sympathetic face. "They were evil, and they left proof."

Alastair was still thinking about this final statement long after Jilly had fallen asleep, succumbing to the drugs which relieved the pain from her burnt skin. He sat with her for a while longer, and the next time she awoke, they talked about anything but the fire. They even joked with one another about how actively they avoided the topic. Jilly began to sound more like herself, and Alastair was sorry to leave her.

"Did the doctors give you any idea when you'd be able to come home," he asked, rising to his feet and preparing to leave.

"I don't know," she replied. "I want to go home now. I want to get things sorted for Mum coming home."

"You're going to look after her at home?"

"Like you and Dawn did for Leo. I wouldn't have it any other way."

"Good for you, Jilly. If I can do anything, anything at all, just shout."

"Thank you, Vicar."

Alastair walked out of the ward but, while he knew he had shopping he had to do, he found his feet led him to the chaplain's door. He knocked and waited as the seconds passed by, before the door was pulled open.

"Alastair," Father Levosky said. "Come in. I have seen more of you in the last two months than I saw of you in the last two years."

"I need some advice," Alastair conceded, sitting on the armchair beside the desk, while Father Levosky sat opposite.

"About Kevin?"

"In a way. It's a bit complicated."

"When isn't it?" the Catholic priest laughed. "I've never been a father in that way, Alastair. You have far more knowledge and experience."

"It's about the curse."

"Alastair," Father Levosky groaned, each of the three syllables containing an equal measure of disapproval. "Neither you nor the child have the devil in you. You're seeking for it because you feel guilty. But Leonard would not begrudge you another child."

"It's not that," Alastair explained. "There was an accident a couple of weeks ago, and another last night. They weren't the doing of the devil or a curse. I think someone is trying to upset and unsettle Kevin."

"But not unsettle you?"

"What do you mean?" Alastair whispered.

"Leonard's photographs?"

"I never told you about that."

Father Levosky opened his hands and shrugged his shoulders, committing nothing to the conversation.

"Who told you?" Alastair demanded.

"Just be careful, Alastair. I suspect Kevin has a past he never deserved. Just make sure you don't become another victim of it."

"Did you know about the fire last night?"

"No," Father Levosky said. "And I don't know who was responsible for defacing little Leonard's photographs. I can't even give you a clue."

"Can't?" Alastair muttered. "Or won't?"

"Both." He folded his arms across his chest and sighed. "You have so many people who care for you, Alastair. And you care for so many more. Tread carefully."

"Someone, not something, is chasing Kevin," Alastair said, eager to dismiss the warning. "I know it, but I can't prove it. But the fire is the key."

"You're not a detective. Have you handed your concerns to someone who is?"

"No. I had the police traipsing around the

house after the first time the photos were graffitied. I don't want the same again until I know something."

"The first time?" Father Levosky asked. "Alastair, you must tell the police."

"That's nothing to do with Kevin," Alastair said, setting his jaw with the same stubborn determination he had seen in Kevin. He laughed as he recognised the boy in himself. "If someone has a concern with me, they can take it to the diocese."

"It sounds like they may not have the patience to do that," Father Levosky cautioned. "I have to repeat it, and I hate repeating myself. Tread carefully."

"Forget the pictures for a minute," Alastair continued, leaning forward in the chair. "Two members of my congregation, therefore of Kevin's new family, have ended up here because of fires. His father and mother, his adopted father, and four lots of foster carers suffered similar incidents. This is like someone taking biblical revenge, or justice. Who would do that, and why?"

"There's nothing biblical about it." Father Levosky leaned forward, so the two of them almost met. "But it does sound like someone is after the boy."

"But why?"

"Have you looked at his past? Before it all began, I mean?"

"He was a baby," Alastair began.

"What about his parents?"

Alastair didn't reply straight away, but fell back in the chair. He gripped his head, then steepled his fingers as he sat forward and faced Father Levosky. "His father was in prison when he was born. That's it. It must have been someone who knew him, who'd been his victim maybe. It would have to be a criminal to do such things."

"Now, can you take it to the police? Now you know, or think you know, who is responsible? It concerns me, Alastair. It concerns me that you can't link the attacks on Kevin's families and friends to the attacks on you. Someone who would blow-up a car won't think twice about intimidating people in the way your house was attacked."

"I'm not intimidated," Alastair laughed, returning his smile to his face. "I just want Kevin to be safe."

"You think you know who broke into your house, don't you?" Father Levosky said, following his words with a heavy sigh. "I have been reading people for forty years, Alastair. I can tell you think you know."

"Do you believe in-?"

"Curses?" he interrupted and watched as Alastair shook his head.

"No," Alastair laughed. "You've made your thoughts quite clear on that one. How about ghosts?"

"You think it's Leonard who did that? Who crossed himself out of your photos and your life? No, whatever I believe doesn't matter. Even if there were ghosts, Leonard would never do that."

"And Dawn? She was so angry. At me, at God, even at Leo."

"You're asking me questions which divide us, Alastair. Didn't we make an agreement to leave doctrine at the door?"

"But I can see every detail of that night. Of all those nights. When I came back from the All Souls service and she was ripping out all the happy endings of Leo's books." Alastair's voice cracked slightly, but he continued to talk. "Or when she had bagged up all his clothes and binned them, because she refused to let anyone else use them. And then the night when I got back from choir practise and-" He paused as he felt his eyes tingle, rising to his feet and walking towards a picture on the wall, which depicted a monk kneeling in prayer. "Recently, I've been scared to open the door. I keep getting Kevin to do it."

"You've convinced me," Father Levosky said, his words causing Alastair to turn around in confusion. "You are definitely a haunted man, Alastair. But Dawn didn't cross out her little boy's face any more than you did."

"Oh," Alastair gasped, looking at the clock on the wall as it chimed the hour. "I've got to get back. Thank you for putting up with me again. One day I'll come here without asking a favour or making ridiculous suggestions."

"Where would be the fun in that?" Father Levosky laughed, observing the smile on the other man's features. He stood in front of the door and waited until Alastair's passive manners gave him cause to clear his throat slightly, reluctant to ask him to move. "I don't want to make you late," the Catholic priest continued, ignoring Alastair's tactful request for him to step aside. "But I won't let you past until you promise you'll go to the police."

"What?" Alastair laughed. "Fine, I'll go to the police."

"About it all?" Father Levosky folded his arms across his chest.

"Okay," Alastair conceded. "As soon as I get back, I'll give them a ring."

Father Levosky stepped out of the way and pulled open the door for Alastair. They parted with wishes of blessings and peace for one another's Christmas celebrations, and Alastair began the journey back to his parish, calling at the shops on the way. He had a home communion that afternoon, and a small service in the nursing home.

After this, he walked round to the church and looked at the carnage from the night before. Jilly had tidied away everything from the play. The church felt damp and more unwelcoming than he had ever noticed before. He walked up to the altar and felt his brow knot into concerned and confused wrinkles. This had been what Jilly meant when she talked about the fire snaking round her. On the ground before the altar, burnt into the carpet in thin lines, was a five-pointed star, with a circle around it. Alastair stood for a moment, puzzling at the care someone must have taken in doing such a thing. From the initial planning, to the painstakingly accurate placing of the flammable lines. Someone must truly hate Kevin. Or perhaps this had been aimed at him.

With a decisive movement, he collected a pair of scissors from the vestry, hacking at the long runner of carpet until he had removed the marked stretch. True to his word, he rang the police, and waited for them to arrive at the church. He detailed everything to them about what had happened the night before, and hinted at his idea regarding Kevin's past. But they were searching for physical clues, not ideas. By the time they had left it was time to meet Kevin from school.

He and Kevin walked back to The Vicarage, Alastair telling him how proud Jilly was of him, and how she was already feeling much improved. He did not mention his theory, nor the image he had found in the church, but when they arrived back at the house, they sat together with a mug of tea and talked as though life was normal. They talked about Christmas, about the school, the play, and the many upcoming parties.

Kevin felt safe and protected as he hugged Alastair that night.

"Goodnight, Alastair," he whispered, and then in a clearer voice, "goodnight, Dad."

"God bless, Kevin," came the reply, which rang with a depth of love and affection Kevin couldn't understand. "Sweet dreams."

Alastair latched the door and felt a huge smile cross his face. It was not his usual facade of a smile. It was so great, he could almost imagine it started from his toes and climbed right to the tips of his hair. Kevin was happy, healthy and safe. And Alastair was determined he would stay that way.

The Last Week

The following Sunday, the third in Advent, found Alastair and Kevin walking along the frosted path to the church. The sun was struggling over the rooftops, but she had no strength in her. Kevin ran from leaf to leaf, or puddle to puddle, crunching the ice as he leapt on them. Alastair swung a CD player in his hand as he walked. It was always difficult expecting the congregation to keep up with the heavily electronic accompaniment on the CD, but with Jilly in hospital and no one ready to fill the breach, it was the only alternative.

He couldn't remember the last time Jilly had missed a Sunday service. It was different in Little Golforth, where they had the whole band. If one person was missing there, the show went on. And Alastair was sure most of that congregation did see it as a show. Here, Jilly was as much a part of the service as he was.

They entered the church through the little door at the back which opened into the vestry. Kevin helped him set up the CD player, and Alastair gave him a list of track numbers. It was far more sensible to leave it to Kevin. Alastair had never been competent with technology. They ran an extension lead from the vestry, the only part of the church's east end which had electricity sockets, out to the choir stalls. The priest frowned at the coil in his hands and was pleased to drop it to the ground. Kevin set a few of the tracks going and tried to find the right volume.

Alastair returned to the vestry and opened the cupboard, pulling out a white robe with a purple stole over the head of the hanger. He shrugged into the robe and was lifting the stole over his head when the door opened. He turned around as Jilly peered around the door.

"What are you doing here?" The words had left his mouth before he had considered their implications.

"I haven't missed a Sunday service in years," she laughed, lifting her hand to a large plaster on the right side of her jaw. "And it's nice to see you, too, Vicar."

"You can't play the organ, you've got your arm in a sling."

"I've got another hand, and I've got feet for the pedals. But if you don't want-"

"Sorry, Jilly," Alastair said, dropping the stole over his shoulders and turning to fully face her. "When did you get home? I could have given you a lift."

"Trish brought me back last night. But, thank you, and thank you for visiting me on Friday. And for visiting Mum so often. And for finding me on Thursday night. And for ruining your coat to save me." Her left cheek showed her embarrassment. "Wow. I've got so much to thank you for."

"I'm just grateful you're okay. You don't have to thank me."

"How's Kevin?" Jilly asked, looking around the room.

"Fine. Excited about Christmas. But he'll be more excited to see you."

"Where is he?"

"Operating the sound system. It wouldn't be working if it had been me who set it up." Alastair smiled across at her as she moved over to the door to the chancel. "I'm glad you're safe, Gillian."

"Me too," she whispered, scrunching her nose as she often did when she found something endearing.

Kevin was watching the people walking into the church without really noticing any of them. His thoughts were all on Christmas, and he felt as though he might explode with excitement before the day actually arrived. The sound from the music player only made him feel more and more excited, and he was so wrapped up in this, he didn't notice the person sitting behind him until he heard someone clear their throat.

"Hello Kevin," Jilly said.

Kevin spun around and looked across at her. She did not look as disfigured as he had imagined. In fact, apart from the plaster across the right side of her face and the sling she wore, she looked exactly the same.

"Alastair said you were going to be fine," Kevin began, smiling back at her. "But I didn't believe him."

"You can always believe him, Kevin," she continued. "He'll never lie to you."

"I'm sorry for the fire," Kevin whispered.

"It wasn't your fault," she answered. "I lit the match."

"You did?" Kevin whispered, feeling confused. He had been certain someone had attacked Jilly with fire because of his curse. But, with this new revelation, more doubt crept into the child's mind. He had spent the last three years of his life and his last three foster homes believing he was in some way responsible for the deaths around him. Helen, his last foster carer, had refused to talk about the subject, but Alastair had been the first person to openly deny the curse.

Kevin hadn't worked Alastair out, yet. He was everything he'd dreamed of having in a father, but there was something Kevin couldn't explain which made him unsure. Jilly, on the other hand, seemed uncomplicated, and he loved her almost as much as he loved Alastair.

"Yes, I did," Jilly replied. "Someone had played a cruel trick on the church. But it wasn't you. You were a star on Thursday night."

The organ music was a little different to usual, but no one commented on it. If they had harboured misgivings about it, the appearance of Jilly at the end of the service explained the cause and excused the idiosyncrasies of the music. Jilly talked happily with everyone, but when she returned to the vestry to hang up the blue robe she always wore to play the organ, she looked more tired than Kevin had ever seen her.

Kevin was tucking the silverware into the safe, listening to the vicar whistling the refrain of the final hymn, when Jilly walked into the small room. Alastair had shown him where they were all meant to sit, and had even drawn him a map to follow.

"I think I'm going home," Jilly muttered, her voice sounding more tired than ever. "It's nice to hear the Vicar making music again. I'm almost tempted to stay and listen."

"Will you come and teach me the rest of Jingle Bells?" Kevin asked. "I want to play it at the Christmas concert, but Miss Downs said she'd only let me do it if I could play it all. I've only got until Friday."

"Well," Jilly said, smiling slightly. "In that case, we'll have to get it learnt."

"Do you want a lift home, Jilly?" Alastair asked, stepping into the vestry. "I can go get the car."

"Jilly's coming back to The Vicarage," Kevin said. "She's going to teach me the rest of Jingle Bells."

Alastair glanced across at Jilly and shook his head. "Kevin, poor Jilly only got home yesterday. I think Jingle Bells can wait until Tuesday."

"It's fine," Jilly said, her smile sinking in weariness. "He wants to do it at-" she stopped as Kevin's eyes widened. "Christmas," she finished.

"We've got to get to Little Golforth this afternoon, Kevin," Alastair continued, trying to give Jilly an opportunity to get some rest.

"I can stay with Jilly," Kevin volunteered. "I don't want to go to Little Golforth."

Alastair looked sympathetically across at Jilly.

"It's fine, Vicar," she replied.

"I tried," Alastair laughed. "We always have enough Sunday dinner to feed an army, so you can have dinner with us if you like."

Kevin took Jilly's hand as they walked back to The Vicarage, calling through the hedge to Mr and Mrs Sinter's dogs. He was in exceptionally high spirits. Jilly was not only alive, but safe from harm, and she had started the fire, so he wasn't responsible. The relief this gave him was substantial, and he couldn't be shaken from it.

Alastair was left to make the dinner while Kevin and Jilly sat on the sofa, reading stories to one another. Kevin laughed every time Jilly made up a silly ending to one of the books from which Dawn had them torn out. But he listened, enthralled, when she read from the Christmas anthology. Alastair listened to them, pausing in his work to look through at them.

It was a squeeze sitting the three of them around the breakfast bar. Kevin relinquished his place to Jilly, but told her to tell him if Ysolde made an appearance. He was still hoping to find her lair, but she visited the apple tree less and less. Afterwards, Kevin did the washing-up and Jilly fell asleep on the sofa. Alastair dried the pots and filed them away into the cupboards.

"Poor Jilly is exhausted, Kevin," he said after he was sure she was asleep. "Look after her this afternoon."

"I will," Kevin promised.

Jilly woke up a short time later, embarrassed

and apologetic for having fallen asleep, but when Alastair waved her words away, she only blushed all the more.

He set off for Little Golforth alone, reminding Kevin to look after their guest and thanking Jilly for looking after the boy. Kevin waved from the door, but as soon as the car had turned onto the road, he bounded into the living room.

"He's gone," he said, smiling across at Jilly. "Can we learn the next part now? I want to play it at the concert, and I want it to be a surprise for my dad."

"Come on, then," Jilly replied with a mischievous smile.

They walked into the study and Jilly lifted up the lid of the piano to reveal the zebra keys. Kevin licked his lips and chewed his bottom lip as he sat on the rickety stool. He lined his fingers up with the notes she had shown him and played through the chorus.

"That's sounding great!" Jilly began, sitting in Alastair's chair and rolling it over to where the piano was. She set her left hand on some of the keys and they played through the song as a duet, before she placed Kevin's left hand on the notes she had just been playing.

"If I play it really well," Kevin said later, trying to make the song sound as good as it had done when Jilly had helped him. "Do you think it might make him want to sing along?"

Jilly smiled across at him, but despite her best efforts even the plaster was not enough to hide her sympathetic look. "Maybe. But if it doesn't, it doesn't mean he isn't proud of you."

"Why won't he sing?"

"He used to love singing. I'm sure I told you this."

Kevin turned slightly on the piano stool. "You told me he stopped singing after a choir practise, but you never told me why."

"It's not up to me, Kevin," Jilly said, sighing as she leaned back into the chair. "Have you asked Ally?"

"Why do you call him Ally?" Kevin laughed.

Jilly's cheeks reddened and she turned back to the piano. "Let's have another go at Jingle Bells. It's sounding really good."

They ran through the song three more times before Kevin sighed. "Can we go and look for hedgehogs?"

"They'll all be sleeping."

"Can we look for Ysolde?"

"It's getting dark, Kevin," she replied, moving over to the window and looking out at the drive. "She'll be sleeping too."

"Can we go for a walk?"

"Okay," Jilly answered, willing herself to find the energy to go out. "Let's leave the vicar a note to tell him where we've gone. Where shall we go?"

Kevin shrugged his shoulders and ran out to pull on his coat. Jilly returned the chair to the desk and looked for a blank piece of paper. She paused as she moved aside some of the papers and found a newspaper article showing a burnt-out car. She leaned forward and read it in interest. It was not recent, but from six years ago. It detailed a crash which had resulted in the death of Liam Given, a man who had left a wife and three children. The journalist explained the driving conditions as perfect, a dry, warm evening. The road was straight and travelled by Liam Given most days on his commute to and from work. As well as the picture of the car, there was a photograph of the man who had died.

Jilly placed the paper down as she read the names of the children. Calum, Fionn and Kevin. She jumped as Kevin appeared at the door, fully clothed and ready to go for their walk.

"Don't you want to go?" Kevin asked. "Alastair was right."

"About what?"

"You're too tired."

"Well, I am tired," she admitted, but as Kevin's face fell she pushed herself up from the desk. "But we can walk up to the church and back if you want."

Kevin nodded, the smile returning, and he ran and collected Jilly's coat. They left a note beside the kettle and walked out into the dimming light. The sun had set, but the sky was still aglow in the west. Standing at the end of the drive to admire it, Jilly hugged Kevin to her, and he held her hand tightly.

Neither of them spoke. As the orange faded to purple, they turned towards the path to the church.

There were no lights on the path and Jilly began to feel nervous. She looked around her, expecting someone to jump out at them. The responsibility of shielding Kevin, and the handicap of having her arm in a sling, made things worse. As they walked past the Sinters' house and the dogs charged to the hedge, Jilly jumped. Her head felt light and it was only Kevin's constant talking which kept her awake. In the past, reaching the church had always given her a safe feeling but, after the events of last Thursday, she no longer felt that the church was a sanctuary.

"Look," Kevin chimed as they walked into the churchyard. "I found this earlier. Let's go and put it on Leonard's grave."

Jilly looked down at a small plant in Kevin's hand. It was more a cluster of leaves than flowers, but the thought was pure, and she smiled down at him. Confronting her own fears, she walked with him to the grave. There was no light at the back of the churchyard, so Jilly relinquished her hold on Kevin's hand and used the torch on her phone.

It was surprisingly peaceful in this corner of the churchyard, and Jilly found herself smiling again. They found Leonard's grave, and Kevin placed the foliage beside the headstone.

"What happened to Dawn Louise Roberts?"

"She died," Jilly replied. "She was so lost after Leonard's death, I think she just forgot how to live."

"I hope I never forget how to live," Kevin said. "Why did she go back to America?"

"Because her parents wanted her to be buried there."

"Did she know she was going to die?"

Jilly forced a smile onto her face, although in the darkness Kevin couldn't have seen it. "No," she replied. "Well, maybe. But she never told the vicar. He was devastated."

"I've lost people," Kevin said, turning to look at her, and resting back against her. "I lost everyone. It's because of the curse. But Mrs Henderson didn't die, and you didn't die. I think

Alastair is protecting everyone from it."

"He's a very special man," she agreed. "But there is no curse, Kevin. I lit that candle, no one else."

They waited a short time, Kevin staring at the grave of the boy he was coming to know so well, while Jilly looked at her father's stone and tried not to consider how soon her mother's name would be added. The last course of chemotherapy had left Hilary Franks weakened beyond the repairs her body was able to perform. She was coming home the next day, and Jilly hoped she could find the strength to nurse her mother in her final weeks.

Alastair returned to The Vicarage in absolute darkness, and at once started panicking. He never left it like this. Even the security light had been switched off, so that he had to try and guess which was the right key for the lock. The second key was the right one and he pushed open the door, lowering his gaze to the floor as he did so, and switching on as many lights as he could before he forced himself to look into the hall.

Everything was exactly as it should have been, except that Kevin's coat was missing from the hall stand. He walked through to the living room and lit the fire, listening in the near silence as the tiny sparks encouraged a cluster of flames to grow. As he moved over to the kitchen and filled the kettle, he smiled down at the note he saw explaining Kevin's absence. The note was in a scrawled hand, which he realised must have been Jilly's left hand. His smile slipped and he shook his head as he sparked the gas alight. Poor

Jilly would not have been able to say no to Kevin. He could almost imagine the conversation in his head, and his imagination was not far removed from the truth.

Instead of standing waiting for the kettle to boil, he set his mug beside it and pulled off his coat, walking back into the hall to hang it up. Next he walked into the study and flicked the light switch. The first thing he did was close the piano lid. There were too many memories in those keys, he was better not seeing them. Next, he drew the curtains closed and then walked over to the desk.

He picked up the phone to find out whether there had been any calls in their absence, but set it down again as his eyes rested on the paper at the top of the pile. He had not left it there, he knew he hadn't. The story of Liam Given's death stared up at him, and he felt guilty for his grateful prayer that Mrs Henderson and Jilly had not suffered the same outcome. Was it wrong of him to think such thoughts when a young man had lost his life and Kevin had lost his family? He pulled open one of the drawers and slotted the paper into it. Reaching over to the phone, he listened to the alternating pitches of the dialling tone which told him he had a message.

Switching to speakerphone so he could tidy through the papers, he stopped abruptly as the message sounded. It was Kevin's voice. He recognised it at once, almost second nature to him. There was no greeting, no friendly word.

"Remember, remember." It was followed by a scraping, whirring sound and a sound like air gently blowing. Then it went dead. Alastair reached forward and pressed the button which allowed him to hear it again. There was something wrong with it. It took him a few renditions of the message to realise what it was. The two words were identical, in tone and inflection.

He looked across at the photo of Leonard which rested on his desk, recalling Bonfire Night when he had found the same message on the frame. Suddenly, the monotonous repetition of the word was masked by Kevin's excited voice, and he heard the boy push open the front door.

"Deleted," the phone announced, as Kevin and Jilly walked to the study.

"Hello," Alastair began, smiling across at them. "Did you find anything on your walk? Jilly," he continued, rising to his feet, "you look exhausted."

"We had a lovely time," Jilly replied, watching as Kevin pulled off his hat. "But I'm ready for home, Vicar. I've got to get the house sorted for Mum coming home tomorrow."

"Jilly," Alastair said. "You can't do that yourself. Kevin and I will come over and give you a hand, won't we Kevin?"

Kevin nodded excitedly.

"I can manage," Jilly said, her cheeks which were red with the cold only deepening in hue.

"No," Alastair insisted. "Hat on again, young man."

He watched as Kevin pulled on his hat and smiled across at him. There was so much life in the boy, so much more than the message on the phone had portrayed. They took the car over to Jilly's house which was as beautiful and idyllic as Kevin had imagined it would be.

It was the old groundsman's cottage for the big house in the woodland beyond. To reach it, they had to drive down a thin avenue of trees on a rickety track which tested the car's suspension to the maximum. Jilly apologised repeatedly, explaining how she usually left the car at the top of the lane and cycled up to it.

"I walked today," she explained when Kevin asked. "I can't really drive or bike like this."

When they arrived at the house, Kevin rushed in. It was a balance between Mrs Henderson's house and The Vicarage. There were children's pictures stuck to the fridge with magnets from exciting destinations.

"Have you been to Turkey?" Kevin asked in amazement. "And Dubai? And the USA?"

"No," Jilly replied. "I've never left the UK. Those are all from John, my brother. He's been all around the world, to every continent. Even Antarctica."

Kevin was amazed. He stared at some of the pictures on the magnets, imagining what it must be like where they were bought.

Alastair wasted no time in returning the diligent care Jilly had shown him over the years. He pulled off his coat and rolled up his sleeves, beginning at the kitchen sink.

"I can do this," Jilly replied, a hint of embarrassment in her voice. "You don't have to."

Alastair lifted his soapy hands from the bowl of washing-up and planted them on his hips.

"You look like Mum," Jilly laughed. "Fine. You win. Thank you."

Kevin was laughing too, as though this image was the most hilarious thing he had ever seen.

But as Jilly and he left the kitchen to go and make up a bed for Hilary Franks, Alastair could hear the boy's voice playing over and over in his head.

"Remember, remember."

He looked down in surprise as his hand caught on a rough edge of one of the pots in the sink. For a moment he had lost himself, trying to understand the reason for the phone call. He picked up a knife from the side and ducked it into the water, grateful he hadn't been cleaning it when his concentration had slipped. He turned as he heard something behind him, and Kevin stepped into the room.

"Jilly's asleep," he whispered, as though he expected to wake her if he spoke normally. "We were making up her mum's bed and she leaned forward on it and fell asleep. She doesn't look very comfortable."

"I told you to go easy today," Alastair said, setting the knife on the draining board and drying his hands on the towel. "Come on, let's finish making the bed for Mrs Franks."

Alastair slipped his shoes off and followed Kevin into the dining room which had a bed-settee. Jilly was where Kevin had said she would be, kneeling on the floor with her head resting on her left arm, her hand still holding the pillowcase. Alastair gently peeled her fingers from the bedding. Except for a sleepy murmur, she made no protest. Kevin watched as Alastair, careful not to catch her scarred right arm, lifted her and carried her into the living room next door, where he set her down on the sofa. They returned and finished making the bed, before

Alastair walked into the kitchen and dried the pots, putting them in cupboards and hoping they were going into the right place. He picked up a small box from the worktop and Kevin watched his eyebrows rise.

"What is it?" the boy asked, concerned about why this change had occurred.

"Nothing," Alastair said, his reassuring smile returning to his face. "There's just no wonder she's asleep after taking these."

Kevin smiled back at him.

They tidied and cleaned the downstairs of the house, but Alastair refused to go upstairs. Kevin couldn't understand this, but followed his directions. Alastair was pulling on his shoes when Kevin broached a subject which had been puzzling him.

"Why isn't Jilly married?"

"I don't know," Alastair whispered in reply, conscious of the sleeping woman through the doorway. "Maybe she never found someone she wanted to marry."

"Why aren't you married to her?"

"What?" Alastair laughed. "Don't be silly, Kevin. I'm already married."

"But Dawn Louise Roberts is dead."

"Yes, she is," Alastair said, gently pushing Kevin towards the door. "But I still love her."

They travelled back to The Vicarage without mentioning Jilly or Dawn, but talking about the last week of term and all the exciting things which would be happening during the holiday. Kevin tried to be as excited as Alastair about the prospect of being in church as Christmas Eve became Christmas Day, but he thought being in a church at midnight sounded frightening. In a final attempt to encourage Kevin to love the magic of Christmas Eve night, Alastair told him a story about animals' ability to speak on the stroke of midnight.

"But it's bad luck to try and hear them," Alastair explained.

"What if I hear them by accident?" Kevin asked.

"That's not bad luck."

"Why do you believe in luck but not curses?"

"Because I believe God has a plan for us, and He wouldn't give up on anyone."

"I wish I believed that," Kevin said. They were pulling into The Vicarage driveway now. The house had its welcoming lights on, and Kevin smiled. It was beginning to really feel like home.

Alastair walked to the door and slotted the key in the lock, twisting it, and pushing the door back. He looked up, expecting again to find Dawn's eyes meeting his own. He could still remember them. Why could he never remember her smile? Why could he not picture her after their winter walks, her cheeks red and her eyes watering in the cold, while her lips still smiled? Why had she become frozen in this bleak way in his memory?

Kevin wandered in, failing to notice the delay Alastair made.

They had a light supper, before both of them climbed upstairs to bed. Alastair decided against checking the phone for messages, still hearing Kevin's voice echoing in his head from the last one. He walked to his own room and waited until he heard Kevin shuffle across the landing.

Walking back to the boy's room, Alastair poked his head around the door and smiled. The space-themed bedding had been replaced with giant reindeer, and Santa rested on the pillow beside Kevin.

"Did you brush your teeth?"

Kevin nodded.

"Washed your face?"

Kevin nodded again.

"Are you ready for sleep?"

Kevin shook his head.

"What's up?"

"I put a plant on Leonard's grave. Do you mind?"

"Mind?" Alastair repeated, surprise in his tone. "Not at all."

"I want him to like me."

"He would have loved you, Kevin," Alastair said, walking into the room and sitting at the foot of the bed. "He would have loved sharing your adventures."

"Do you only love me because you loved Leonard?"

"What do you mean?"

"No one's ever done so much for me."

"I'm glad you came to live with me, Kevin. And in some ways you do remind me of Leo. But I love you because you're you, not because I loved my son. Thank you for visiting his grave."

"Do you ever go?"

"Yes."

"When?"

"When you're at school," Alastair replied, rising to his feet. "Are you ready for sleep now?"

"Will you tell me a story?"

Alastair nodded and sat down again, holding Kevin's little hand in his own. He told him about the Stones of Plouhinec, when the animals talked at midnight, and the beggar learnt of buried treasure. He felt a little hand, thinner than Kevin's, take his free hand. Turning, he expected to find Leonard standing there, but he was alone with Kevin.

"Goodnight," he whispered, leaning forward and kissing the boy's hair.

Monday was met with a giddiness Alastair was not prepared for. Kevin was so excited he could hardly eat his breakfast, and he danced down the small lane to the school. In the evening, they decorated the tree which Alastair had bought that day. They set it in the hall, next to the hall stand, so it was a welcoming sight. For the sake of Kevin, Alastair pretended it was for the visitors to the house, but in truth he wanted anything which would distract him from the belief that Dawn would be waiting there.

Their first visitor did not arrive until Tuesday, after the morning church service, when Jilly appeared at the door. She had taken off her sling and the dressing on her face had been changed. It was not enough to shake her smile, though, and she blushed as Alastair opened the door.

"Hello, Vicar," she chimed. "Firstly," she continued, before he had the chance to say anything in reply to her greeting. "I'm so sorry about the other night. I think it was the tablets."

"I'm sure it was," he replied, stepping back to let her in. "And you have no reason to be sorry. I didn't think you'd be here today. How are you, and how's your mum?"

"I'm fine," Jilly answered as she tugged her hat from her mass of red hair. "Oh, your tree looks lovely."

"Kevin did most of it," Alastair said, smiling across but unable to shake his concern at the fact Jilly had avoided the question about her mother. "I'll stick the kettle on."

"I'd better get on," Jilly called as Alastair walked through.

"I'd rather you just sat for a minute," came the reply. "Did you walk up again?"

"Yes, but-"

"Come and have a drink, Gillian."

She stepped into the kitchen. "I'll just do some of the washing-up, then," she began. She turned in surprise as he took her hand and led her back to the living room.

"Sit down, Jilly. You can have a drink before you start. I don't even think you should be here."

Jilly didn't argue but looked around the room, feeling as if she were seeing it for the first time. There were little clues of Kevin's influence on Alastair and the house. The horse which looked like a zebra had made its way onto the coffee table, while there was a picture of Kevin and Alastair from the Little Golforth Carol Service last Tuesday night next to the picture of Leonard and Dawn. There were also Christmas decorations all around the room. Never grouped together, but dotted throughout, wherever there was a surface to put them.

"How's your mum?" Alastair asked again as he came and sat down opposite her, handing her a cup of tea as he walked past.

"Okay, I suppose," Jilly whispered, taking a

sip and thanking him for the tea. "She was asleep when I left. She slept nearly all day yesterday. I just sat beside her," Jilly continued, lifting her eyes to meet with his. "I just watched her all day."

"Is there anything I can do to help?"

"No," she replied with a smile which made Alastair's heart break. "Trish is there now. She's much more capable than me."

"In some things," Alastair replied, sitting back in his chair and sighing. "Not long after we first came, Dawn told me someone had stopped her on the church path. She said they'd asked if they could do anything to help us settle in. Then, three years later, the same person offered quiet support when we found out Leo had leukaemia. She was sure that, if the time ever arose when that favour could be returned, we would and should return that support."

"I thought it was so exciting to have an American in the village," Jilly replied, her smile deepening. "In The Vicarage, no less."

"It must have been a dull disappointment to find your vicar was a Scot."

"Well," she said, teasingly. "Not too great. But you don't owe me anything, Vicar. I just always seem to be the sadder part of myself in your company, and I'm sorry about that."

"I like to think you feel comfortable enough to share your worries with me."

"I do," she replied, but her cheeks burnt the moment she had said these two words. "Does everyone else speak so candidly to you?"

"Some people," he replied, his smile becoming gentler.

"Actually," she continued, encouraged by this tone and gesture. "There is something I wanted to talk to you about, but it comes with a massive apology attached."

"Oh," Alastair whispered, unsure he wanted to know where this conversation was heading.

"On Sunday," she began, setting her mug down next to the wooden horse and lifting her hand to stop him from saying anything. "I was looking for a blank piece of paper on your desk. Just to write you a note. I didn't mean to pry, or see anything I wasn't meant to. But I've hardly been able to stop thinking about it. I don't know if it's because I feel lucky last Thursday didn't turn out the same way for me; which is terrible. But I just keep thinking of Liam Given and his little family. And I keep wondering why you had it on your desk. And I'm sorry I looked. I know I shouldn't have done."

"Was there a question in any of that?" Alastair asked, the smile around his words making Jilly return the gesture, and she shook her head. "Liam Given was Kevin's adopted father. The last time he had someone he could call Dad." Alastair chewed the side of his mouth for a moment, trying to weigh up how much he wanted to share, and trying to decide how much Kevin would be happy for her to know. "He's sure he's cursed."

"I know," she replied. "He told me he thought it was his fault what happened last Thursday. Is he so sure because of what happened to Liam Given? Surely he can't remember it, he'd only have been two at the time."

"It's followed him round. But I'm trying to

make him see that there is no curse. And I think he's starting to believe me."

"You don't believe in curses?" she asked, a teasing light appearing in her eyes.

"No. I don't."

"Do you believe in luck?"

"Why do I feel like I shouldn't answer that?"

"I believe in luck," she replied, getting to her feet. "And I believe that you're as lucky to have Kevin as he is to have you." She collected her cup from the low table and walked towards the kitchen. "Any one person dying is terrible, but it can hardly constitute a curse. Liam Given wasn't the only one, was he?"

Alastair shook his head, but remained silent.

"Is someone doing this on purpose? How many times has it happened?"

"Too many to be bad luck."

"Then you think he is cursed?"

"No," Alastair said, the smile returning to his face. "I think someone, a very tangible person, is doing this. I just don't know why. He's the sweetest kid. Why would anyone want to hurt him so much?"

"He wants to hear you sing," Jilly blurted out. "He's learning to play the piano so that you'll be inspired to sing again."

"Oh no," Alastair muttered, standing up so that he was looking down at the photograph of Leonard and Dawn. "I've no inclination to sing. I lost it all."

"I know," Jilly whispered back. "But he hasn't shared your past. Maybe you should tell him. He'd understand, I'm sure he would."

"No," Alastair replied, turning to face her and

shaking his head. "He'd be terrified."

"He took flowers, well, leaves really, to their grave the other day. He's not doing that for Leonard, or Dawn. He's doing that for you."

"I haven't sung in two years, Jilly. I'm pretty sure he'd be disappointed to hear me now."

"I don't think he'd care if you were tone deaf and permanently flat. He wants you to sing because singing makes him happy. He wants to know you're happy too."

Alastair was considering the words of this conversation long after it had ended. Jilly struggled on through the day of housework, refusing to stop despite Alastair's insistence that she should. Finding nothing he could say to dissuade her, Alastair helped with all the chores, although he did have to drive to Little Golforth to visit one of his housebound parishioners. He and Jilly shared a late lunch together, during which they discussed Ysolde, watching where she leapt and swung through the branches of the tree, like a miniature Tarzan in red fur.

By three o'clock, Jilly was ready to return home. Trish would be going to collect Benji and Tom from the school, and neither sister wanted their mother to be alone. Alastair insisted on driving her back, and the eight-minute car journey was completed in silence. It would not have taken much longer to walk and, still feeling guilty for looking through the papers, Jilly wished she had done. When they reached the house, she turned to Alastair and smiled, pulling her woolly hat over her mass of hair.

"Thank you for the lift, Vicar."

"You're very welcome. Tell your mum I'll call

round soon."

"Oh, I forgot," Jilly hissed. "That's terrible, I can't believe I forgot."

"It's okay," Alastair said, taking her hand and watching as her large eyes turned up to him. "Sorry," he said quickly, letting go of her and turning to look out of the window. "I'll maybe wait to call on her."

"No," Jilly replied, snatching his hand in both of hers. "Mum wanted Communion, but she can't leave the house. I was meant to ask you."

"Of course, I will," he smiled across at her, wishing she would let go of his hand but not wanting to slide it free from her grip. "Is Thursday okay?"

Jilly nodded as she let go of his hand. She would be out on Thursday, and he knew that. "I'll probably see you on Friday. At the School."

"Thanks, Jilly," he whispered as she climbed out of the car.

"Just-" She paused and looked into the car. "Just be safe, Vicar," she finished.

Somehow her words felt almost like a threat to him, although he knew they were meant as a comfort. Smiling across, he assured her that he would, and watched as she flushed crimson before rushing over to the house door. He turned the car and drove back to The Vicarage, hardly concentrating on the road but feeling embarrassed by his behaviour.

He pulled into the drive and looked down at the clock, jumping as he realised he only had three minutes to get to the school. Without collecting his coat and scarf from the house, he rushed along the path, through the churchyard, and arrived at the school gates as the bell was ringing.

Kevin remained unaware of Alastair's hurried arrival, his conflict regarding his behaviour towards Jilly, and his plan to actively avoid the organist wherever possible. All the boy could think about was Christmas, which was only a little over a week away.

On Wednesday afternoon, Alastair arrived at the school gate with a minute to spare, and waved across to Jilly where she stood with Kate Humphries and Leona Johnson, but remained standing where he was. Kevin came running out, Benji beside him, and they both stopped to talk to Jilly before Kevin rushed over to Alastair.

"Why are you standing here?" Kevin asked.

"I'm waiting for you," Alastair replied with a smile.

"But you usually wait with Jilly. I wanted to tell you both at the same time."

"Tell us what?"

"Miss Downs has said that I can play Jingle Bells at the party on Friday. And you'll come and listen, won't you?"

"I wouldn't miss it for anything," Alastair said, smiling with a pride he hoped was enough to cover the knowledge of Kevin's ulterior motive. "Shall I ask Jilly to come over tomorrow night for a last-minute practice?"

Kevin nodded. They walked across the playground to where Jilly was still waiting for Tom.

"Jilly," Alastair began, feeling Leona's eyes causing the back of his neck to prickle. "Can I have a word?"

"Of course," she said, smiling across at him with infectious enthusiasm. They walked a few steps from everyone else, Kevin staying to talk to Benji. "What is it?"

"I'm so sorry for my behaviour yesterday."

"What?" she laughed. "What behaviour?"

"When- when I dropped you back at your house," Alastair muttered, feeling unsure that he should have mentioned it again as she seemed to have forgotten.

"You mean because you took my hand?" she said, her smile only deepening as he nodded. "It was a gesture of comfort," she continued. "I promise you, I viewed it as nothing more than that."

"Thank you," he sighed, relieved by how readily she had accepted his apology and true motives. "Could you come around tomorrow and help Kevin with the piano?"

"Tomorrow night?" Jilly asked. "Yes, I'll pop over. But aren't you over at Little Golforth tomorrow night?"

"No, the youth club is finished for Christmas," Alastair said, feeling the tension of the past twenty-four hours melt away.

She smiled back at him and nodded, her expression suggesting she felt just as relieved. Kevin rushed over to Alastair as he held his hand out, and they walked back to The Vicarage with a renewed spring to their steps.

When they arrived back, the first thing Alastair did was crawl under the Christmas tree and flick on the lights. Every other year he had left them on all day, but Kevin had been insistent that they be switched off whenever there was no one to oversee them. Given the boy's history with fires, Alastair had agreed, more through a hope of avoiding worrying Kevin than any feeling of threat. But it did have the benefit of allowing Alastair the satisfaction of hearing Kevin's excited gasp each time the tree sparkled again, as though it was the first time he had seen it.

They had a cup of hot chocolate, with cream and marshmallows floating on the top, during which Kevin related his time at school. There seemed to be no lessons, only making cards, gifts and decorations.

"And I'd like to make a gift for Mr Samuels," Kevin finished. "It's his last day tomorrow. And for Miss Downs, because her last day is Friday."

"Then you should," Alastair agreed. "What did you want to make?"

"Coconut ice," Kevin said with certainty.

"Okay," Alastair replied with surprise.

"Isn't it a good idea?" Kevin sounded unsure. "Miss Downs said it used to be her favourite sweetie when she was little, and I thought I could just make twice as much and give some to Mr Samuels."

"It's a perfect idea," Alastair said, placing his arm around the boy's shoulders and hugging him tightly. "I was just expecting you to want to make a picture, or something. You really do think these things out, don't you? I'm so proud of you, Kevin."

"I know what I'm making you for Christmas," Kevin replied eagerly.

"Don't tell me!" Alastair laughed, setting his mug on the arm of the sofa so he could cover his ears.

Kevin's face creased with laughter, and Alastair smiled across at him.

"We'll have to visit the shop first," Alastair continued. "I'm sure you need condensed milk for coconut ice, and I haven't got any."

They had an adventure going out to the shops, returning to The Vicarage in the dark. Alastair had to follow the cable of the tree lights to the socket, feeling faint with the sickening feeling it gave him, but it was worth it to hear Kevin's excitement as the reds, ambers, greens and blues sprang to life.

The rest of the night they spent making coconut ice. Kevin's favourite part by far was helping clean up at the end, when he scraped out the bowl and ate the last pieces of the coconut mixture before handing it over to Alastair to wash.

By Friday, Kevin was nervous and excited in equal measure. He gripped his book bag as he walked out of the door, checking for the fourth time that the sheet of music was still safely in there. Jilly had visited last night to go through Jingle Bells with him once more, and they had shared a meal together, all three of them talking excitedly about Christmas. But despite his elation at the impending arrival of the holidays, Kevin had been sad to hear Jilly talking to Alastair about Mrs Franks. She had cried, resting her head in her hands to try and hide the fact from the priest, but Alastair had let her lean against him as she wept. Neither of them knew he had seen.

But now that was yesterday, and Kevin's mind was pointing forward, not back. Christmas was on the horizon, and he couldn't wait to share it with Alastair. It was not that he had never enjoyed Christmas before, but Alastair spoke about the festival as though it had all the magic the television adverts told him it did. Alastair hardly ever talked about presents. His excitement was not focused on what he would get, but on the experiences they would share.

The school morning had been reserved for the children's party. The afternoon was an opportunity for the children to share their festive spirit with family and friends. In Kevin's mind, Alastair would be so impressed with the rendition of Jingle Bells, he would feel sure he wanted to sing again. There was dancing and games all morning, culminating in a visit from Santa Claus, who arrived on a sledge pulled by a team of six mountain dogs. To many of the children, this was equally as exciting. But Kevin, believing entirely in the spirit of Christmas, had something in particular he wanted to discuss with Santa. Each child was allocated two minutes, and Kevin was determined not to waste a moment of his.

"I'm Kevin," he announced, walking into the corner of the hall which had been arranged as Santa's Grotto.

"I know," Santa replied, his voice low and his words accompanied by a jolly laugh. "Kevin Alderman."

"How do you know?" Kevin asked, more in awe than mistrust.

"I know every boy and girl." He tapped his knee and waited until Kevin walked over and sat on his lap. "What would you like for Christmas,

Kevin Alderman?"

"That's it," Kevin said, his face becoming serious. "I don't want to be Alderman, I want to be Roberts. I really want Alastair to actually be my dad."

"Ah," replied Santa, slightly awkwardly. "That's an unusual request, Kevin."

"I know I can't be Leonard. But I've lost lots of people, and he's lost his son and his wife. I thought that we could be a family."

"He's a lucky dad to have a son as thoughtful as you."

"I want him to sing again, too."

"Oh, I'm sure he will. When he hears you play Jingle Bells this afternoon."

"How did you know?"

"I know all about you, Kevin. I'm sure Christmas will bring you and your dad together. Christmas is an amazing time. Full of magic, and light, and hope. None of these things are missing in your life, because you bring them all to other people. What else would you like for Christmas?"

"I'd like Jilly to be happy."

"Anything I can put under the tree for you?" Santa asked, trying to gain a more conventional answer.

"I don't know. Whatever you think I should get."

"Okay, Kevin," Kathryn interrupted, stepping into the grotto. She was dressed as an elf, but there was no mistaking her as anyone but the school secretary. "Did you get a chance to talk to Santa and tell him what you'd like?"

"Yes. Goodbye, Santa."

"Goodbye, Kevin. Here's a little gift for you." He handed Kevin a book-shaped parcel, wrapped in paper with holly on.

"Thank you," Kevin chimed, stepping out of the tent grotto and walking back into the hall.

Next, there was a Christmas dinner provided for all the children and staff, but Kevin was too nervous to eat much of his. Everything, all his hopes and wishes for Christmas, had been pinned on his performance this afternoon.

He watched as the school hall began to fill with people. He saw Alastair walk in alongside Graham and Mrs Henderson, and Jilly walk in with Trish. Daniel must have been spending the afternoon with Hilary Franks. Kevin suspected Tom would rather have had his father there than his aunt, but his friend was too quiet to ever suggest such a thing.

He patiently sat through the performances before his, some singing, some dancing, some reading Bible passages or reciting poems. He was the only one who had chosen to play the piano. His hands shook as he carried the sheet of paper over to the instrument and, as he sat down on the piano stool, he forgot what all of the keys were, and what all of the marks on the paper meant. They danced before his vision, and he felt his eyes brim with tears. Everything depended on this performance, and he couldn't remember what he was doing. He chewed his lip as he looked across at the expectant faces in the audience. Jilly was smiling encouragingly, and nodding to him as though she expected the gesture to help in some way, but it only made him feel more foolish for forgetting.

He looked across at Alastair. He didn't look expectant. He didn't look angry or sad. He looked proud. His smile almost reached his ears, it was so wide. Kevin stopped chewing his lip, scrubbed his hands across his eyes, and began playing.

It was perfect. Everyone applauded him and he blushed as he snatched his sheet from the piano's music stand and scurried back to his seat. He enjoyed the other performances far more now his was over, but it didn't compare to the ringing of the early bell after Alastair had led them all in prayers. Kevin jumped into Alastair's arms, and the priest picked him up from the floor, kissing his cheek.

"I was very proud of you," Alastair began. "You played it perfectly."

"I forgot all the notes," Kevin admitted, hugging his arms about Alastair's neck. "That was why I didn't start for ages."

"I thought you were checking all your audience were paying full attention. Come on, let's get home."

They paused long enough for Kevin to be congratulated by Jilly and Trish, before they walked out into the onset of the premature night. It was already getting dark, the streetlights were on, but they turned in the opposite direction and took their little path back to The Vicarage. Alastair had set Kevin down in the school playground, and now the boy leapt and ran as happily as any child could. He was a far cry from the timid, withdrawn boy who had arrived only two months ago. He was bright, excited and eager.

They sat in front of the fire that night,

watching a Christmas film and talking about the excitement of all that the next week might bring. Christmas day was a week from now. The school had closed at the earliest ever time, but there were still several events coming up. Monday was the Christingle service, which Alastair talked about as though it was an amazing event. Wednesday was Nine Lessons and Carols. And then Thursday would be the most magical event of the year: Midnight Mass.

Kevin had already fallen asleep by the time the film ended so Alastair guided him up the stairs and helped him into bed. He mumbled incoherent words, and the vicar smiled down at him. He could not have imagined loving any child as much as he loved Leonard, but Kevin was proving him wrong.

He slipped out of the room and walked down to the study. For several minutes, he stood staring at the closed piano. He tried to bring himself not to let the boy down, to sit at the piano and play a tune he could sing along to, but he hadn't sung a note for two years. Somehow, in that time, he had come to associate singing with his loss of Dawn. And it was her piano.

He walked the three steps to the stool and sat down, lifting up the lid. For a while longer, he just touched the keys, playing a tune without any note sounding. One of his fingers tapped down with more force than he had meant it to, and gradually his hands played out the flowing tune of Greensleeves. He took a deep breath and willed the words to come.

"What-?" he faltered on the first word. Those eyes, Dawn's eyes, stared out of the darkness, looking down on him judgementally. Why had he chosen to go the choir practice at all? He should have stayed. He should have been here. Then, perhaps, she would not have gone.

"No," he muttered to the empty room. She had already gone. She had been gone from the moment she returned home and found Leonard dead in his father's arms.

"What child is this?" he sang, his voice shaking but determined. He had the chance to be a father again, and his son had conquered all the fears which had chased him every day of his life, solely to encourage these sung words from Alastair.

The more he sang, the stronger his voice became, and he lost himself for a moment. He stopped abruptly as he heard footsteps in the hall, and he turned to the study door as it opened.

"Dawn?" he whispered. "Oh," he said, smiling across as Kevin's bright sparkling eyes met his.

"I heard you singing," he said, excitement trying to beat back his tiredness. "It worked."

"What worked?" Alastair reached out to the boy, and Kevin came and stood beside him, resting his sleepy head on Alastair's shoulders. "You played so well today, you rekindled a long, long buried interest I had."

"That's what worked," Kevin explained, hugging Alastair tightly. "And Jilly was right," he continued sleepily. "You have a very nice voice."

"Thank you," Alastair replied, with genuine appreciation. "Come on. I'm as tired as you look and sound. Time for bed, for us both I think."

They switched off all the lights, put the fire

guard in front of the dying embers, and Kevin checked the gas hob three times to make sure it was safe. Finally, two tired people trudged up the stairs to their own beds, and both fell asleep almost at once.

Part Seven

Christmas

The morning was barely dawned when Kevin woke up. He lay in bed, his eyes still closed, listening to all the sounds of the world. There was the regular, and surprisingly rapid, tick of the clock. It was like a metronome into which everything else fitted. There was the sound of the water in the pipes, a clear indication that Alastair was already up. By the continued noise, he was probably having a shower. And then, entirely unwelcome on the first morning of the holiday, there was the phone ringing.

Kevin slotted his feet into his slippers and padded out of the room, along the landing where he carefully avoided the rough part of the balustrade, down the stairs and into the study. The phone stopped ringing the moment he reached out for it. It began again almost at once.

"Hello?" he asked, picking up the receiver and

pressing it to his ear.

"Vicar?" asked a voice on the other end. "Sorry, I think I must have got the wrong number."

"No. But Alastair's upstairs. Shall I try and find him?"

"No need, Kevin. It's Trish. I'll ring him back later."

Kevin said goodbye and set the phone down, walking out into the hall where Alastair was just coming down the stairs. He was still dressed in his dressing gown and was towel-drying his hair. He moved over to the tree but stopped as Kevin rushed forward and snatched his arm. Alastair turned to face the boy's terrified eyes and smiled gently.

"Don't," Kevin stammered. "Not with wet hands. Helen said you shouldn't touch anything electric with wet hands."

"She was right," Alastair said. "But don't worry," he continued, taking Kevin's hand. "Mine's dry, see?"

Kevin let go of Alastair and watched as the lights on the tree lit up.

"Trish called," Kevin murmured, pressing his nose up to one of the baubles.

"I thought I heard the phone," Alastair continued, walking through to the kitchen and lighting the gas hob for the kettle. "Did she want me to ring back?"

"She said she'd ring back later."

"So," Alastair began purposefully. "What's it going to be for breakfast?"

"Not toast?" Kevin asked.

"It's a special day. Don't you want something different? I can do beans or eggs or bacon."

"Can we have all three?" Kevin asked, a cheeky tone to his voice.

"Well," Alastair said. "I suppose it is a very special day."

Kevin grinned across at him.

"I'll just go and get dressed first."

"Me too," Kevin replied, following Alastair upstairs after switching off the kettle.

By the time Kevin came downstairs again, the kitchen was filled with exciting smells, and he leapt onto the high stool at the breakfast bar. He watched as the meal came together, and Alastair had hardly set the plate on the surface before Kevin began eating. They sat beside each other and ate in silence.

"Is Jilly coming today?" Kevin asked, running his finger along the plate to collect the last of the tomato sauce.

"No. She's got to look after her mum. Mrs Franks is really ill."

"I know," Kevin said, moving over to the sink. "Benji and Tom know too, but their mum thinks they don't."

"How do you know?"

"Benji told me. He heard his mum saying it would be a miracle if she lives until New Year."

"I believe in miracles," Alastair replied, tipping his own breakfast pots into the sink and collecting the tea towel to dry while Kevin washed. "It's a shame you won't have the chance to know Mrs Franks. She is a really strong lady."

Kevin went and collected the wooden horse from the table. As he did so, he looked across at the picture of Leonard and Dawn. He felt as though he knew Leonard so well now, but his mum was still shrouded in mystery.

"I hope I never forget how to live," he mused.

"What do you mean?" Alastair began, confused by this sudden announcement. "I don't think Mrs Franks has forgotten how to live, I think she's just sick."

"No. Not Mrs Franks." Kevin watched as Alastair came and sat in the armchair, facing the boy. "Why did you think I was Dawn last night when you were singing? I thought Dawn was dead."

"She is," Alastair replied, trying not to wince each time Kevin carelessly tossed her name into the mix.

"Why did she go to America when she died?"

"Kevin," Alastair began. "Do we have to talk about this?"

"No. I just wish I knew. I want to know why you thought I was a dead lady."

"I sang with Dawn," Alastair explained. "After so many years of making music together, it seemed odd not to have her there."

"But if you both sang, why did she forget how to live?"

"What do you mean, 'forget how to live'?"

"That's what Jilly said. She said that was why Dawn died."

"Okay," Alastair said, holding his hands up as though he was surrendering. "Dawn couldn't get over the fact Leonard died. And that he had died when she was not even here, it was too much for her. She blamed me."

"Why?"

"Because he died in my arms. Right there," he continued, pointing out of the French windows to the apple tree. "He wanted to pick an apple, but he didn't have the strength to."

"That's why you don't pick the apples anymore," Kevin said, feeling pleased with himself for solving this conundrum, but Alastair's tale was only just beginning.

"Yes. I only use the windfall now. I can see his little hand reaching out whenever I try to pick one."

"But you sang after he died," Kevin replied, shivering as though he was cold, but the heating was on and the room was warm.

"I did. But Dawn had lost her interest in it. She was lost without Leo, and she couldn't see her way out." Alastair rose to his feet. "That's enough, Kevin. I don't want to talk about it anymore, and I don't want to scare or upset you."

"Did you kill her?"

"What?" Alastair choked, turning back to the boy and having to remind himself that Kevin was only a child. "No! I loved her. Absolutely and totally. But she'd drifted away from who she was. Forgot how to live, as Jilly said. When she told me she wouldn't be here after choir practise, I thought she was just saying it to make me give up the choir, like she had done."

"She left you?" Kevin asked, trying to keep up with the man's words.

"Don't worry about it, Kevin. Yes, she left me. And I didn't sing from then until last night." Alastair smiled down at the boy and sighed. "There isn't always a scary story behind bad things, sometimes it's just sad. Horribly, cruelly sad. But then you came along. You're my happy ending, which Dawn could never find without

Leonard."

"Why did she go back to America? Was it because Leonard was dead?"

"No. It was because her parents wouldn't help me fight the diocese to have her buried with her son."

"Who is the diocese?" Kevin asked, struggling around the word. "Why wouldn't they let her?"

"Because suicide is a crime in the eyes of the church."

"She killed herself?" Kevin whispered, his face paling and his white hands gripping the fabric of the sofa.

Alastair nodded. "I didn't want to tell you. I didn't want to scare you."

"While you were singing, she killed herself?"

"I got back from the choir practise and found her hanging in the hall. But she'd warned me," he whispered. "If I left her, she would leave me. And she did."

"So it was your fault?" Kevin murmured. "I can't believe you killed her. No wonder you never sang."

"I suppose," Alastair whispered, feeling the work of the last two months crumble in his hands as Kevin backed away from him. "I didn't kill her, Kevin," he continued. "I loved her."

"No wonder you and Jilly aren't married," Kevin began, chasing after his own train of thought and agenda. "She knows, doesn't she?"

Alastair nodded as he felt all his self-recrimination intensify. There was no escaping the boy's words. Kevin rushed upstairs and didn't return for several minutes.

When he did reappear, Alastair tried to engage

him, listing so many things they could do, but Kevin had his heart set on hunting for Ysolde, and he made it clear he wanted to do this alone. Alastair watched him squelching through the muddy ground, not particularly looking for the squirrel, just pleased to be away from the priest.

A little later, Alastair called him in for lunch, but Kevin called back to announce he was still full from breakfast and didn't want any.

Alastair watched the boy through sad eyes. He hadn't told Kevin about Dawn because he hadn't wanted to frighten him. It was bad enough for Alastair to imagine her emotionless eyes staring across at him each time he entered the house, the blue baler-twine suspending her from the balustrade.

He could remember that moment when he had returned, still singing, after the choir practise. He could remember the feel of the words ending abruptly on his lips. For a handful of seconds, he had just stood there. She was dead already, he could see that. But since then, he had questioned his judgement, not only about going to the rehearsal in the first place, but about the length of time it had taken him to come to his senses and cut her down. He rubbed his fingers across his palms, recalling the lifeless feel of the rough cord in his hands. The coroner had said she died instantly, the height breaking her neck. That was why her eyes had continued to stare out at him as he had walked in through the door.

Alastair jumped back to the present as the phone rang. He glanced out of the window again, his gaze resting on Kevin who was stretching up to try and reach inside a thin crack in one of the tree trunks. After the third ring, Alastair remembered Trish had been going to call and he rushed into the study to catch the phone before it rang off.

"Hello?"

There was silence.

"Trish? Is that you? Are you okay?"

A soft grinding whir purred through the phone. Alastair felt his gaze drift to the picture of Leonard on his desk. This sound was becoming almost too familiar. Leonard stared back, frozen in time. Perhaps encouraged by his son's gentle gaze, or pushed by desperation because Kevin had come to think he was the monster Dawn had accused him of being, Alastair spoke back.

"I don't know what you want. I don't know who you are. But if you want to talk, why don't you talk?"

There was a click over the speaker of the phone, and Kevin's voice began. It was stilted, as it had been last time, with all the wrong inflections and a cacophony of tone and pitch. But the words made the sender's intentions clear.

"You. Want. A. Family. But. I'm. Kevin. Alderman. I. Can't. Be. Leonard. Roberts. I. Know. You. Lost. A. Son. And. A. Wife. Too. I. Don't. Want. You. To. Be. My. Dad. You. Know. Whatever. It. Could. Be. To. 'Ve. Lost. A. Son. I. Really. Want. That. To. Be. Again. Goodbye."

Alastair lowered the phone. The final word was repeating on a loop, with no alteration. After listening to it several times, he slammed the phone down and stumbled backwards from the table. He didn't believe in curses, he reminded himself repeatedly, but as he shakily walked back through to the living room and looked out into the damp, dull day, he felt sick as he realised he couldn't see Kevin.

Trying to remain calm as he raced to pull on his shoes, leaving them unfastened, he ran out into the garden. Each step he took across the lawn found his feet sinking half an inch into the muddy ground.

"Kevin?" he called out, repeating the name as he rushed through the trees. He didn't know how many times he called, but the sky was growing darker. His stomach grew more tense with every step, and his shoes skidded as panic quickened his pace. Finally, he found little boot prints leading round to the front of the house and he followed them onto the drive. There were large puddles here, and the onset of drizzling rain made it impossible to know the boy's direction.

Alastair stopped calling out and peered through the grey curtain of fine rain to try and find any trace of Kevin, but there was none. He could hear his frantic breaths catching in his throat, making strange strangled noises as he tried to hold back his emotions. Prayers, pleading and desperate, flooded his head. Having to make a decision, and praying he made the right one, he ran towards the church. The mud splattered up at him as he skidded down the path. It had never seemed this long before. The church was locked, all three doors of it. He raced to Leonard's grave, looking down at the greenery which Kevin had placed there, but there was no sign of him now.

Alastair let his tears fall with the rain as his mind raced. He had to find him. Someone wanted to harm the boy. Someone wanted to frighten and harm his son. But where would he go?

A little hand rested on his arm, snatching his sleeve to try and get his attention. He turned, hoping to find Kevin, but it could only have been a trick of the wind as it whirled in tiny tornadoes in this part of the churchyard. It did, however, carry a smell with it. A familiar smell, but one he associated with a little earlier in the year. His nose tingled as he tried to identify it. The rain had stopped, and the wind was carrying the smell to him from the west. From The Vicarage.

"Fire," he hissed.

He ran faster than he had ever run before. He slipped repeatedly, and at the end of the path one of his shoes got stuck in the mud so, as he ran up the drive, the gravel stabbed through his sock and into his foot. He didn't notice. He didn't lessen his speed but raced forward. Blue lights spun through the lane as a fire engine appeared, and Alastair spared the briefest thought to question how they had got here so quickly. It all pointed to one unthinkable thing: Kevin was inside.

There were flames visible through the window and, as he pulled open the door, more rushed out to meet him. He lifted his hand to his face to shelter from the fire and called out.

"Kevin!"

There was no response. Lifting his hand to his mouth to try and limit the smoke he inhaled, he stepped into the house.

Everything was burning. The tree was a pillar of orange, melted ornaments dripped into colourful stains on the charring carpet. The balustrade, with its rope-burnt wood which Jilly had religiously polished, was a mass of orange and yellow tongues. He walked cautiously towards the stairs, checking each step tentatively. Past the study doorway, where more flames were building. How had it spread so quickly? Every room in the house must have been ablaze.

He caught a movement of darkness in his eye corner as he stepped past the study, and he turned slightly towards it.

"Kevin?" he began, trying not to breathe in too deeply.

Something heavy struck the side of his chest. Winded, he lurched forward, unable to control his involuntary instinct to draw a deep breath and combat the air which had been struck from his lungs. This action acted as a chimney to the fumes which billowed from the burning house, and he gripped at his throat, struggling to breathe in anything but smoke.

"You lost another son, Vicar," a deep, rasping voice announced. "But Kevin Alderman is my boy, not yours."

Alastair felt another blow strike him, and he collapsed to his knees. His desk lamp was dropped to the floor beside him.

"But he likes you. So I've given you a chance. I called the fire brigade the moment I lit the spark. Good talk, Vicar."

Alastair would have replied, but he had neither breath nor voice. He watched as the figure moved towards the French windows, and let himself out. A thousand points of light, more brilliant than the flames, filled his sight. Perhaps they only seemed brighter because of the darkness pushing in around them, funnelling his vision as he tried to breathe. There was no sign now of the arsonist, only towering flames which destroyed his world while he lay, helpless, in the middle of it.

Kevin had heard the phone ringing in the house and watched Alastair go through to the study to answer it. Seizing this opportunity, he had walked from the garden, running in his wellington boots, out to the drive and along the road. He couldn't bear to spend another night in the house now that he knew someone had died there. He had told himself that Leonard's death had been natural, cruel but coldly logical in the child's brain. There was nothing comforting in the knowledge of Dawn's death. He started to imagine that she had been haunting the house, that everything which had moved or any unexplained sound which had been made, had been caused by her.

He hadn't meant to argue with Alastair, but he couldn't bear the thought of staying in that house, and he knew he would not manage to sleep there anymore. He walked past houses with pretty lights and trees in their windows. The Sinters' dogs were sitting in the front window, staying out of the rain. Mrs Henderson's house was lit up with brilliant white lights which shifted slowly to blue, and then back again. Mr Samuels' house was dark and empty, and Kevin wondered where the man would be spending Christmas.

He walked on along the road, avoiding the church for fear of ghosts, and found that his feet stopped at the end of the long track down to Jilly's house. She would understand. That must have been why he had subconsciously reached this point. He began traipsing down the road, flicking the rain from his face with the back of his hand.

By the time he reached Jilly's door, the rain was lessening. He lifted his hand to tap on the door, waiting a few seconds before he tapped it again a little harder.

"Kevin," Jilly said with a smile as she opened the door. The dressing on her jaw had been removed, allowing the gesture to cover her face. "You look frozen. Come inside." She stepped back and watched as the boy walked past her. "Are you all alone?"

Kevin nodded.

"Come on, I'll get you a drink to help warm you up."

"Dawn killed herself," he announced as he followed her into the kitchen.

"I know." Jilly turned to face him, setting the kettle on the halogen hob as she did so. "She forgot how to live, like I told you. Is that why you came to see me?"

"I was scared," Kevin whispered, shuffling to stand beside her, grateful of her tangible arms around him as she soothingly ran her right hand over his hair.

"Couldn't you talk to the vicar?"

"I-I," he stammered, realising how foolish he had been. "I argued with him. I blamed him."

"Oh, Kevin," Jilly sighed. "Poor Vicar. Dawn blamed him, the bishop blamed him, he even blamed himself. Did you have to blame him too?"

"I didn't mean to," he sobbed, hugging tightly to her. "I was scared. I didn't want to sleep in a house where someone died."

"Imagine how much worse it's been for Alastair," she replied. "He's been doing it for two years. But you were helping him, Kevin," she continued, leaning back and smiling down at him. She switched the kettle off as it boiled, but instead of pouring a drink, Jilly guided Kevin towards the door. "Come on, we'll sort this out. And if you don't want to sleep in The Vicarage tonight, you can come back and sleep here. But I think you owe the vicar an apology."

Kevin nodded and took her hand as they walked out. The rain had stopped now, but the ground was wet, and the terrain hampered their speed.

"This was going to be the best Christmas," Kevin mumbled. "I was going to be Kevin Roberts."

"You already are," Jilly said, guiding him up the track to her car.

"But that was what I asked Santa for. And Alastair sang last night. He actually sang."

"You see," she said, slowing down to turn onto the lane where The Vicarage was. "He needs you as much as you need him. You've got to be strong for him, like he's… Oh God!" Jilly pulled into the lane and gasped at the blue lights which filled it. She applied the brake and climbed out of the car without turning off the ignition. Kevin scrambled out and rushed forward, but Jilly snatched his sleeve as they reached the driveway.

They were stopped by one of the firemen, who gently gripped Kevin's arm as he struggled to get past.

"Is he in there?" Jilly asked, hugging Kevin as the boy's body suddenly became rigid. "Where's the vicar?"

"Someone's gone in to get him out," the fireman replied.

"Are you sure he's in there?" Jilly sobbed. "He might have gone out."

"No, he's definitely in there," came the unwelcome reply. "It was the weirdest thing. He actually watched us pulling up, and then ran in."

"This is my fault," Kevin muttered.

Neither adult could stop Kevin running forward as another fireman carried Alastair from the building and over to the ambulance which stood waiting. Jilly was only a step behind the boy and lifted her hand to her face as she looked down at the vicar. He was covered in sweat, and soot marked his features. There seemed to be no life in his body, and Jilly listened to the paramedics' words without understanding them.

Kevin watched silently as the doors of the ambulance closed them out, and the vehicle pulled away, lights flashing and sirens blaring.

"Where are they taking him?" he asked, turning to face Jilly. "Where's he gone?"

"To the hospital," Jilly replied, surprised by how calm her voice sounded. "We'll go and meet him there."

Having to be strong for Kevin was the only thing which held Jilly together as they walked back to the car. When she got there, instead of driving to the hospital straight away, she rang Daniel and explained the situation, asking him to take the twins and check on Mrs Franks. Then she turned the car in the road and sedately journeyed into town.

It wasn't fast enough for Kevin, but when they arrived at the hospital it felt too soon for him to face the product of what was certainly his fault. Jilly dragged him from the car and gently pushed him through the doors of the A&E department. She announced to the receptionist why they were there, Kevin wincing as he was referred to as Alastair's son. The woman at the desk directed them to a seating area, assuring Jilly someone would come and collect her and Kevin.

"You are his son," Jilly said later, sitting on the plastic chair which was as painfully sterile as the rest of the room. "He wouldn't have run back into that house if he didn't think of you as his son."

"I wish I hadn't blamed him," Kevin sniffed. "I wish I hadn't been so horrible."

"You were scared, Kevin. It doesn't excuse it, but it does explain it. Alastair will understand."

"I think he might be dead."

"No," Jilly said with a smile she hoped would convince herself as well as Kevin. "Someone would have told us if that were the case."

The night was complete, and the hospital had fallen quiet, when a nurse walked over to them. Kevin had cried himself to sleep against Jilly's side, while Jilly had thought over every event which had happened since Kevin had arrived, trying to think of anything she could have done differently, blaming herself for ever mentioning Dawn to the child.

"You're here because of Reverend Roberts?" the nurse asked.

"Ally, yes," Jilly replied. "Is he okay?"

"He's stabilised now. I'll take you to see him if you want." She waited as Jilly shook Kevin awake. "You must be his son, Kevin," she continued. "You should be really proud of your dad. One of the firemen said he was shouting your name as he rushed in. There aren't many people would run into a burning building. It's stupid and dangerous, but he must really love you to have done it."

Kevin scrunched his nose to try and stem the flow of tears, but nothing could stop them as they streamed down his face. They walked down corridors, through doors, up stairs, and along more corridors. Finally, the nurse turned back to them and smiled.

"It's not really visiting hours, but we try to make slight concessions on this ward. Just please keep your voices down so you don't disturb other people."

Kevin nodded while Jilly stared at the initials on the double doors into the ward. ICU. She ushered him through, and they followed the nurse to one of the beds. Kevin leapt forward as he recognised Alastair, but stopped as his gaze took in all the machines and tubes which surrounded him. Jilly thanked the nurse and turned to face the man on the bed.

Every fibre of her being told her how wrong this image looked. There was no smile on that placid face, that was the first thing. Instead, his features looked perfectly at peace. The sweat and soot had been washed away, and he looked as though he might wake up at any moment.

Kevin watched as Jilly talked to the nurse and two police officers who stood against the glass partition, as far from the boy as they could be. He couldn't hear their words, and didn't want to, certain there could be no happy outcome for the man who he desperately wanted to be his father. Instead, Kevin's fingers hovered over an intravenous which was buried in Alastair's hand, and he turned to Jilly as she walked over to him.

"Is he alive?" Kevin whispered.

"Yes." Jilly pulled off her scarf and set it on one of the two chairs. "He can hear you. Why don't you tell him what we were going to say?"

Kevin nodded and put his little hand on Alastair's shoulder. "I didn't mean what I said. I don't blame you really. I don't want to go," he sobbed, resting his head against Alastair's chest. "I want to stay with you."

Jilly watched as Kevin climbed onto the bed and curled up beside Alastair, dragging the unconscious man's arm around him, hugging him tightly. She felt unable to move him, but made sure the drip was still secure. Kevin fell asleep there, and Jilly stood over them, wishing and praying that there was something she could do.

"Look how much he needs you, Vicar," she said after a while, holding Alastair's hand. "You have to get through this for him. He'll end up back in the system again. He doesn't deserve that." She rested his hand on Kevin again, and leaned forward to kiss the priest's forehead. "We all need you."

She sat down on the chair where she had draped her scarf and coat, and felt her eyes brim. Confident that both Kevin and Alastair wouldn't see, she let her tears fall. She stroked her hand down Alastair's arm, whimpering desperate words. She begged him to wake up, her whole body trembling with the force of the tears, until she fell asleep under the weight of them.

She woke up to Kevin's voice.

"It's Sunday," he muttered. "What will they do at church?"

"Oh," she gasped. "I've got to get back."

"Don't leave me here," Kevin pleaded, scrambling off the bed. "What if he doesn't wake up?"

"Don't think like that, Kevin," she replied. "Life must go on. He would tell you the same thing."

She hugged him tightly, leaning forward to kiss him. They both turned as a deep voice boomed out.

"I didn't believe it when they told me. Who would do such a thing?"

"Father Levosky," Kevin stammered. "It's my fault."

"No it's not," said the priest, anger ringing in his voice as he stepped forward to the opposite side of the bed. "It's the fault of whoever did this."

"It's the curse," Kevin sobbed.

"You don't know what happened, do you?" Father Levosky asked, sitting down and taking Alastair's hand.

"I argued with him. I blamed him for his wife's death."

"I argued with him about that, too." The priest

paused and watched as Jilly pulled her coat on. "Are you going, Miss Franks?"

"I have to get back to play the organ," she explained.

"Don't go, Jilly," Kevin begged.

Jilly hesitated but, after a moment, she pulled off her coat and scarf. Father Levosky smiled across at the pair.

"What did happen?" Jilly whispered. "You seem certain it wasn't anything to do with Kevin. How do you know?"

"Actually," the priest replied. "I'm certain it is to do with Kevin. But not a curse like he believes, nor a haunting. A real person. Alastair is far too sensible to get trapped in his own house. And he's not solely here because of the fire."

"What do you mean?" Jilly asked, watching as Kevin's eyes widened and knowing her own were doing the same thing. "That there was someone else in there?"

"According to the x-ray he's got two broken ribs. Someone must have done that to him." He turned to Kevin. "Your curse, as Alastair knew, is from a very tangible person. He put himself in harm's way to protect you. I told him he should contact the police," the priest muttered. "But he's as stubborn as I am, so I can't fault him on that."

Jilly looked down at the sleeping man with renewed appreciation. She placed her hand on his own and squeezed it gently, wishing more than anything that he would at least return the gesture. But Alastair didn't move. She listened as Father Levosky spoke to Kevin, but she never let her eyes stray from Alastair.

"It can be a scary place," the priest agreed as Kevin told him how frightened he was that Alastair might never leave the hospital. "But it's less frightening when you know what everything does. That tube," he continued as Kevin's fingers rested on the one which fed into Alastair's mouth. "That is helping him breathe. The machine it's linked to is like a pretend lung. He can't do it by himself at the moment. That's why it's called 'life support'."

"Will he forget how to live?" Kevin whispered.

"We'll have to see when he wakes up," the priest replied. "It's difficult to know what damage might have been done to his brain."

"Brain damage?" Jilly interrupted.

"It just depends on the oxygen supply to the brain, so they tell me."

"So he might not remember me?" Kevin asked.

"No, I'm sure he'll remember you. We might just have to give him time."

"What is this for?" Kevin asked, tracing the tube which disappeared into Alastair's hand.

"That's to help him sleep. And while he sleeps, his body heals. It's pretty strong stuff."

"What is it?"

Father Levosky shrugged. "I don't know." He looked across at Jilly's expression as she watched Alastair's unchanging face. "Have you eaten since you arrived? Or drunk anything?"

"I got some juice from the machine," Kevin replied.

"Let's go get Miss Franks something," Father Levosky said, rising to his feet and offering his hand down to the boy. "I don't think she's remembered to eat or drink anything."

"Oh," Jilly whispered. "I'm fine."

"No, you're not," the priest answered, smiling slightly. "I've heard it said that people in comas hear everything which is going on around them."

"She knows that," Kevin chimed. "She told me earlier."

"Then I think we'll go, Kevin, and get Miss Franks some breakfast." Jilly felt her cheeks bloom as the Catholic priest smiled across at her, and she lifted her hands to her burning face in an attempt to hide it. "Come on, Kevin," Father Levosky continued. "Let's go down to the canteen and see what we can find. Most of its quite inedible, but since you haven't eaten for hours, you'll probably manage to stomach it."

Kevin smiled at Jilly, who returned the gesture, before following Father Levosky. They walked through corridors which all looked the same to him, but his guide knew exactly where he was going. The priest seemed in no rush to complete the chore he had set before them, and he talked about anything Kevin had a mind to discuss. If the conversation ever strayed to the topic of yesterday, Father Levosky would answer with certainty, that there was no man who was less inclined to bear a grudge than Alastair. Somehow this only made Kevin feel more responsible.

When they returned to the ICU ward, it was to find Jilly sitting beside Alastair, a faint smile on her face, and a look of contentment. Kevin was surprised, then, to find that Alastair had neither moved nor woken. Father Levosky thought nothing of this, but watched as the young woman gently set Alastair's hand back on the bed and gratefully accepted the cheese sandwich and coffee they had brought her. The priest departed a few minutes later, but assured both Kevin and Jilly that he would check in on Alastair whenever he was able.

Jilly took Kevin back to her house and he spent the next few days living with Mrs and Miss Franks, although every day he visited the hospital. If Jilly was able to take him, she would stay a while, but sometimes Trish took him in and he would stay for her shift, returning to the village in the evening.

The Christingle service was led by Graham Henderson in the vicar's absence, and the Nine Lessons and Carols was a combined effort by the people of the church, but all felt the loss of Alastair Roberts as far more than a figurehead, but as a friend and a guiding light. The church, however, was packed.

On Monday, Sally-Anne had appeared at the hospital. Kevin was sitting on the side of the bed, dangling his feet lifelessly towards the floor. They were too short to reach. His hand rested beside Alastair's, and his fingers tapped the priest's, hoping to encourage a gesture in return, but none came. Jilly was sitting reading on the chair at the other side of the bed. The book was open in her hands, but she hadn't turned a page in ten minutes, staring over the leaves of the book to watch the man and boy before her.

"Hello Kevin."

The sound of familiarity in an unfamiliar voice made Jilly turn to the newcomer.

"This is my fault," Kevin sniffed as he looked across at Sally-Anne. "I don't want to go."

Kevin watched as Sally-Anne offered him the same sympathetic smile she had done on too many other occasions. She turned to Jilly and smiled.

"Sally-Anne Brown," she announced, as Jilly rose and shook her offered hand.

Jilly's round face smiled back, surprised by how gentle the woman was in her approach. She had imagined a strict, cold individual, incapable of a smile. "I'm Gillian Franks," she said after a moment. "Kevin's been staying with me since the fire."

Sally-Anne nodded slightly, and she glanced back at Kevin, whose eyes challenged her to take him away from the man beside him. Turning back to Jilly, she gestured towards the reception desk of the ward.

"Can we speak, Ms Franks?"

Jilly's eyes widened a little, bracing herself for whatever the woman was about to say, before she nodded. She had to do this, for the sakes of Alastair and Kevin. She had to talk to Sally-Anne to protect the vicar's family.

"Kevin," Sally-Anne continued. "We'll just be over by the desk."

"I'm not leaving Alastair," Kevin replied firmly, tears filling his eyes. He watched as Jilly followed Sally-Anne and tried not to think over all the other times this had happened. He watched the exchange between the two women, unable to hear their words, but imagining what they might be saying. His little hands clenched into fists, which gripped the papery sheet of the hospital bed.

"I wanted to be Kevin Roberts," he sniffed,

staring at Alastair as though it was his fault. "I don't want to go."

Jilly and Sally-Anne were gone for several minutes and, when they returned, Kevin lifted Alastair's hand gripping it tightly in the hope the man would not let him go.

"I'll see you in the new year, Kevin," Sally-Anne said with a smile.

"I can stay?" Kevin asked in disbelief, smiling across at Jilly who nodded.

"We'll see how things go. I hope Reverend Roberts makes a full recovery."

"He will," Kevin replied, letting go of his hand and straightening out his own fingers. He watched Sally-Anne leave, saying goodbye to her and feeling confused that he was able to.

On Christmas Eve morning, Jilly asked Trish to look after their mum in the hope of travelling into town and taking Kevin to the hospital. She had tirelessly gone from tending Mrs Franks, to looking after Kevin, to her role as organist, but she had found a handful of minutes on most days to visit Alastair. She had always worn her smile, feeling she owed it to him to do so. She and Kevin had arrived by half past nine in the morning, sitting beside the bed and talking to one another.

Kevin jumped as Jilly's phone rang, and watched as she rummaged through her chaotic bag to try and find it. It was not a clever phone like Alastair had. It was purely practical, solely for ringing and messaging.

"Oh, it's Trish," she whispered, her eyes widening as she checked the name on the screen.

Kevin watched as Jilly whispered into the

phone, her face becoming pale and her voice rising in pitch. He walked over to her and took her arm.

"Is it Mrs Franks?"

"Yes, Kevin. She's just been brought into hospital again," she said, her voice trying to return to its normal pitch. "Why is God doing this to me?"

"Would you like me you come with you, Jilly?"

She looked down at him in surprise. "Yes, please, Kevin. You sounded just like him. You sounded just like Ally."

"I want to be like him," Kevin whispered. "I want to make him proud of me."

"Oh Kevin," she began, hugging Kevin as tightly as he did her. "He's already proud of you."

"Do you think he'll wake up, Jilly?" Kevin sobbed into her Christmas jumper. "I think he's going to die. I think he's forgotten how to live."

"No," she said. "He's going to live. He has to live." She knelt down in front of him and rubbed her thumbs over his cheeks, wiping the tears away. "I'm going to find my mum, but you can stay here with your dad if you want. Just don't wander off."

"No. Alastair wouldn't want you to go alone." He held his little hand out, and she took it in her own.

They hurried out of the ward, rushing to find Mrs Franks. Jilly tried not to convince herself it would be the last opportunity she had to see her mum alive, but that gnawing suspicion continued to grow in her. Kevin walked beside her, feeling pleased to be a rock for her at this time, and wishing desperately that Alastair would wake up to see him.

Neither of them noticed Father Levosky, who watched them as they left Alastair's bedside. He was dressed in his usual long black cassock which stood out from the rest of the white hospital, but their emotions were high and had built an impassable wall around them. Father Levosky stood a short distance away, watching his friend. Since the first time he had met Alastair Roberts, a grieving father even while his son lived, he had considered him to be amongst the best of people. Of course, their religious beliefs differed from one another but despite their jobs, or perhaps because of them, they found this a cause to celebrate and discuss, not divide. Alastair had been able to unburden his worries, his sorrows and his misgivings, while Father Levosky had enjoyed the company of an individual who could challenge him academically and theologically.

Now, as he watched Jilly and Kevin disappear, he stepped forward to the bedside feeling he had to address his concerns to the man before him. He sat down on the chair and watched the machines as they continued to beep and whir. How many of these beds had he sat beside, praying for and with the people who lay there, so many of them strangers to him? Was it right that it felt infinitely harder to express his thoughts to God when he knew the man he prayed for? All the same, he muttered the words of a prayer, forming the sign of the cross about him.

"You're not an idle man, Alastair," he said, leaning forward and taking his hand. "You have lain in that bed long enough." He sighed as he watched the neutral expression on his friend's face. "You're needed here. By Kevin; by Jilly; by all your parishioners. You've got to wake up. God's plan for you is not yet done." Father Levosky relinquished his hold on Alastair's hand and sat back in the chair. "Please, God, he has not finished his work yet," he muttered.

He had watched so many people, whose faith was as strong as his own, slip away. He had stood or sat by bedsides where families had joined in prayers with him. He had prayed alone when there was no one left to grieve the passing of the individual. But as his brow furrowed into its usual consternation, he considered how he had never been more sorry to see a life pass.

Having duties to fulfil and other patients to visit, a short service to perform in the hospital chapel and sacraments to administer, Father Levosky had left Alastair's side a short time later. Before leaving the hospital that evening, he returned once more to the ICU to find Jilly asleep with her head resting on Alastair's side, while Kevin had once again curled up on the bed. The breathing tube had been removed from Alastair's mouth, but the drip remained in his left hand.

"Christmas peace be with you all," he muttered, watching the simultaneously heart-warming and heart-breaking scene before him. Neither Jilly nor Kevin moved, but Father Levosky smiled across as Alastair's brow creased slightly. He walked forward and placed a hand on his friend's arm. Alastair's eyes opened a fraction and he turned his head awkwardly to face the priest.

"I have heard it said," Father Levosky began, his smile deepening, "that only fools and heroes run into burning buildings. I never had you down as a fool."

"Kevin?" Alastair muttered.

Father Levosky lifted Alastair's hand and set it on the boy's head. He watched as Alastair smiled weakly before he continued. "Then again, it was the father of a fireman who told me, so perhaps he was biased."

"There was," Alastair began, his voice sounding distant to his own ears, "someone in the house."

"Well, you're safe now, with your two guardian angels."

Alastair looked confused, but let his head roll to the other side as Father Levosky pointed across.

"It's been a long time since I've seen such devotion in one human being to another. She cares very deeply for you."

Alastair lifted his hand slightly, having to concentrate on the movement as he rested it in Jilly's fiery curls.

"Merry Christmas, Alastair," the Catholic priest added, making the sign of the cross before him. "God bless you."

Alastair's eyes drifted closed as Father Levosky walked away, a smile on his face and a prayer of grateful praise in his heart.

There were no windows in the room Alastair woke up in. There was no way of telling what time it was, except for by the dimmed lights. There were strong, white lights a little further away, but he could only see them on the edge of his vision. He ran his left hand over Kevin's hair and smiled down at the boy, thanking God he was safe. His memory was patchy, and he couldn't remember what had happened to bring him to this point, or even when this point was. Frowning, he looked down at the intravenous which was taped to his hand. There had been someone in the house. Someone who wanted Kevin. And Alastair had been frightened that Kevin could have been there.

He tensed the fingers on his other hand and found they were nestled in a mass of curls. Jilly lifted her own hand in her sleep, and it rested on his arm. Even in the dim light the runs of tear-marks were visible, and without thinking about what he was doing, or questioning whether it was right or wise, he lifted his hand from her hair and ran it down her cheek.

She woke up with a start, gasping for breath as she pushed herself backwards, deeper into the chair she was sitting in. She looked sleepily around her, trying to remember where she was, before she looked down at the watch she wore and sighed.

"Merry Christmas, Kevin," she said, reaching across to rest her hand on his back. He remained asleep. Putting two fingers together, she kissed them and set them on Alastair's lips. "Merry Christmas, Ally."

"Merry Christmas, Gillian," Alastair whispered, opening his eyes once more. "How is it Christmas already?"

"Vicar?" she squeaked, pulling her hand back and hiding it behind her back. "I didn't know you were awake. I knew you'd wake up. I knew you would." She smiled down at him, and stretched over to Kevin, but stopped as Alastair spoke.

"Let him sleep, Jilly. I missed Midnight Mass," he continued, his voice labouring over each word.

"Me too," she replied. "Mum's- she's not too good at the moment."

"I'm so sorry, Jilly," Alastair said, reaching his hand out to her. She took it. "What can I do?"

"What can you do?" she whispered, laughing about the words. "You can get better, Vicar. You can give Kevin his Christmas wish, and be his dad. But you can't do anything for mum."

"That's not quite true," he answered, his eyes closing and his words slurring. "And I heard Kevin's voice. 'I don't want you to be my dad,' that's what he said."

"He was scared," she said, gripping his hand in both of her own and watching as he fell asleep once more. She smiled. The gesture wasn't directed at anyone or anything, it was just the relief at this perfect Christmas gift. Jilly felt more giddy than she had ever felt on Christmas morning, and she began flicking through all the contacts on her phone, sending Christmas messages, despite the fact it was still four o'clock in the morning. She had never done it before but today felt like the right time to reach out to people.

Trish would be with their mum, she understood what was going on there so much more than Jilly. Mrs Franks had contracted pneumonia and Jilly, feeling she should have better tended her mum, couldn't bear the weight of that responsibility. But Trish was the nurse, not her. She had looked after her mum as well as she could, but this fact could not assuage her guilt.

Jilly felt the smile slip. She sent a message to Trish asking her about their mum and telling her about Alastair. Staring at her phone, she waited expectantly as the minutes ticked by, looking at the blank screen. She rose to her feet and began pacing the floor, wondering if she could find her way back to her mum's bedside. But she couldn't leave Kevin.

It took Trish almost an hour to reply, and her message was brief but welcome. Hilary Franks' condition had stabilised, and Jilly felt the smile return to her face.

Despite spending Christmas in the hospital, neither Jilly nor Kevin could remember ever having a Christmas they were more grateful for. Kevin spent as much of the day as he could at Alastair's side. The boy was unsure whether Alastair really couldn't remember the conversation they had shared or if he only pretended it for the sake of the boy, but when Kevin apologised he was only met with the same gentle smile he had come to love. Jilly had left the pair to go and visit her mum.

Alastair was moved from the ICU two days later, much to Kevin's relief as he saw it as an indication Alastair would be returning home to him soon, wherever home might be. The move did mean that he was now expected to observe the visiting times, so he spent several hours in the company of the hospital chaplain.

Each night, he went back with Jilly to her house, and each day they would return to the hospital. Jilly would wait long enough to check on Alastair's health before she left them to visit her mum. Mrs Franks was making a surprising recovery, and Jilly was hopeful her mum might be able to return home for New Year.

Part Eight

New Year

Alastair had always appreciated the outdoors. For as long as he could remember, he had spent free minutes walking through the landscape, gardening, or just watching the clouds moving overhead. It came as a great relief to him when his new hospital bed was beside a window and he could gaze out at the stormy clouds which promised snow but only shed rain. Although Kevin visited him every day, Alastair missed the constant company he had promised himself he would have over the Christmas period.

He spent his solitary time trying to remember what had happened before he awoke in a hospital bed. It frightened him that his memory had so many holes, and he found himself repeatedly telling himself who he was. He had lost track of days, both before and after Christmas, before he finally had the opportunity to address this concern.

Kevin had gone back to Jilly's house for the night, an arrangement which seemed to suit both of them, and the lights in the ward were dimmed to try and maintain a sense of day and night for its inhabitants. Alastair stared out of the window, trying to catch a glimpse of the stars, but the interior lights were too bright for the tiny, distant specks to compete with.

"So, they're letting you go tomorrow?"

"So I'm promised," Alastair replied, smiling across as Father Levosky entered the room. "Jilly's going to give me a lift back."

"Where will you stay?"

Alistair shifted slightly, grimacing as his chest ached. "Something happened to The Vicarage, didn't it?"

"There was a fire, Alastair." Father Levosky pulled up the chair Kevin had occupied for most of the day. "Don't you remember?"

Alistair nodded slowly. "Someone rang. It was Kevin's voice, but it sounded like a recording, badly put together."

"What did it say?"

"That he didn't want to be my son. And that he wanted me to lose another son."

"That's not something the boy would ever say," Father Levosky agreed. "I know you quarrelled, but he still loves you."

"I'd be worried if we didn't argue," Alastair laughed. "I'm not giving up on him. I don't care what happens, I won't let him down."

"Then you love him too."

"I went to try and find him, but I found Leo

instead. No," he carried on. "I'm sure it was Leonard."

Father Levosky tapped his finger on his chin.

"I'm not going mad. I ended up at Leonard's grave." Alastair smiled at the look of open relief on his friend's face. "And I smelt the fire. The fire brigade were already arriving. He said he'd called them."

"You were right, then? It is someone from Kevin's past?"

Alastair nodded, another piece of his memory fitting into place. "He said Kevin was his boy. But-"

"Alastair," the other man interrupted. "You must tell the police."

"I told them last time."

"But this time someone broke two of your ribs."

"Kevin's parents both died in fires. Who's trying to claim him as their own?"

"You can only do so much for the boy yourself. You must have some help, some protection." He watched as Alastair nodded. "We can't live in the past, Alastair," he sighed. "That's why it haunts you. Because you will not let it go. Kevin told me what he said, what he accused you of. And I know why his words stung so much. It's because you still blame yourself."

"If enough people tell you something, you start believing it. Like Kevin and his curse. My boy died in my arms, I can't find blame in anyone else."

"Because there is none," Father Levosky stated. "But Dawn was wrong to blame you. The fact is, no one was to blame for Leonard's death, and only Dawn is to blame for her own."

"I shouldn't have left her," Alastair whispered, suddenly feeling the intensity of the pain from his ribs double. "Why could I talk other people out of these things but not my own wife?"

"Because she knew you too well." Father Levosky shifted the coat he carried on his lap and watched as Alastair screwed his eyes closed. "You shared the bitterness of Leonard's death and she could not hear you telling her that you had found a way to see through your grief. But you were not to blame." His lips turned up in a smile, unseen by Alastair. "There is someone who's never apportioned blame to you."

"I appreciate your friendship," Alastair began. He stopped as he opened his eyes and looked across at the Catholic priest. "You don't mean yourself, do you?"

Father Levosky grinned. "Two people, then."

"Gillian Franks?"

"We can't live in the past," he repeated. "And that girl loves you."

"I made a promise before God-"

"Pah!" the other man interrupted, rising to his feet and pulling on his long coat. "If you don't love her just say so, but don't pin this one on God. Have and hold, love and cherish, unto death. You did that, Alastair. And if I'd had the love of a woman as deeply as the love Miss Franks has for you, I would never have taken the road to ordination. You're not bound to the vows I am. God bless you."

Alastair smiled across, returning the blessing, and watched as Father Levosky walked out, sharing a joke with the man who sat at the ward reception desk.

He couldn't sleep. He was tired of sleeping. A thousand questions, each raised by his discussion with Father Levosky, milled in his brain. The part he continued to consider was what the intruder could have had meant when he had referred to Kevin as his boy. All manner of scenarios, ranging from a Fagin-esque character to an overzealous uncle, ran through his head.

There was a tired dawn out the window when he finally felt his eyes fall close, only to be opened shortly afterwards by someone snatching his hand and shaking his arm. He blinked awake and stared across at Kevin whose grin covered his entire face. Alastair reminded himself of a time when he had doubted such a sight was a possibility, and smiled back.

"You can come home today," Kevin chimed, failing to acknowledge the exhaustion on the man's face. Jilly, who stood behind him, lifted the boy's hand and smiled across at Alastair, her red hair spilling out from beneath the rib of her bobble hat. Recalling Father Levosky's words, Alastair felt his cheeks burning as though he was a schoolchild.

"Only if you're feeling up to it," Jilly added, mistaking the cause of his flushed complexion.

"No," he replied, affixing his faultlessly patient smile to his face as he turned to Kevin. "I'm ready for home."

He was discharged later in the day, much to Kevin's great delight. Jilly had to gently remind Kevin that the vicar had broken two ribs and couldn't be pulled around like a ragdoll. On one occasion, she had to remind Alastair, too. She smiled across at Kevin as the boy reached for the passenger door handle.

"No, Kevin," she said. "I think we should let the vicar have the front seat."

"No, it's fine," Alastair replied, desperate to sit down again, and sensing it would take twice as long to get into the passenger seat as it would the backseat. Jilly offered him her hand and smiled across as he thanked her.

"So," she began as she sat behind the wheel. "Are we all going back to my house?"

"Yes, please," Kevin replied.

They pulled out from the hospital carpark and Jilly smiled across at the boy.

"Did you tell the vicar what you thought about Christmas?"

"Not yet," Kevin said, lifting his finger to his lips and pointing into the backseat. "He's asleep already."

"Poor Vicar," Jilly sighed, smiling as she watched him in the rear-view mirror. "Where he's from, New Year is almost as big a celebration as Christmas."

"What do you mean?"

"Today is a special day for him, and tomorrow too."

"But what do you mean 'where he's from'? Isn't he from the same place as you?"

"No," she said with a slight laugh. "I've only ever lived in the house I live in now. I never met him until I was twenty. He's from Scotland."

Kevin twisted around in his chair to look at Alastair. "I hope he likes what I made him," he whispered. "It seems so sad now."

"He'll love it, Kevin."

When they reached the village, Jilly pulled up outside The Vicarage. "I'll just be a moment," she whispered. "Wait in the car with the vicar."

"It's not safe to go in there," Kevin hissed.

"I haven't got any clothes for him."

"But all his clothes will have burnt away," Kevin persisted as she opened her car door.

"You're right," Jilly conceded, sighing heavily. "But there's only John's clothes in the house, and they won't fit him any better than mine will."

Kevin laughed, the noise pulling Alastair back to consciousness. He looked across at the building and took a sharp breath.

"I thought I'd lost you, Kevin," he muttered, reaching his left hand forward and resting it on the boy's shoulder.

"I'm so sorry."

"I didn't say it for that," Alastair said, squeezing the boy's shoulder before he let his hand drop. "I just want you to know, I won't let anyone hurt you."

Kevin scrambled out of the car and opened the door where Alastair sat. He wrapped his arms about Alastair's neck and hugged him tightly.

"I wanted you to be my dad. I told Santa that's what I wanted, and it worked."

Alastair held the child in his left arm and, despite this being the extent of the embrace, Kevin had never felt safer.

"The diocese are sending someone in the new year to get the house sorted," Jilly said, as Kevin got back into the car and they drove towards her house. "Apparently the structure's fine. Somehow."

"Did they find any trace of-?"

"The police?" Jilly asked. "I don't know. But I do know they're treating it as intentional, the fire and the attack."

Alastair nodded and looked out of the window. The drive down the track to Jilly's house was excruciating and, by the time they reached the pretty groundsman's cottage, Alastair felt like he might be sick. He struggled to maintain his smile but, as Kevin helped him out of the car and over to the house door, he hugged the boy tightly, overwhelmed by the relief of knowing he was safe. Jilly unlocked the door and ushered the two of them into the living room.

"Grab a seat, Vicar. I'll get the kettle on."

Alastair walked in and smiled at the room he had just entered. It was perfect. The tree in the corner next to two windows, rising to seven feet and almost brushing the ceiling; the star, which was attached to it, scraping the plaster; a cluster of presents safely nestled beneath the tree's lowest branches, in an array of different papers, each tied with raffia ribbon; pastel coloured lights which shone from the central trunk, catching the bold, bright colours of the tinsel and the baubles. There were stockings still hanging from the fireplace, but these all hung limp, while the mantle shelf itself was lost behind a garland of real evergreen.

"It's beautiful in here, Jilly," he called through, as loudly as his tired voice could manage. "Magical."

Kevin and he sat on the sofa, the boy pulling his feet up and snuggling into his side. Alastair rested his head on Kevin's hair and smiled. He turned as Jilly appeared in the doorway.

"Marshmallows and cream?"

"In tea?" Alastair laughed.

"No," she replied. "Kevin and I have a special Hogmanay planned. To make up for the fact you missed Christmas."

"I didn't miss it," Alastair whispered. "I had all I could pray for." He kissed Kevin's hair before he lifted his chin towards her. "How is your mum?"

"She's much better, thank you." She beamed across at him. "The doctors are amazed, and I'm amazed too. They just wanted to keep her in for observations, or whatever they call it these days. But she was very pleased to hear you were on the mend."

"I'm glad she's doing well," Alastair replied.

"She's a very special lady," Jilly whispered. "I can't bear to think of a life without her."

"You don't have to," Alastair pointed out. He looked at Kevin as the boy tilted his head up.

"When can we open the presents?"

"You waited to open your presents?" Alastair asked in disbelief.

Kevin nodded, while Jilly wrinkled her nose across at him and returned to the kitchen. Alastair listened as she hummed and sang Christmas carols while she made the drinks, uncaring of who listened.

"I'm afraid I haven't got anything to give you, Kevin."

Kevin's face fell and Alastair felt his own expression drop to match the despondency. "Everything I'd got lined up as gifts were in The Vicarage. Along with everything I had of everyone else I loved."

"All I really want is to be Kevin Roberts. Can

you make it happen?"

"You're already Kevin Roberts," Alastair replied, hugging the boy even tighter. "I won't ever give up on you. I'm going to find who's doing this, and the police will lock him away. You and me, we'll be able to have a boringly normal life as father and son."

"I don't want it to be boring," Kevin giggled.

"Uncomplicated, then," Alastair laughed.

They both silently watched the tree until Jilly arrived with a Christmas tray and three giant mugs of hot chocolate, topped with a skin of melting marshmallows. They sat and talked as though the events of the last week and a half had never happened.

The afternoon darkened into evening and Kevin began to get restless, walking over to the present pile, sighing, and walking back again. Alastair felt reluctant to open them, feeling he had failed the boy in providing nothing for him.

When it reached seven o'clock, Jilly nodded across at Kevin who sat down on the pine needles which scattered the carpet and pulled out all the presents. Jilly shook her head as Kevin picked up one addressed to Alastair.

"I think we'll leave that one until the end."

Most of the presents were for Kevin, ones he had collected and saved from school friends, from Santa, and from members of the church. There were a handful for Alastair, but none for Jilly. Far from being upset about this, Jilly loved watching the other two open their gifts. Her smile deepened every time Kevin squealed with excitement, and she blushed as the boy thanked her for her own gift of piano books.

"You should keep learning, Kevin," she said, returning the hug he gave her after opening them. "And your dad can sing along, too."

Alastair smiled sleepily across at them both. "Only if you learn easy songs," he replied.

"Can we give him my present, now?" Kevin asked.

Alastair watched with curiosity and trepidation as Jilly pulled out the present she had put to one side. It was a large, flat cuboid, indistinct in shape, and could have contained anything. Aware of the fact Kevin was clearly proud of this gift, Alastair tried to prepare himself for whatever was in the parcel. He thanked Kevin for it as he handed it over. The tag, cut from an old Christmas card, read: "To Dad, love from Kevin xx". Kevin sat cross-legged on the floor in front of him but, unable to wait patiently, knelt up and rested his hands on Alastair's knees.

"I did it," he explained, as Alastair pulled off the papery ribbon. "Well, I helped do it."

Alastair tore off the paper, laughing slightly as he was confronted by a cardboard box. "Are you sure this isn't pass the parcel?" Kevin laughed as though this was the funniest thing he had ever heard. Alastair opened the box, rolling his eyes in a comedic fashion as he pulled out a bubble-wrapped package. He smiled across at Kevin, and tore through the bubble-wrap. Lowering his eyes to the object in his hands, he gave a slight gasp, and Kevin's face fell as tears bloomed in Alastair's eyes. Before he had time to check himself, they spilt down his cheeks.

"Don't you like it?" Kevin whispered, glancing across at Jilly who smiled and shook her head slightly. "One of Jilly's friends is a painter. She did most of it."

Alastair ran his fingers across the glass of the frame. "It's perfect," he smiled, trying to lean forward to the boy, but he scrunched his eyes closed as his chest felt like it was about to cave in. Kevin sat beside him on the sofa and leaned up to kiss Alastair's cheek. "My boys," Alastair whispered, looking down at the painting of Kevin and Leonard. "You would have loved him, Kevin. And he would have loved you."

"I know," Kevin replied, trying to establish a maturity in his voice. "I want to be his brother."

Jilly watched the pair, feeling that this gift meant more to Kevin than anything else he had opened that evening. And she knew it was right that it should do.

"Are you going to tell your dad which bit you did?" Jilly prompted.

"I took pictures of the pictures for Rosemary to copy from, and I helped her choose the frame. And I helped her frame it."

"Well, it is a very nice frame," Alastair replied, smiling down. "I thought I'd lost every trace of Leonard in that fire."

They stayed long enough to have another drink, but as the clock on the wall chimed nine, Jilly stood up.

"It's time you got going. I'll give you a lift."

"Aren't we staying here?" Kevin asked, and was met by Jilly's cheeks blushing.

"Not tonight, Kevin. The bishop has very kindly paid for you to stay at a B&B. At Leona's."

Alastair shot Jilly a sideways glance. "Leona Johnson?"

"Yes," Jilly replied with a teasing smile. "I understand she has a lot more room in her house after the divorce. Perhaps the bishop is listening out for wedding bells."

"He can keep listening," Alastair remarked.

Jilly nodded and smiled. "Let's get you safely there, then," she answered. "Can you collect all your things, Kevin?"

Kevin and Alastair safely tucked their gifts into some bags, all except for Kevin's new piano books which Jilly said he could leave on her piano. She loaded their bags into the boot of her car and returned to the house. Standing at the door to the living room, unnoticed, she watched them for a time. It was oddly satisfying to see the vicar behaving with Kevin as he had done with Leonard. He was a natural father. A smile tugged at the corners of her mouth, and she coughed purposefully.

"Come on. I just sent Leona a message to say we're on our way. She'll be expecting you," she added playfully, grinning across at Alastair.

Despite Jilly's best efforts to soften the drive back up the track, by the time Alastair reached Leona's house, he just wanted to go to bed. After spending ten days lying in a hospital, today had been utterly exhausting. He lay back on the bed and stared up at the lamp above him. Kevin had a room across the landing from his, and he could hear the boy singing songs to himself, too awake to fall asleep. Alastair tried to lift his right hand, to rest it on the space where, a little over two years ago, Dawn might have lain beside him.

He must have fallen asleep then, the first time he had not stayed awake to welcome in the new year for as long as he could remember. The next thing he knew was that someone had come into his room. It was daylight outside, but he couldn't make himself wake up. He heard the latch on the door as it closed and shuffling footsteps walked over to where he lay. Recalling where he was, hearing excited voices downstairs as his hosts celebrated New Year, he forced his eyes to open. He was not entirely convinced that he wasn't going to find Leona in the room with him.

"Are you still alive?" a nervous voice asked, and Alastair smiled across at Kevin. "It's almost afternoon."

"Do we have plans for today?" Alastair mumbled.

"I want to go to Jilly's. Benji and Tom said they have a party at three o'clock every New Year, and Jilly said we could go."

"Great," Alastair replied, through gritted teeth, tipping his head back on the pillow again.

"Don't you feel well enough to go?" Kevin asked.

There was something about the boy's tone which made Alastair start. He silently rebuked himself as he sat up awkwardly, reminding himself that it was his duty to be concerned for Kevin, not the other way around.

"No, I'm fine," he lied. "I'm sorry I slept so long."

"Father Levosky said the hospital kept you asleep so you could heal yourself."

"Well," Alastair replied, smiling at the boy. "He's a very smart man. Go across to your room, and I'll see you in a minute."

Kevin nodded and left the room, leaving

Alastair to struggle out of bed. He looked longingly at the bath in the en-suite, but his chest ached so much there was no guarantee he would be able to get into it, far less out again. Instead, he washed and shaved, leaning on the handbasin and staring at the man who looked back at him in the mirror. He almost didn't recognise himself. His face was drawn, his eyes dark and his cheeks seemed to sink right back into his skull.

He closed his eyes and remembered the words his attacker had spoken. *I've given you a chance.* The rasping voice echoed in his head until he felt overwhelmed by it. And with it came the sudden realisation. This man, whoever he was, would stop at nothing until he got Kevin. How many more lives would it cost? Was it better to unite Kevin with him if he was the boy's flesh and blood?

He opened his eyes and stared at the mirror once more, hating himself for the thoughts which had passed, uncontrolled, through his head. He had promised Kevin he would keep him safe. He was not sure, when he had made the promise, whether he had realised just how difficult it was going to be. But he loved Kevin, and his paternal drive to protect the boy overshadowed every doubt he had. He believed God had sent Kevin, and he would not lose another son.

Alastair jumped as his hand skidded on the basin and laughed slightly as it awoke him from his darkening thoughts. He grabbed the shirt he had been wearing yesterday and slotted his hand through the sleeve, looking down at the crumpled garment and wishing he had something else to wear. Pulling on his trousers, he walked across the landing, knocking on Kevin's door. He looked like a rebelling teenager, unable to twist and tuck his shirt into his trousers. It was these little things, things which were second nature to him, which he hated being unable to do almost as much as he hated having lost his home.

"Kevin's downstairs, Vicar," Leona said, smiling across as she walked out of Kevin's room carrying a basket of cleaning products. Her gaze looked him up and down, and her lips pursed into an amused expression. "I didn't have you pegged as the type to wear your shirt tails out, Vicar."

Alastair smiled across at her, feeling embarrassed and uncomfortable, a feeling which only doubled as she rested her hand on his arm.

"But I'm really glad you're safe, Vicar. Really glad. I hope they find whoever did this."

"I'm sure they will, Leona. Thank you."

She watched as he walked towards the stairs before she called after him. "If you need a hand with anything, anything at all, just give me a shout."

Alastair thanked her again and tried to descend the stairs even faster.

He and Kevin began walking up to the church. Alastair kept pausing under the pretence of admiring something or pointing out an unusual display of Christmas lights. He was not sure if Kevin fell for any of these, but the boy was always pleased to stop and be told something totally mundane. When they reached the church, Alastair sat down on the soggy wood of the bench and stared up at the building.

"It's been here nine hundred years," he muttered, his smile never fading. "And before that, there was a timber church. I think it's a comfort to know it's endured so much."

Kevin nodded as he sat next to him.

"It's not what we endure that matters, Kevin," Alastair continued, but he knew he was directing the words at himself at least as much as the boy. "It's the witness we bear."

Kevin's forehead creased, unable to follow Alastair's words but not wanting to challenge him on them.

"Can I ring Jilly now?" Kevin asked after a short silence. "I'm too tired to walk all the way down to her house."

"Have you got a phone?"

"Jilly gave me one and put her number in it. And Father Levosky gave me his number, too."

"They're the best friends you could hope for."

Kevin brought his phone out of his coat pocket and showed Alastair how to use it. Alastair clicked Jilly's number and waited as it rang.

"Hello Kevin," her cheerful voice sounded. "I'm just putting the goose in the oven."

"Hello Jilly," Alastair replied.

"You're not Kevin. Just pretend you didn't hear that last bit. It's meant to be a surprise."

"Got it," he laughed. "Well, when you've finished whatever you're doing, Kevin wondered if you could pick us up. I'm all set for walking, but he's exhausted after opening all those presents yesterday."

Kevin smiled and nodded as Alastair grinned across at him.

"I'll be there in about ten minutes."

"We're at the church."

"Vicar," she began. "You're not meant to doing much walking. You're out on my recognisance."

"See you soon," Alastair said quickly, lowering the phone and ending the call.

Perhaps driven by the discovery that Kevin and Alastair were sitting outside in the cold, or perhaps because it had taken her less time than she had pre-empted, Jilly arrived at the church in six minutes. She was wearing bright red wellingtons and stomped her way up the path, her thick curls being blown in all directions by the wind.

"I was meant to pick you up from Leona's," she said, worry sounding in her voice. Kevin looked guiltily across at her, while Alastair rose to his feet, smiling with his customary expression. "I only just got back from town."

"Why were you in town?" Kevin asked. "I thought everything was closed at New Year."

"The hospital isn't," she explained. "The doctors said Mum could get home tomorrow."

"Jilly, that's wonderful," Alastair exclaimed. "I'm so pleased for you."

They spent a fun-filled New Year together. Benji, Tom, Trish and Daniel all joined them for dinner and games, which lasted long into the evening. The three children played happily together, while Alastair listened to Trish trying to explain her mum's condition. She was trying to justify the medical turnaround in Mrs Franks' situation, but no matter which way she addressed it, it made little sense.

"Don't question miracles," Alastair cautioned. "And don't try to explain them."

Daniel laughed nervously. The man was fearless as he travelled the world for his work, but the topic of religion unsettled him. Alastair had never quite understood where his beliefs sat, but he always seemed embarrassed and uneasy when the vicar spoke with openness.

"So He does work times other than Sundays?" Trish remarked, unimpressed by Alastair's explanation.

"If you know where to look," Alastair replied, his patient smile never fading.

"You sound just like her," Trish groaned. "You sound just like Mum."

"Is that such a bad thing?" Jilly demanded as she entered the living room with a bottle of wine.

"New Year," Daniel announced.

He looked pleadingly across at Alastair, who turned the conversation quickly, lamenting his attire and apologising for it. He was happy to have the others laugh over the topic, pleased to keep a civility between the two sisters at any cost.

Jilly disappeared a little while later and, at the end of their festivities, explained her absence.

"I've collected up a couple of John's shirts and things. They're a bit bigger than yours, but it beats having to wear one shirt continuously. I think you lost quite a bit of weight while you were in hospital, Vicar," she added, looking with a concerned and critical eye. She blushed as she realised he was watching. "You've got to forgive Trish, Vicar," she pleaded.

"I've learnt to get quite good at forgiveness," Alastair replied with a smile.

"But you can't forgive yourself?"

"That's a little more complicated." He sighed and reached his hand out to the door to support himself. "When we walked past the Post Office today, I spotted there's a house available to rent, out on Smithson's Close."

"Are you really that desperate to get away from Leona?" Jilly laughed.

Smithson's Close was an attempt at a sheltered housing project, which had closed ten years earlier. The houses were tiny and the families who lived there were regarded with distaste and mistrust by several people in the village.

"I just need my own space."

"Away from gossip?" she suggested.

"I suppose," Alastair agreed. "But I just want to have a chance to rebuild the relationship I had with Kevin. I feel like he's missed out on the Christmas I promised him."

"And you're blaming yourself for that, too?" Jilly's hand twitched towards his, before she turned the action into zipping up the bag she had put the clothes in. "Mum said," she faltered. "She always said I blamed myself too much. I don't want to see you go the same way."

"Thank you, Gillian. Isn't it terrible what people do to other people? I can't help measuring myself against the things I try to achieve for others, it's just who I am. But, along with that, comes the knowledge that, if I fail, the blame can only rest with me. I wanted Kevin to smile, properly smile, and after a month he did. I want Trish to acknowledge God in her life instead of confining Him to a church. I want Ms Johnson to happily marry someone and have the love she needs. I want your mum not to suffer, but have her health restored or her pain ceased. For Mrs Henderson to see more of her son, Philip. I invest in every single member of my congregation. I know it's selfish, but I can't believe one of them has chosen not to do so for me."

"What do you want for yourself?" Jilly asked in a tone which made Alastair question her reason for asking.

"I want to see those things happen. And-" he paused as her eyebrows raised, looking expectantly across at him. "I want you all to be happy."

"Well, I can't speak for anyone else," Jilly said with a smile. "But I'm happy."

"Twelve hours over seven visits."

"What?" she laughed.

"That was how long it took you to talk to me when I first arrived. And I've treasured every word since, because I know what it cost you to speak them."

Jilly gasped, the sound turning into a laugh. "It was one week and two days before I spoke to anyone else." Her cheeks burnt, but she forced herself to finish her words. "I don't blame you for anything. In fact, I'm grateful to you. You've given my family dignity and support, and you did the same for your own family. For Leonard, Dawn, and now for Kevin. We all know it. Even Dawn did, deep down."

He returned her words with a nod and a smile but could find no words of his own to address her with.

They did not see Jilly the following day, although Kevin, Benji and Tom gathered with Alastair in the church. The vicar had to get things ready for the service tomorrow. It was strange how different the building felt now they were out of Advent. All the excitement had turned to exuberance, and the church seemed tired and drawn. Every job took twice as long as normal, but the sounds of the three children playing hide-and-seek made the time pass merrily. The last time he had missed a Christmas in church had been when he had been eighteen, half his life ago. Perhaps it would be another eighteen years before he missed another. He tried to imagine where he might be by then. Kevin would be an adult, a thought which made him wonder what path the boy would choose. All the thoughts and expectations he had considered for Leonard's future returned as he thought about Kevin's.

Tom was looking for Kevin and Benji, searching through all the pews. His gentle footsteps were far lighter than either of the other two boys. Kevin hid in the foot well of the organ, on the shelf where Jilly put her feet when she wasn't using the pedals. Alastair had seen Benji hiding behind the enormous spray of flowers in the west doorway. No one ever used the west door anymore. Some people might have found the game sacrilegious, but Alastair loved hearing them play as he set the components in place for tomorrow's Eucharist.

He looked across at the organ as Kevin's phone rang. Tom looked too and rushed forward to find him. Kevin was not impressed, but answered the phone, handing it over to Alastair.

"Hello Vicar," Jilly's voice began. "I've just got Mum home, and she wondered if you'd be able to pop over."

"That's great," Alastair answered with absolute sincerity. "Graham's leading tomorrow's service in Little Golforth, so I can get around tomorrow afternoon if that's any good." He watched as Tom ran to the west door as he spotted Benji's coat. Kevin ran with him.

"Yes, that's perfect," Jilly replied. "See you tomorrow."

She ended the call and Alastair lowered the phone, calling across to the boys. "Time to start stopping. Your mum will be here soon, boys."

The following morning, Alastair and Kevin departed from Leona's house bright and early. It was a dull day with no rain or snow, but the threatening promise of something yet to come. Kevin happily skipped towards the church, all of the horrors of the last two weeks fading from his mind. Alastair watched him run on ahead, happily greeting everyone he met.

When they reached the vestry, Jilly was already there, pulling on her blue robe. Kevin bounded into the room and swirled around, holding his coat out as though he thought it was a cloak.

"Can I wear a robe one day?" he asked Jilly as she clipped her lace collar about her neck.

"We haven't had servers in months. Why don't you ask the vicar if you can serve?"

"What does serving mean?" Kevin asked as Alastair walked into the vestry, only just catching him up.

"It's helping your dad out at the front of the church," Jilly replied. "You're maybe a little bit young. When will you be ten?"

"Next year," Kevin replied.

"Maybe then." Jilly watched as Alastair lifted the cassock out of the cupboard and shrugged out of his coat. Her brother's shirt hung limply from Alastair's slim body, and she smiled slightly. "Would you like a hand?" she asked, seeing him struggling to don the vestments.

"Thank you," he replied. "How's your mum, Jilly?"

"In very high spirits," Jilly laughed. "I think she's pleased to have proved the doctors wrong. And I'm pretty sure she's equally pleased to have proved it to Trish."

Alastair lowered his head as she reached to place the stole about his neck. "And how are you?"

"Relieved, happy, grateful," she smiled up at him. "Can things just go back to normal now, Vicar? I love adventure as much as the next person, but I'm tired of all these misadventures."

"I know what you mean," Alastair sighed. "I just want to get back into my own house. But I spoke to the owner of the Smithson Close house, and he said I could get in tomorrow if I wanted. I don't think he wants it standing empty."

"In that neighbourhood, I'm not surprised," Jilly laughed. "Are you sure you want to go there?"

"It's only temporary," Alastair replied.

He didn't offer any further words, but he had one very clear reason for wanting to go somewhere as obscure as the old sheltered housing. While Jilly was celebrating life returning to normal, he was less sure it would be able to. Whoever had come after him with the intention of finding Kevin was not going to give up just because it was a new year. This man had more deaths to his name than anyone Alastair had ever met and, by moving into the last place anyone would expect to find him, he could buy a little more time in the hope of him being caught.

After the service, Kevin was invited back to Trish's house for the afternoon, while Alastair joined Jilly in her drive back to the groundsman's cottage. He was eager to see Hilary Franks again, not having seen her since before Christmas, and stepped into the house taking in a deep breath as he smelled the fragrance of Sunday dinner. It transported him back through time, and he stood for a moment trying to remember all the memories attached to that scent.

"Mum," Jilly began, squeezing past him to walk into the living room. "The vicar's here."

Alastair followed her in as she invited him to do so.

"I'll get the dinner sorted," Jilly continued. She grinned broadly. "I'll leave you two to it."

"Vicar," Mrs Franks said warmly, holding her hands out to him. "Thank you for coming. You'll stay for dinner, won't you? You're as thin as a rake."

"I really came to offer you the sacrament, Mrs Franks," he replied, smiling across at her as he sat in the armchair next to her corner of the sofa.

"Jilly told me what happened," she went on, ignoring his words. "Have the police caught the man who torched your home?"

"If they have done, then they haven't told me."

"You should ask them," she stated. "They have all the right intentions but not always all the right drive."

"I don't want to talk about me, Mrs Franks," he said. "How are you feeling?"

"Vicar, you never want to talk about yourself. But I am the one whose time is running out, and I want to talk about you."

"I'm not a very interesting topic of conversation," he warned her.

"That is certainly not true." She gave a feeble laugh. "You suit that shirt much better than John did."

"Have you heard from him?" Alastair asked, determined that this conversation would not be about himself.

"No," she sighed. "He'll come back when I'm gone. That much I know. I love him, very dearly, but I know what he is."

"What do you mean?"

"He'll throw my little Jilly out to sell the house. Will you look after her for me?"

"I promised you once before that I would. What's changed since then?"

"You've changed," Mrs Franks continued. Alastair smiled and shook his head as he realised she had managed to turn the conversation back to him.

"Not really," he replied. "I'm just-"

"You're a father again," she interrupted. "And to a lovely, loving boy. He came to visit me in hospital, you know?"

"No, I didn't."

"You should always have been a father, Vicar. You've got such a desire to see God and goodness in people." She watched as he opened his mouth to speak, but she held up her hand, silencing him. "I don't want Jilly thrown out of this house.

I was going to leave her the house in my will but, when she's grieving, John will convince her of anything."

"I can try and guide her, but-"

"I'm going to leave the house to you."

"What?" Alastair gasped, leaning forward. "You can't mean that, Mrs Franks. You have three children. You should leave it to them."

"I want you to look after Jilly's interests here. John will throw her out, and Trish would not be far behind. But you've seen something in my little Jilly, haven't you? The same strength I love to watch. But despite it, or perhaps because of it, she's fragile."

"I'll make sure Jilly is safe and has her home, this home, to return to every night."

"She thinks very highly of you, Vicar."

"You're going to make me blush, Mrs Franks," he said, smiling across at her.

They talked a while longer, Alastair grateful of the conversation and Mrs Franks grateful of the company, before Alastair performed the short service of home communion. He was unsure whether Jilly was listening at the door, or whether it was simply fate which caused such perfect timing, but the moment they had finished their ritual, Jilly called out that it was dinner time.

"Doctor's orders," Mrs Franks replied when he asked her if she would be going through to the kitchen. "Movement."

Alastair offered her his arm and guided her through. She leaned heavily on him, thankful for the support, but Jilly rushed in and helped her mum, explaining to Mrs Franks that Alastair was still nursing his own injury.

They shared a meal together, Hilary Franks eating next to nothing, but pleased to be in the company of Alastair and Jilly. They laughed, talked and ate, celebrating this communion with quiet appreciation.

"You must forgive Trish, Vicar," Mrs Franks said at length. "She has the mind of a sceptic but the heart of a believer, and she finds herself torn between the two. It shouldn't be a surprise. Her father was just the same."

"Poor Trish," Jilly muttered. "She's going to be left holding the baby if anything happens to you."

"What baby?" Alastair asked, confused by her use of the phrase.

"Me," Jilly answered, as though it were obvious. "So, I've got to keep Mum alive," she continued, smiling across at her mother.

"Don't tease," Mrs Franks said, and Alastair felt as though he was caught in a conversation he didn't fully understand.

At the end of the afternoon, Jilly drove Alastair back to Leona's house, calling in at Trish's to collect Kevin. As Alastair was leaving, Mrs Franks had taken him aside. For the first time since he had arrived, she looked frail. Her skin looked grey in the fading light, and it was drawn over her skull like taut elastic. She was hunched forward, and shuffled rather than walked.

"She jokes, Vicar," she whispered, taking his hand in her own. "But there's no doubt of the terminal nature of my cancer. The more she shrugs it aside, the harder it will be for her to bear."

"I promise I'll do all I can to see she's safe," Alastair replied.

Mrs Franks nodded her head and thanked him, waving him off in a manner which suggested she might never see him again. Alastair ducked into the car and smiled across at Jilly. He could understand the cares and worries her mother bore for her. In many ways she was as fragile as Mrs Franks had said and, after the darkest times of her breakdown, her mother was justified in worrying about her future. But as she chatted happily to him, joking and maintaining her smile which was almost as well-trained as his own, he reminded himself of the strength Hilary Franks had spoken of. Alastair knew that, in light of her faith, she was as strong as either her brother or sister. He tried to convince himself that this was why Mrs Franks had singled him out to help Jilly, because her faith would help her get through the sorrow of her mother's death.

But, as he lay awake that night, listening to the noises which echoed through the B&B, he felt more and more certain that her motives were not solely geared towards her daughter's spiritual wellbeing.

When he did finally fall asleep, he dreamed he was walking into the church, through the great west door. Jilly was playing the organ, but it sounded discordant, and everyone who sang was out of key. The voices stretched as though he was about to pass out. He placed his hands over his ears, but the sound still penetrated. Raising his eyes, he stared in momentary disbelief at the hanging bodies which dangled from the rood screen, Dawn, Leonard, Jilly. He rushed forward to them, not wasting a second as he had done when he had found Dawn two years ago, struggling with the knots in the baler-twine, and feeling the horrible, sickening nausea of the cord passing through his fingers. He looked down at the three pairs of eyes, each staring accusingly back at him, and clamped his hand over his mouth.

He faltered as a question entered his head. It was not the one he knew he should be asking, but as he stared at Jilly's face, lifeless and cold, he frowned. If Jilly was here, who was playing the organ?

Alastair looked across, his gaze resting on that same grey figure who had stepped out of the flames in The Vicarage. Kevin sat on the shelf at the man's feet, where he had done when he had been playing hide-and-seek yesterday. There was smoke coming out of the organ pipes and Alastair lifted his hands to try and stop the smoke from entering his lungs. Without turning to face him, the man spoke.

"Kevin Alderman is my boy, not yours."

Alastair tried to reason with him, but the organ was now bursting into flames. He tried to snatch Kevin away from it, but the boy fought him back, desperate to stay with the other man, whatever the cost. Alastair opened his mouth to speak but crashed forward onto the choir stall as he felt something strike his back.

He leapt awake, turning to look at the clock beside the bed. It showed 2:54. Gripping the right side of his chest, he tried to steady his pounding heart. It was a dream. It meant nothing more than his subconscious playing over his fears and worries. He climbed out of bed and walked to the window, staring down into the village. Nothing moved. Everything and everyone was asleep except for him. He gripped his hands together, steepling his index fingers and tapping them thoughtfully. God had brought Kevin to him for a reason, but what if the reason was so that Alastair could return the boy to this man. But this stranger was an arsonist, a murderer. Alastair was not sure he could let Kevin anywhere near such a man. Staring at the church tower, remote and dull from this part of the village, he turned his thoughts heavenward, praying earnestly that God would show him the route through this chapter of his life, and give him the strength to end this horrific cycle of deaths which haunted Kevin.

As he returned to bed after a few minutes, he realised he had to find out who had started the fire in The Vicarage. Whatever the outcome of their second meeting, Alastair knew the alternative would be that he would live a life haunted by this man as surely as he was haunted by Dawn's death. If nothing else, he owed it to Kevin to ensure he found the truth.

Part Nine

Epiphany

Alastair and Kevin moved into their rented house on Monday. Kevin approached it as an adventure, the same way he had tackled everything in the new year. Since Alastair had woken up on Christmas Day, nothing had dampened his spirits for more than a moment. The curse had been lifted, and it had been Alastair who had ended it, surviving the fire which Kevin knew had been meant to kill him. Kevin was not entirely sure that there had been anyone in The Vicarage as Alastair and Father Levosky believed, but it made little difference to the boy. The fire had come, and Alastair still wanted to be his dad. It was the end of the cruel events which had continually chased him. He had a family, a man who loved him, and Kevin loved him equally in return.

The house was small, with two tiny bedrooms,

a bathroom, a kitchenette and a living area. None of the rooms were large, but as soon as Alastair had set the painting of Kevin and Leonard on the sideboard, it began to feel like home. The only thing Kevin disliked about the house was that Alastair would not let him go outside by himself. There was a communal garden, shared with five other homes, but Alastair had made it clear to Kevin that he was not to go there without him. Aside from annoying and disappointing the boy, it made him fearful. But the memory of what had happened last time he challenged Alastair caused him to hold his tongue.

He missed Ysolde and, on Tuesday morning, he asked Alastair if they could go back to The Vicarage garden and look for her. Kevin was surprised when Alastair readily agreed to take him in the afternoon.

They walked together to the church for the usual Tuesday morning service. It was the first time Kevin had ever attended this event, and he sat beside the silent organ, wishing for any hint of music. The church seemed bland and cold without the organ filling it, and he huddled into his coat, wrapping it tightly around him.

The congregation was small, only eight people, all sitting at the back and, except for Mrs Humphries, all were old enough to be Alastair's parents. This observation, as Kevin leaned forward to watch an old man stagger forward to the lectern to give a reading, made him wonder why Alastair never mentioned his parents. He wondered whether the vicar's parents were dead, like his own, or perhaps they lived in Scotland still, and Alastair never had the opportunity to visit them. Kevin might have adopted grandparents he didn't know about. He had heard Sally-Anne telling Helen about his real grandparents, who wanted nothing to do with him, and wondered what it might be like to have some who really did care.

After the service, Kevin met Alastair in the vestry. The man's faultless smile was only marred by a hint of concern as Kevin plodded in.

"What's wrong?" he began.

"Can we go and find Ysolde now?" Kevin replied, accompanying his words with a heavy sigh.

"I'll just go and have a word with each of the congregation, then we can go home and grab some lunch. We'll go and find Ysolde after that." Alastair watched as Kevin nodded. "Will you tidy the altar for me?"

Kevin smiled and nodded again, with more enthusiasm. He loved the trust Alastair placed in him with this job, and rushed out to the chancel. Alastair smiled as he walked down through the nave and spoke with each of the congregation in turn as they left.

"Is that your boy, Vicar?" asked Mr Greene, who walked out with the aid of two sticks. His wife followed. "He's not grown much."

"Yes, that's Kevin," Alastair replied with a gentle smile as Mrs Greene chided her husband. "Not Leonard."

"Sorry, Vicar," Mrs Greene began, looking up to check her husband's words had not offended the priest. Alastair's smile remained constant. "He's getting more mixed up than ever, these days."

"You've nothing to apologise for, Mrs Greene," Alastair replied. "It's just wonderful to see you both again, and wonderful that he's feeling up to walking. Did you have a quiet Christmas?"

"Lilly came," Mrs Greene said. "And she's a little one of her own now."

"Freddie, isn't it? Did you see him, too?"

"You remember everything, Vicar." Mrs Greene took his hand in both of her own. "I thought being a Grandmother was the most wonderful thing, but being a great-grandmother is just as special." She beamed across at him. "He's a little rascal. I'll bet your little one keeps you on your toes."

Alastair nodded, his smile deepening.

"I'm glad you're back, Vicar," she added, before he could make a comment of his own. "Safe and well." She looked down the path to where Mr Greene was struggling with a car handle. "Poor Peter," she clucked. "He had a green car when we were courting and now he thinks all green cars are his."

"Have you got any help, Mrs Greene?"

"No," she replied stubbornly. "And don't you worry about it. We can manage just fine. You enjoy little Kevin's holidays."

He watched as she walked briskly down the path to meet her husband, prising his hand from the car door's handle and leading him over to their own white car. Alastair smiled across at Mrs Humphries as she stood before him.

"Thank you, Vicar," she began, her face unusually gentle. "I didn't get a chance to talk to you on Sunday, but I wanted to wish you all the best for the new year."

"Thank you, Mrs Humphries," Alastair replied. "And the same to you and all your family."

"Have you heard from the police?" she asked, her voice quiet as though she thought someone else might hear, although she was the last person to leave the church.

"Not yet. I'll give them a ring later."

"It was Jack who got you out, you know," she said. "He said something was off about it, that it couldn't be an accident."

"I didn't know," Alastair whispered, trying to remember the man who had found him in the burning vicarage, but confronted always by the image of his attacker. "But I'm so grateful he did."

"So am I, Vicar," she replied, smiling across at him before she walked along the church path.

Kevin stepped up to Alastair and his wide eyes stared expectantly.

"Can we get some lunch and find Ysolde now?"

Alastair wrapped his left arm about the boy, hugging him close and trying not to think about what might have happened if Mrs Humphries' husband had not carried him safely from the fire. He guided Kevin back into the church where the boy helped him out of his cassock, and he hung up the vestments.

They walked back to their tiny house, talking about nothing in particular, just pleased to be sharing the walk. Eager to go hunting for the squirrel as soon as possible, Kevin helped to butter the bread. Alastair pulled open the fridge door.

"What would you like in the sandwich?" He looked at the contents of the fridge and frowned.

"I think it might have to be jam, I'm afraid."

"Jilly gave you some meat on Sunday," Kevin ventured, squeezing past him to pick up a little foil-wrapped package. "Can we have that?"

Alastair nodded, a gesture which lit Kevin's thin face with a broad grin. They ate their beef sandwiches at the tiny table in the corner of the sitting room, and Kevin talked excitedly about returning to The Vicarage garden. Any misgivings Alastair felt on behalf of the boy, worried he wouldn't want to revisit the burnt-out shell of his home, faded when he heard the enthusiasm in Kevin's voice.

Kevin washed the pots while Alastair dried and filed them away, but before they left their little house, the vicar made a phone call. He had bought a new phone, putting his new number on the weekly news sheet which had been handed out on Sunday and today. Now, he was able to not only receive calls from his parishioners, but could also ring out without Kevin knowing who he was talking to.

He walked through to the kitchen and looked out of the window at the grey day beyond. His phone call was to the police station. He discreetly took himself away from Kevin, not wanting to alarm the boy.

He waited on hold as he was passed from one person to another, before he finally managed to get an answer to his question. It was not an answer he was prepared for, nor one which he had ever considered as a real possibility.

He was in a daze as he ended the call and stared blankly out of the window at the communal garden. There had been fingerprints on the lamp, apparently, rubbed and distorted, but enough of them to give a match. And it was a match to records they already had, records which had been closed for almost nine years.

Alastair jumped as Kevin poked his head around the kitchen door and smiled, blissfully ignorant of the truth Alastair had just learnt.

"Can we go yet?"

"Yes," Alastair replied, his smile having returned the moment he had heard the latch of the door. "I'll just grab my coat. You'll need yours, too. It's getting colder out there."

He looked down at the loose shirt he wore and shook his head. He had met John on a handful of occasions, and the man had dwarfed Alastair. Grabbing his coat from the back of the sofa, he eased his right arm into the sleeve. Moving was getting easier, but he still struggled to lift anything in his right hand and was constantly aware of the gripping ache when he tried to twist around. He longed to get his own clothes but, being unable to drive, he would have to wait until Kevin was back at school and take the bus into town.

Kevin sat by the front door and pulled on his wellingtons, before Alastair pushed a knitted hat down about his ears.

"Did you get the nuts?" Alastair asked. "Poor Ysolde is not used to having no food. I hope she remembered her instincts and stored some."

"Me too," Kevin agreed, collecting the bag of peanuts and taking Alastair's hand as they left the house.

Their walk was quite a long one, past the other primary school, on towards the butcher's shop, then a turn up to the church. From here, Alastair let go of Kevin's hand and watched as the boy ran on ahead, squelching through the mud of the little path, and calling through the hedge to Mr Sinter's dogs. The first drops of rain began to fall as they walked along the path. The smells of the cold day seemed to intensify, and Alastair felt an equal amount of sorrow and determination as he walked onward, towards what he knew was his home.

When they reached The Vicarage, Alastair called Kevin back. It was already a construction site. A huge skip was parked on the driveway beside his car, and Alastair tried not to think about the things which filled it. His things, mementos of his life. He jingled the spare set of car keys in his pocket. After having locked himself out of the house on one occasion four years ago, he had learned the value of relocating the second set of keys. Since then, he had always kept his spare keys in the old anorak he left in the vestry cupboard and, on Sunday, he had taken the scruffy jacket out of the church. But his doctor had told him not to drive for six weeks, leaving the car as useless as all his other possessions.

Trying to ignore the work of the contractors, whilst smiling and waving across at them, Alastair guided Kevin around to the back of the house. The apple tree stood timelessly guarding the garden. He walked over to it, resting his hand on the branch which had been such a turning point in his life. Kevin didn't notice this, but ran around the garden looking for Ysolde. He lined peanuts along any branch he could reach, peering into the holes in the trees and looking for any sign of the squirrel.

Alastair watched Kevin running through the garden, content and safe. He pulled out his phone and, dialling a number he knew by heart, he lifted it to his ear. The line rang out, three times, four times, five times, before it clicked through to the answer machine.

"Hello," Alastair began, looking over his shoulder to make sure he was alone. "I was right, sort of. It's not a curse, it's a person. And it's not just any person, it was-" he pulled the phone away so that he could double-check the number he had just rung. He spun around as Kevin called out to him, the faintest hint of guilt on his features. Pressing the picture of a red phone, he ended the call.

"Come and look! Dad, come and look!"

Alastair slotted the phone into his pocket and walked over to where Kevin stood. Kevin's smile plastered every inch of his face. It even seemed to make him glow. He was pointing at an old tree, wizened and stunted, at the back of the garden against the wall.

"Keep watching," he said, hugging Alastair's arms about him. "I think I found her."

Alastair watched as a tiny face appeared from behind the trunk of the tree, watching them as intently as they watched her. Kevin tightened his hold on Alastair and squirmed with excitement.

"Look a bit higher, Kevin," Alastair instructed. "It's not just Ysolde you've found. Look, there's Tristan, too."

"Hello, Kevin," a cheery voice called. "Hello, Vicar."

"Jilly," Kevin called, running to the mouth of the driveway to meet her. "We've found Tristan."

"That's very exciting," she agreed, smiling across at Alastair as he walked over. "I'm surprised to find you here, though."

"We came to feed Ysolde," Alastair said, but Kevin talked excitedly over the top of him.

"We brought her peanuts because we haven't fed her since before Christmas. I thought she might have gone, but instead she fetched Tristan."

"She's very lucky to have you caring for her," Jilly said, smiling at Kevin and pulling the bike helmet off her head, hanging it from the handlebars. Somehow, her mass of curls sprang back into shape. "Are you both still coming for dinner tomorrow? I know the cider is off-limits, but I've got great plans for the food."

"Yes," Kevin chimed.

"How are you finding your new house?"

"Dad won't let me go outside on my own," Kevin moaned. "But I like it otherwise."

Jilly smiled across at Alastair, whose gaze was on the basket at the front of her bike.

"How are you feeling, Jilly?" he asked.

"Fine, thank you," she muttered, confused by this question coming so far into the conversation. She looked down into the basket and realised why he had asked. "Mum's having an off-day," she explained, resting her hand on the green cross of the pharmacy bag. "She didn't want to get up this morning. I'm just looking for things which might help her." Jilly tugged her helmet on again and clipped it closed under her chin. "Just give me a ring when you've got an idea of times for tomorrow," she said, scrunching her nose at Kevin. "And don't stay out in the rain too long."

"You sound just like him," Kevin laughed, pointing at Alastair.

"I suppose there are worse people to sound like," she replied as she looked across at the priest. "Not many, maybe, but a few."

She waved to them as she pushed herself onto the saddle of her bike once more. She loved the freedom of riding her bike. It was something her father had taught her to do, the only time she could remember him teaching her anything. She smiled and waved at people as she rode through the village, a far cry from the girl who, ten years ago, had confined herself to the four walls of the groundsman's cottage. Switching on her bike lights, she continued down the lane towards the start of the track which led to her house. She didn't need the light to see by, but the road was used by heavy farm vehicles, and she wanted to make sure they saw her.

There were no tractors on the lane that afternoon, although she was not the only person on the road. She squeezed the brakes on the handlebars and waved across the road to the man who was walking towards her.

"Mr Samuels!" she called, and watched as he turned to face her, a smile crossing his face.

"Gillian, what are you doing out here?"

"I live out here," she replied, crossing the road. "Just down there." She pointed down at the lights of the house which looked remote. "What are you doing here? I thought you'd moved out."

"Yes, I have," he smiled, the gesture softening

his usually gruff voice. "But I got to quite like the village, so when they were looking for folk to help out down at the big house, I volunteered."

"You're walking all the way down there?" Jilly asked in disbelief.

He nodded.

"No," she said, and grinned across at him. "Come on down to my house. You can have a cup of tea to warm you up, you look frozen, and then I'll give you a lift to the big house."

Mr Samuels tried to dissuade her, but she couldn't let the former caretaker wander along the long lane by himself in the rain. He pushed her bike for her, and they walked down the lane, discussing the village and the people who lived in it. Jilly laughed at all his jokes, and he smiled back at her, enjoying one another's company. She had spent her whole life in the village, but Kenneth Samuels had lived all over the country, and had visited several other places.

When they got to the house, Kenneth looked uncomfortable and peered over his shoulder as though he expected someone to be there. She pushed the door open and encouraged him inside, but he shook his head.

"I thought you were the vicar's lady."

Jilly felt her cheeks burst with colour and shook her head. "I'm my own lady," she whispered. "Who told you I was anything else? The vicar is still faithful to the vows he made to his wife. Did you know he used to be married?"

"No," Kenneth answered. "I just assumed he'd adopted the boy because he wanted a family. That vicarage was a big house for one man on his own."

"He had a son, too. But Leonard and Dawn both died. He's had his fair share of heartache, and all undeserved."

"You are his lady, aren't you?" Kenneth said, a twinkle in his eye.

"No," Jilly protested. "Everyone in the village will tell you just what I've told you. Come on," she added. "I don't want to leave the door open. It's not good for Mum. Anyway, who's going to see you out here?"

Kenneth reluctantly walked up the two steps and pulled his hat off, gripping it tightly. He looked uncomfortable, but Jilly ushered him into the living room and knelt down to get the fire going. There were enough embers for it to take and, as she pulled open the grate, smoke billowed up the chimney.

"I'll just go check on Mum, then I'll pop the kettle on."

She walked out of the living room and to the back of the small house, into the room which used to be the dining room but was now arranged as her mum's bedroom. There was a small circular table in the kitchen, and the family were so rarely together for a sit-down meal that the large dining room was now obsolete. Hilary Franks was sleeping on the sofa bed, her mouth twitching slightly as though she was trying to smile. Jilly smiled down at her, wishing, praying that her end was not as imminent as the doctors had suggested it might be. She looked down at the mobile phone she had given her mum, checking it still had charge, and hoping she had no need to use it.

Finally, she went back through to the living

room and found Kenneth sitting on the edge of the armchair. He still gripped his hat, and Jilly shook her head slightly, remembering her manners.

"Let me take your hat and coat," she said. "You won't feel the benefit of them when you go out again otherwise."

"Why are you being so nice to me?" Kenneth asked, a note of suspicion creeping through his disbelief. "It's been a long time since anyone invited me into their home."

"Haven't you got any family?" Jilly questioned, collecting his hat and coat. "Any friends?"

"I had one very good friend," he confided. "But she left me."

Jilly tried to find some comforting words to soften the pain the man clearly felt at the conversation she had forced on him. "In this village, you'll find people are mostly friendly, and we welcome company. Didn't you find that at the school?"

"Yes," he replied gently, in a voice so low it sounded like someone scraping their foot on gravel.

"There you go, you see," she said, happy to find a smile returning to his face. She walked out to the hall and hung up his coat, setting his hat on the round handle of her dad's walking stick. She jumped as the phone rang on the hall stand next to her, and she reached out to answer it, hoping that it hadn't disturbed her mum's sleep. Still thinking about this, she lowered her voice and whispered into the phone.

"Hello?"

"Jilly?" asked the voice at the other end. "Is

that you?"

"Hello, Kevin," she laughed. "Sorry, I'm trying to keep quiet, so I don't wake Mum."

"We're about to go home," his little voice explained, not needing any more explanation than she had already offered for her strange reception. "And Dad wondered if there was anything you wanted for tomorrow, because we'll be walking straight past the- Look, she's back!"

"Pass me the phone, Kevin," Jilly heard Alastair's voice say. "You see where Ysolde goes."

There was a pause before Alastair's voice spoke again.

"Hello, Gillian."

"Hello, Vicar," she replied, blushing as she remembered what Kenneth had said.

"We're going to be going right past the shop, so if you want anything for tomorrow we can pick it up for you."

"That's lovely, but I think I'm all set, thank you, Vicar." She jumped as Kenneth reached past her to collect his coat. "No, don't go," she said quickly. "I'm going to make you a cup of tea. You need something warm before you head out into the cold."

"Sorry," Alastair's voice stammered. "I didn't know you had company. If you think of something just send me a message and we'll get whatever you need,"

"It's Mr Samuels," Jilly said, feeling a certain air of victory as she managed to hang the man's coat up once more. "He's got a job up at the big house, helping out with the renovations."

"That's great," Alastair replied, his tone speaking of absolute sincerity. Jilly wasn't sure why, but her smile fell at how readily he had accepted the fact Kenneth Samuels was in her house. "We'll see you tomorrow, Jilly."

"I'll come and pick you up at three," she said, suddenly afraid to let him go.

"Sounds perfect. See you then."

The phone rang off and she set the receiver down. She looked up at her reflection in the mirror on the hall stand and jumped as she found Kenneth's eyes staring back at her.

"Oh, Miss Franks," he said, that mischievous twinkle glistening in his eyes. "I think you *are* his lady."

"No," she muttered, pushing her hands on her cheeks. "It's all just rumours. He was very good to me when he first arrived here, I am just trying to return his kindness." She sighed and turned to face him. "Tea," she said, smiling across. "I'll get the kettle on. It takes a while, I'm afraid," she called over her shoulder as she walked into the kitchen. "I prefer these kettles you boil on the hob, not those electric ones. They always leave a scummy mush on the tops of drinks."

She filled the kettle and set it on the halogen hob before returning to the living room where Kenneth had retaken his seat. She was pleased to find he looked much more relaxed, leaning back in the chair and gazing admiringly at the tree and decorations which would all be coming down tomorrow. Jilly rushed to the hearth and kicked the vent closed as she watched the flames roaring up the chimney.

"It always seems a shame to take them down," Kenneth mused, pointing to the garlands. "To end that which brings beauty and cheer."

"Yes," Jilly agreed. "When you put it like that, it's true. Christmas has always been my favourite time of year, but this year I feel like it's passed me by a little bit."

"Your decorations don't suggest it." Kenneth replied. "And a real tree, not one of those horribly plastic ones. I feel the same way about plastic trees as you do about plastic kettles," he laughed. "And I love the bonfires you can have with real trees. It's like nature feeding back into nature."

"I don't know," Jilly sighed, feeling suddenly that she had sounded ungrateful and trying to make up for the fact. "I think it was just strange spending so much of the festive period in hospital. This is really not a happy topic," she laughed. "I'll go get us a drink."

She walked through to the kitchen and lifted two mugs down from the hooks under the cupboard. One had a sheep on, the other a Christmas tree. She dropped a teabag in each and turned to the doorway as Kenneth appeared.

"What do you have in your tea?" she asked. "Sugar? Sweeteners? Milk?"

"Leave the tea for a moment, Gillian."

Jilly looked across at him in surprise, feeling suddenly nervous. "Sorry," she whispered. "I think I just get carried away sometimes."

"You don't have to be sorry," he laughed, sounding as nervous as she felt, but there was an eagerness to his features. "But there is something I'd like to know."

"What?" she whispered, stepping backwards. Kenneth didn't advance, she noticed, slightly relieved by this. She jumped as the kettle began boiling, shrieking out its shrill whistle. Kenneth laughed as he did the same, and reached for the kettle, pulling it from the hob and pouring the water into the two mugs. Jilly felt suddenly foolish as he did this. All the terrible things she had imagined running through his head, and he probably only wanted to know where the bathroom was.

"Sorry," she laughed, shaking her head slightly. "What did you want to know?"

"I want to know where Alastair Roberts lives," he said flatly, snatching her wrist and pulling her over to the cooker. "Where are you picking him up from tomorrow?"

"Let go of me!" she screamed. "Please, let go of me!"

Instead of releasing his hold on her, he pushed her hand towards the red glow of the halogen hob, flicking the dial on once more. "Where is Alastair Roberts?"

"Why?" she whimpered. "Don't, please."

She pushed herself away from the oven with her free hand, but Kenneth only dragged her forward again. She could feel the heat rising from the hob and she curled her hand away from it, trying to twist out of his grasp.

"Where is he?" Kenneth repeated, pushing her hand down.

Jilly heard herself screaming, a cry so instinctive that she hardly knew she was the one who made it. She sobbed as she heard her mum's frail voice calling through, and she tried vainly to escape the man's hold on her. As he pulled her hand away from the hob once more she felt her head go light, relief running through her that he had not pushed it as far as the glowing surface. Her vision blurred into a hazy white light, and she realised she was on the verge of either being sick or passing out. Kenneth snatched the back of her head and pushed her face towards the red ring.

"Do you know what he is?" Kenneth demanded, while Jilly sobbed, each of her tears turning to steam the moment they hit the hob. "He's a kidnapper, a thief, a charlatan."

"No," she wailed. "No, he's none of those things. He's-" she screamed again as he pushed her face down, stopping with her cheek only an inch above the red glow. She tried to reach the controls which would turn off the ring, but her right hand was stinging and would not follow the commands her brain tried to send it.

She stopped screaming as Kenneth pulled her upright once more, turning her so she faced him. "Why does everyone want to take him from me?"

"What are you talking about?" she sobbed, screaming once more as he snatched her right wrist.

She turned to the doorway as she heard the sound of breaking glass.

"Help me!" she yelled out, her voice turning to a scream as she felt Kenneth squeeze her burning hand. "Oh God, please help me!"

There was the sound of the latch on the front door being turned, and Kenneth gripped her in front of him as they faced the doorway. He pulled a cigarette lighter out of his pocket, an old-fashioned one which could be refilled and with a lid which he flipped open. Jilly struggled in his grip, trying to wriggle free, but he held her tightly. She felt tears stream in torrents down her cheeks as she recognised Alastair. She stared across, never more pleased to see him.

"I think you should let her go," Alastair said. His smile was no longer on his face, and he carried his hands up as though he was surrendering.

Kenneth flicked the flint on the lighter, and Alastair realised with a horribly predictable acceptance that this had been the sound he had heard so often over the phone. The man moved the lighter flame towards Jilly's tight curls. Alastair watched as she tried to lean away from this. He stepped forward but stumbled back as Kenneth dropped the lighter to the tabletop, snatching a knife from the rack and slashing it towards the priest. Alastair felt the same dull ache which was becoming commonplace now as he made his pre-emptive manoeuvre.

"You don't want Jilly," Alastair said, as calmly as he could. He looked across at her large eyes. "You don't really want me, either. You want Kevin. You want your son. Let her go, and she can fetch him." Alastair held out a set of keys. "He's in the car. Jilly can get him. But if you hurt her, you won't ever see your son again, Harry."

"Harry?" Jilly whispered.

In reply Alastair only nodded, but he released a shaky breath as the other man let go of Jilly, who stumbled forward. Alastair caught her as she fell, the force jolting his arm.

"Are you going to be okay?" he whispered, stroking his hand down her face, but never taking his eyes from the man before him. She nodded. "Go and get Kevin, and check your mum's alright. I wouldn't put anything past him."

Jilly nodded, taking the car keys and moving cautiously over to the doorway. Alastair reached across to the hob and turned the dial to switch it off. He looked across at Harry Alderman, seeing him clearly for the first time. This was Kevin's father. He didn't understand how, when he was meant to have died in a road accident years ago, but the prints had confirmed it.

"You know what it is to lose a son," the man's voice grated. "Imagine losing him, not once, but eight times."

"I know what it is to long for a child, to miss him. I know how strongly a paternal instinct can drive the heart. But you've killed so many people, and those murders can't be counted as equal to wanting to see your son. If you'd stayed in prison, you'd have been out by now. You could have had Kevin back."

"You've manipulated my boy, Vicar," he spat, making the title sound like an accusation. "You stole him away like all the others before. Melanie never even told me he existed. Then when I found out, she wouldn't let me see him. Then that perfect family."

"Liam Given?" Alastair whispered, feeling unbelievably tired but reminding himself of the importance of hearing this man's confession. "You killed him too?"

"Yes," came the reply. "And all the others in between. It was going to be great fun with you. The pentagram in the church; the little threats over the face of your angelic boy; using Kevin's words on you."

"Fun?" Alastair whispered, the word tasting

bitter in his mouth.

Harry barked a laugh. "And it worked. Replacing Mr Sinter, becoming invaluable to the school and a favourite of my own son. But then the unthinkable happened." He reached his hand to his pocket, laughing as Alastair jumped as he pulled out his phone. Flicking on a recording, Alastair listened to Kevin's voice as it announced: "I don't want to be Alderman, I want to be Roberts. I really want Alastair to actually be my dad."

"I told that to Santa," Kevin's small voice trembled from the doorway, and both men turned to face the boy. "Mr Samuels, were you spying on me?"

"Kevin," Alastair said, watching as two men in police uniform entered after the boy. "This is the man who's been chasing you. This is the man who invented, and became, your curse."

"Why?" Kevin asked, leaning against Jilly and watching as the officers handcuffed Harry's hands. The man seemed almost content to allow them to restrain him, but as Kevin's eyes filled with hurt tears, Harry stepped forward to the boy.

"He's not your father," Harry spat, using his elbow to indicate to Alastair, who leaned against the worktop. "You're my boy, Kevin, not his! I didn't escape that truck and swim out that river so you could be another man's son! You're mine, Kevin!"

"Mr Samuels is your father, Kevin," Alastair explained, while the other man struggled against being led from the room.

One of the officers stopped to speak to Jilly in

the doorway, but Kevin barely noticed. He never took his eyes from Mr Samuels as he was led out of the house, and his gaze was met with more anger than love in the caretaker's fierce eyes.

"I've got to check on Mum," Jilly was explaining to the policeman, her voice trembling a little. "She might be hurt."

"You've her to thank," he replied. "I believe it was Mrs Franks who called 999."

"Thank God she did," Jilly replied, tensing her right hand which still felt as though it was burning.

"Do you want to get that looked at?"

"No," she replied, her voice suddenly much clearer. "I'm just going to go see Mum."

She saw the police to the door before hurrying to the back of the house to check on Mrs Franks. She spared a brief glance for Kevin and Alastair in the kitchen as she rushed past, but Kevin was still staring after his father.

Jilly stumbled into the dining room to find her mum struggling to her feet. She rushed over to her, hugging her tightly while Mrs Franks made gentle, soothing sounds to her youngest child. The old woman's cheeks were damp with relieved tears as Jilly poured out an explanation of what had happened.

Alastair could hear Jilly sobbing as she spoke to Hilary Franks. There was no noise in the kitchen to obscure her heartbreak. Kevin moved to the window and looked out as the police car drove up the lane. He only spoke when the vehicle was out of sight.

"I don't understand," he whispered. "I thought my dad was dead."

"And he's been safe, since then, because of it," Alastair replied, just as softly. "You thought the curse was because no one wanted you, but in fact it was because so many people wanted you. What your dad did, all the fire, the fear, was terrible. But, however wicked his actions, he had his reasons."

"What reason?"

"Because he loved you. He really wanted to know you, and for you to know he is your dad."

Kevin shook his head. "You're my dad. I don't want any other dad."

Alastair held his arms out to the boy, who stepped forward and leaned his head against him. He felt as though his chest was on fire as he hugged Kevin, but he didn't want to let go of him. "I told you there were no such things as curses."

Kevin pulled back and looked up at Alastair. "You said you'd protect me. And you did."

Kevin's eyes filled with fear as he looked at Alastair's expression.

"Kevin, what happened? Are you hurt?"

Lifting his hand to his face, Kevin looked down at the red stain on his fingers. He felt panic grip him and he ran his hand down the side of his head, but he couldn't find any cut. Alastair kissed Kevin's hair, trying to calm the boy, his eyes searching for the source of the blood.

"Jilly?" Kevin screamed, his voice making Alastair jump. Kevin's eyes filled his tears, and he pointed across at Alastair. Jilly ran through, staring in confusion at Kevin's bloodied face and accusatory hand gesture.

"Oh," Alastair whispered, looking down at the

baggy shirt he wore which was now plastered to his body by his own blood. He looked across at Jilly as she ran forward, snatching a tea towel and pressing it against his chest.

"Oh, God," she whispered, looking down at the discarded knife on the floor. "I didn't think it reached you."

"It's okay," Alastair replied, trying to return the smile to his face, but now he knew the wound was there, he couldn't shake his own anxiety about its outcome.

"Can you walk to the car?" Jilly asked. "Can you get that far?"

"Of course I can, Jilly. I didn't even know it was there until Kevin pointed it out. Will you look after Kevin?"

"Nope," Jilly replied firmly. "You're looking after Kevin. Come on, let's get you to the car, an ambulance will take too long."

Between her and Kevin, they managed to persuade Alastair to the car, before Jilly rushed back to explain what was happening to her mum. In tones which would bear no refusal, she called Daniel and ordered him to call in on Hilary Franks. She rushed into Alastair's car and scrambled into the driver's seat. Kevin sat in the back beside Alastair, pressing the towel against the long cut on his chest.

"I'm fine," Alastair repeatedly protested.

Every jolt the car made caused Alastair's chest to feel like it was about to implode. Kevin's voice repeatedly told him he was going to be okay, but as he begged Alastair to stay awake, his voice began to morph into Leonard's. But where Kevin's tone was frantic and pleading,

Leonard's was soft and gentle. He lifted his left hand, resting his head firmly on the heel of his palm and gripping his hair tightly in his fingers. By the time they turned out of the track, he had lost Kevin's voice entirely.

Jilly had always been a cautious driver, always driving five miles below any speed limit. But as they turned onto the road into town and Alastair's voice became a slurred, garbled sound, Jilly forgot speed limits even existed. Kevin watched as the man's hand slid down by his side and the boy let the towel fall.

"I think he's dead," Kevin's voice trembled. "Jilly, I think he's dead."

Jilly glanced in the rear-view mirror and licked her lips. He couldn't be dead. God wouldn't let him die.

"Just keep that towel pressed on, Kevin."

"Why did Mr Samuels want to kill him? If he was really my dad, he would have wanted me to be happy. And I was happy with Alastair."

"I'm just so glad you arrived when you did," Jilly replied, unsure she had an answer to offer to the boy. "How did you know, Kevin?"

"Alastair said something about a big house, and he told me to get in the car. He didn't tell me where we were going or why."

"He can't be dead," Jilly whispered. "God, please don't let him be dead."

They reached the hospital in a time which Alastair would have struggled to better. Jilly parked at the A&E entrance and rushed around to try and guide Alastair out of the car, but the man was a deadweight, and even with Kevin's eager help, she couldn't move him. She ran into the hospital, reaching out her bloodied hands and calling desperately for help. Two porters came to help and, between them, they set the unconscious priest in a wheelchair, pushing him into the rooms beyond the double doors. Both Jilly and Kevin, each covered in Alastair's blood, stood absolutely still in the middle of the waiting room.

"Where is he?" boomed out a voice behind them. Kevin turned to face Father Levosky, but Jilly continued to stare at the doors through which she had last seen Alastair. She had her hand held out slightly, red with blood, and every move she made was like a jolt. She looked down as Father Levosky took her hands.

"This doesn't look good," he whispered. "Miss Franks, what happened? I got the message he left earlier, then I heard his car registration being called across the tannoy for being parked across the restricted bays. I take it you drove?"

She nodded.

"Would you like me to go and move the car?"

She nodded again, handing him the keys.

"Kevin," Father Levosky began. "Why don't you go and sit down over there with Miss Franks?" He pointed to a row of empty seats.

"He saved me." Jilly looked into the eyes of the Catholic priest. "I didn't even know he was hurt."

"If he had cause to save you, Miss Franks, there can be no blame laid at your feet."

He left them, going to park the car before returning to find the same stunned silence, although they had taken the seats he had suggested. Every time a green-clad orderly, or a doctor or nurse walked through the doors, Jilly rose to her feet. Eventually, Father Levosky walked over to the desk and asked for any update on Alastair's situation.

Within two minutes, a nurse came through to them.

"Mrs Roberts?" she began.

"Oh, no," Jilly replied, blushing, while Father Levosky only enhanced this embarrassment as he added,

"Not yet."

"How's my dad?" Kevin demanded. "Is he alive?"

"He's alive," came the comforting reply. "Are you Leonard or Kevin?"

"Kevin," the boy replied.

"You can come through and see him if you'd like, Kevin."

He nodded, and the three of them followed her as she guided them through the double doors.

"Is he going to be okay?" Jilly asked.

"We've got him hooked up for a transfusion at the moment. He's in and out of consciousness, but that's normal in his condition, and we're measuring his response to the treatment very carefully."

The nurse pulled back a curtain as though she was performing an amazing magic trick, to reveal the sight of Alastair asleep on the bed. To Kevin and Jilly there could not have been a greater trick.

"Don't touch the bags," the nurse said, as Kevin's finger followed the tube of blood. Softening her voice as the boy jumped, she continued. "He's going to be fine." She turned to Jilly and smiled. "You've got to be related to Trish Macauley, are you?"

"She's my sister."

"You're Gillian?" the nurse smiled. "She's always talking about you. You did a good thing, getting him here so quickly."

Jilly smiled, unsure how to respond to such words, and watched as the nurse left, pulling the curtain closed. The noise, peculiar and unusual, made Alastair's eyes flicker open. All three of his visitors took a step forward and Alastair felt uncomfortable as he looked at them all.

"I've got to stop doing this," he murmured. "Father," he continued, reaching out his left hand to the priest. "I was right."

"I know." The deep voice sounded full to admiration. "I got your message. Harry Alderman, wasn't it?"

"Yes," Alastair whispered, as nodding proved too difficult. "Kevin's dad."

"I only need one dad," Kevin said. "And it's not Mr Samuels, or Mr Alderman, or whatever he was really called. I want it to be you." Kevin leaned forward and kissed Alastair's cheek.

"Next time, Alastair," Father Levosky began. "Go to the police. My nerves are too well shot to deal with another incident like this."

"There won't be a next time. Harry Alderman is gone." Alastair's tone was desperate.

"Kevin," Father Levosky said. "That game of chess is still waiting to be finished. Did you make a New Year's Resolution to beat me?"

"I was winning," Kevin squeaked.

"Shall we go finish it?"

Kevin nodded.

"We'll be back soon," Father Levosky said, guiding the boy past the curtain, and smiling slightly as he glanced back.

Alastair's eyes were closed, and Jilly watched him for a moment before she turned to leave.

"Jilly," Alastair muttered, not opening his eyes. "Thank you for getting me here."

"Me?" Jilly laughed in disbelief. "Don't thank me when I owe you so much thanks. I thought I was going to die today. Thank you for saving me, again. How did you know?"

"Know what?" he began, opening his eyes.

"To come. To find me. How did you know?"

"I've been asking Lord Dalton to get involved since I first arrived. He told me last summer—Jilly?" he interrupted himself, reaching his hand towards her.

"I'm here," she whispered, leaning forward and taking his hand, carefully avoiding the clip on his middle finger.

"He was leaving the big house. He'd lost interest in it. There was no way he was renovating it." He smiled across at her. "And I knew Harry Alderman was out there. There was no one else he could be."

"Can life get back to normal now?" Jilly asked, looking down at his chest.

"Not quite," he whispered, turning to look at the bag of red liquid. "Jilly, I don't feel right."

"I'll go get a nurse," she said quickly.

"No," his stammered, turning back to her. She was surprised to find tears in his eyes and, as they spilt, she wiped them away from his face. "I'm scared."

"You're going to be fine," she said soothingly.

"The nurse said you would be."

"I don't know what I would have done to him if he'd gone through with his threat. I'm scared of what I might have done to him. I was so scared when I saw you there."

"Not as much as I was relieved to see you. I was terrified, but he didn't do me any permanent harm. Just make sure he hasn't done any permanent harm to you. We can get back to living our lives, calm and simple. Can we please?"

"No," he whispered, his eyes closing once again.

"Ally," she sobbed. "Don't leave me, Ally."

"Leave you?" Alastair's voice trailed, and he struggled to lift his hand to her, laughing slightly at his own feebleness. "Gillian Franks, I can't bear to lose you. Kevin loves you almost as much as I do. He'd love you to be his mother, and I desperately want you to be my wife."

"You've got someone else's blood in your veins, Vicar. It's confusing your heart."

"I can't bear to lose you, Jilly," he repeated. His smile, diluted in weariness, returned to his face, and Jilly found herself smiling back at him. "A twelfth night epiphany. Will you marry me, Jilly?"

"Really?" Jilly whispered. "I don't know whether or not to believe you."

"I've never lied to you. I'm not lying now."

Jilly looked down at him and leaned forward, kissing his forehead. "Then, yes."

She watched him slip out of consciousness once more. Holding his hand in both of her own, she gently rubbed her thumbs across it, feeling an inescapable smile cross her face. It was odd to sit in such a place and wonder if she could ever be so happy again. But it was made all the stranger by realising that she didn't really care. This was not going to be her adventure alone, but Alastair's and Kevin's too. And whatever the future held, it was their future.

Books by Virginia Crow

Caledon

"Go out and tell all those you meet, Caledon has risen. Caledon will be protected and defended. And to you who would cause her harm, be prepared. A new fight has come."

After the destruction of the Jacobite forces at Culloden, Scotland is divided, vulnerable and leaderless, with survivors from both sides seeking to make sense of the battles they have fought against their fellow Scots.

James Og flees Drumossie, seeking the protection of his uncle's house in Sutherland. It is here that James learns that the Northern Highlands hold a secret power only he can wield: Caledon. When Ensign John Mackay begins hunting Og's family, James realises he must harness this power to defeat the enemies of Scotland.

But, as the ageless Caledon awakes, so too does an ancient evil. When it allies with Mackay, the small Clan of Caledon faces enemies at every turn, discovering that even those closest to them may seek to destroy them.

Day's Dying Glory

Aside from living together in a comfortable home in the Scottish Grampians, Major Tenterchilt's three daughters seem to have little in common.

Influenced by her mother, Arabella aspires to be a wife and a lady, Imogen wishes to teach, while Cat always endeavours to be the son her father never had. The Major's sole stipulation is that they marry military officers.

As the girls' idyllic existence falls apart around them, they must overcome tragedies and challenges to find their place in a world where betrayal and secrets threaten everything they hold dear, and where no one is quite who they seem.

Day's Dying Glory is a story of how sisterly love can overcome anything, and a thrilling coming of age novel set during the Napoleonic Wars.

Beneath Black Clouds and White

Despite adoring his family and enjoying frequenting gaming tables, Captain Josiah Tenterchilt's true love is the British Army and he is committed to his duty. As such, he does not hesitate to answer the army's call when King Louis XVI of France is executed.

Accompanied by his wife to Flanders, Josiah finds his path crosses with a man who could not be more different from him: an apprentice surgeon named Henry Fotherby. As these two men pursue their own actions, fate and the careful connivance of a mysterious individual will push them together for the rest of their lives.

But it is a tumultuous time, and the French revolutionaries are not the only ones who pose a threat. The two gentlemen must find their place in a world where the constraints of social class are inescapable, and 'slavery or abolition' are the words on everyone's lips.